Seeking Samuel

By Minette Bryant

Outer Banks Publishing Group
Raleigh/Outer Banks

For information contact Outer Banks Publishing Group at

info@outerbankspublishing.com

FIRST EDITION – October 2020

Library of Congress Control Number: 2020945701

ISBN: 978-1-7341687-7-8
eISBN: 978-0-4639933-7-8

For Emma because she asked me to.

The water's cold
The fire is hot.
The night is bold
But I am not.
The Sultan's wife,
That crocodile,
She spits me out,
I fall a mile.
I look around
This endless ride,
And see tin soldiers
Side by side.
I think they'll save
Me from the sea.
But I am wrong.
They fall with me.

-Trista Maybrey, 4th grade

Chapter One

Thursday began with the call from Pillar Loans telling me, coolly, that they were not going to be able to close on my loan after all. It had been six weeks since I was "conditionally approved" and now, less than 48 hours from my flight to Maine for the closing, they were backing out.

The woman on the other end of the line introduced herself as Megan, a name that sounded remarkably innocuous for the news she was delivering. If you're going to have a position in your company for someone whose sole purpose is to rip the rug out from under people at the last minute, it seems you would scour through the applications and resumes for someone with a name like Helga, or Edwina, or something harsh-sounding. Jacosta. It wouldn't matter what this person's qualifications were prior to hiring...just the sound of their name on the phone would strike a note of apprehension in the person receiving the call, and then the news wouldn't come as a total shock. You can't expect people to prepare themselves to be emotionally eviscerated by someone named Megan. It was just cruel.

Perhaps because I was not able to prepare myself for this, I didn't actually believe it was real. Fumbling for words that sounded in any way adult-ish in this moment, I asked, "Why? What happened today, after six weeks of being approved?"

"I do understand your concerns," Megan said, in a voice that said, *this part is scripted. Most of my job is scripted.* "Now that we finally have the appraisal, we just aren't going to be able to close."

"But...I'm flying to Maine on Saturday. I'm supposed to close on Monday morning. This is my life..." I knew I sounded ridiculous...pitiful...grasping. I was determined not to cry in front of Megan.

"I do understand your concerns," Megan repeated, indicating that she did not, in fact, understand my concerns. Actually understanding was not part of her script. "Let me see if I can connect you to someone who can help you."

And then Megan was gone, and I was listening to an on-hold message that was far too loud in comparison with the live-attendant volume. A cheery man expressed with overblown sincerity that his company was dedicated to helping men and women just like me to achieve the American dream...except he was a little late in his reassurances. Megan had already made that clear. I listened to this cheery man fully express his American

Dream promise twice through and he was beginning a third oration when he was cut off.

"Hello, Miss Maybrey, my name is Kelly, and I'm a customer relations agent. It sounds like you're having some difficulty."

Kelly. How could I trust a Kelly at this point? Where was my Helga, who would tell it to me straight?

"Hi, Kelly," I began, having no idea how this sentence would end, "I'm being told, here in the proverbial eleventh hour—more like the twelfth hour—that my loan is being rejected. I've been conditionally approved for six weeks. You guys have every piece of paper that defines every aspect of my life. I fly to Maine on Saturday and I'm set to close on Monday. What could possibly have happened?"

Before she could begin her answer, I started my new line of defense. "Megan said it was something in the appraisal, but I've read every page of the appraisal, and it shows that the property appraises for eight thousand more than the asking price, so how can that be a problem?"

"I do understand your concerns, Miss Maybrey," (*oh boy*) "But it appears that the Executive Leadership is worried about the accessibility of the property. It looks like it can only be reached...by a boat?"

That sentence had begun as a statement and ended as a question. I felt like Kelly had been thrown in here without all the information, and now she was needing for me to explain to her why her company was rejecting me.

"It's an island," I said, knowing I sounded patronizing. "It's always been an island. The address is Number One, Simple Island. It's an island."

Kelly didn't answer right away, so I continued, trying to sound less condescending. "But it's so close to the mainland that at low tide, you can literally just walk out there. Twice a day, there's about a four-hour window when you can just walk across."

I was actually surprised at how confident I sounded in this explanation. I had never been there. I had never even been in Maine. I had never knowingly experienced low tide, and I had never walked across to Simple Island, or any island. I knew these things from photographs and reports in the real estate listing, and from stories I could read online about people who lived on islands close enough to the shore to walk at low tide. I had studied these things so thoroughly over the past two months that I felt like I had been there...and this is where the confidence in my voice came from. In that moment, I was more confident in that information than in any of the other scattered pieces of my life.

Kelly returned to her script. "The Executive Leadership is concerned about accessibility because, in times of hardship, people tend to default on a second mortgage, and the accessibility of this property might make it difficult to resell."

I experienced a moment of mental gymnastics. This was like a child's dot-to-dot puzzle which had just completely abandoned the original picture and added random dots all over the page and then rapidly connected them with no interest in creating a real image.

I heard the patronizing tone creep back into my voice. "With that kind of reasoning, how does anyone get a loan for anything? *'What if they die in a car accident and their kids don't want the house—the color of wallpaper they* might *choose* might *make it harder to resell...'"*

Kelly was silent, so I plowed forward. "Look...this property has been an island since I first put in the application. Everyone knew that. You have paperwork to show every dusty corner of my life. You see my income from my business, you see that I've never had a foreclosure, or a car repossessed. I paid off my student loans. This isn't really a second mortgage for me...my ex-husband has paid me half the equity in our home, because he is keeping it, and that equity is the down payment I'm making on Simple Island. You have no reason to suspect that I'm going to default. It is grossly unfair for this to be taken away from me now because some guy in a suit somewhere doesn't understand what an island is. There's a Simon and Garfunkle song I could recommend if that would be helpful."

"I understand your concerns, Miss Maybrey. I really do. I'm here to be your advocate, and I'm going to talk to Executive Leadership with all of this information and see what we can do."

"Thank you, Kelly," I said, knowing I sounded exhausted at 9:30 in the morning.

When I pushed the button to end the call, my phone immediately buzzed with an email from my real estate agent, Lisa. She was forwarding me an email she had already received...from Megan...telling her that the loan was not going to be moving forward. Sorry for the inconvenience. Have a nice day. Lisa hadn't written anything in her own email except for five question marks. I had the feeling she was probably driving. I had the feeling Lisa spent most of her time driving.

The phone didn't even sound like it had rung before she answered, and because she knew it was me, she didn't even say hello.

"Oh my god you must be livid! Did they tell you why?"

"I think they've just realized that it's an island."

"Just realized? The listing is called 'Simple Island' for Chrissakes!"

"Well, maybe they just thought it was a clever name."

"Oh my god. What are you going to do?"

Before I could formulate an answer, Lisa jumped in again. "Don't cancel your flight! Come on up, visit the island, we'll figure this out!"

I tried to tell myself that her concern was for me, for my life, for my busted future...not just that she was counting on making this sale. "I'm not cancelling anything," I assured her with a sigh. "I refuse to accept that this is suddenly over. I'm going to get in touch with the bank you recommended in the first place. I'm guessing they have more experience with this kind of property."

"Yes! Do that! Call Linda at Maine Federal! Oh my god..."

"I'll let you know how it goes," I said, and then hung up, glad to get the road noise out of my ear.

I did make the call to Maine Federal, and Linda was every bit as friendly and helpful as Lisa had predicted. It turns out that the second time you apply for the same loan, everything is much easier, because I already had a file folder on my laptop with all the documents it had taken me days to gather the first time. Click click click click click...send. Linda told me that they did have a special program just for this kind of property, and that the only hold up there might be was whether the bank could accept the appraisal I sent, as they hadn't actually commissioned it themselves.

"Well," I said, resignedly, "I just paid four thousand dollars for that appraisal...last week...so hopefully they will make an exception."

"I will do my best for you!" She assured me. So, now, between Kelly and Linda, I had two people promising to do their best for me...which felt like it meant very little.

Simple Island was my only plan. I had to get out of Dallas...I had to get out of this house, which I had sold to Jason for half the equity. He was living with his girlfriend until I had the chance to move out...I had promised him I'd be out by the end of April...so then he and his girlfriend could move in. So they could cook together in my kitchen, watch TV together in my living room, sleep together in my bedroom.

I thought about all of that for a minute...like running my tongue across an ulcer inside my cheek. I discovered that it didn't hurt as much as it used to. It was still an open, gaping sore, and it still hurt like hell, but it didn't feel like it was going to kill me. Not like it used to. That was a good sign, and I needed good signs today.

Funny how signs work, signifying the beginning of things, the end of things, the points of interest along the way. When I looked back, I could see so many signs that I had missed. Signs that Jason wasn't quite *with* me like he used to be. We still talked, went out sometimes, we still made love maybe once a week...at least I had thought of it as "making love" but I guess for him it wasn't anymore. We managed finances together, talked about big decisions, took turns walking the dog...but Jason wasn't really *with* me. I knew it, but I ignored it. He was going through a phase, he was just past forty and dealing with his mortality, he'd talk about it when he was ready. He'd be back.

I guess I'd been missing those signs for over two years. But the first sign I didn't miss was so confusing that I couldn't even process it. We were in the car, headed to the grocery store, and I realized I didn't have a Chapstick in my purse. I dug all around in the dark caverns of my bag, and finally gave up. Maybe there was one in the glove box.

I pulled the camouflaged handle on the dash, and the door sprang open, practically hurling the little blue object into my lap. I stared at it, blankly. Knowing what it was, and yet not being able to process it, as it was so completely out of place in my life.

"What is this?" I asked, turning to Jason and holding it up for him to see. He didn't take his eyes off the road. He didn't look at me. I could see his jaw working in what I later realized was his moment of deciding whether to make up a story or just tell me the truth.

"Pacifier," he said.

Not "It's a pacifier" or "Why, that's a pacifier you've got there!" ...just "Pacifier" which somehow served to make my question a really stupid one. Of course it was a pacifier. Just because I don't have children doesn't mean I don't recognize this iconic invention.

"Right..." I fumbled for a second. "But what is it doing in the glove box?"

I waited for the perfectly reasonable explanation. He had carpooled with a coworker who laughingly discovered the blue binky in her handbag and asked if she could store it in his car for the day so that she didn't look like she had "Mom brain" to her office mates. He had picked up a woman and her child who'd been stranded by a flat tire, and when he dropped them off at the service station, she inadvertently left the pacifier behind. There had been a baby shower at work, and he had won the prize for pinning the most clothespins on the cloth diaper, and this little blue pacifier had been his prize...not wanting to hurt anyone's feelings, he had accepted it, and stashed it here in the glove box. It could have been there for weeks, months. How long since I'd opened that compartment?

"Jason," I repeated, "Why is this in your glove box?"

"It belongs to my son."

So...truth won out. Jason and I had been married for eleven years, and he had long ago accepted that I couldn't have children. I had carried the twins for Jon and Bobby, but that c-section had messed me up pretty bad, leading to a hysterectomy before I was thirty, so there would be no children with my own biological material. Jason knew this. Obviously, I knew this. So, who was this son who had a blue pacifier in the glove box?

I didn't have to ask. Jason ploughed ahead, letting the momentum and the relief that comes with the end of secrecy propel him forward.

"I have a son. His name is Luke. He just turned two. We've been trying to break him of the pacifier, but it's hard. He's pretty stuck on it." Jason smiled, then, to himself...suddenly a proud Daddy, both amused and stupefied at how stubborn toddlers can be.

Knowing the answer would rip me open, I asked anyway: "Who is 'we'?"

There was no point in being hesitant this time. Clearly, Luke had a mother, someone who was comfortably co-parenting with my husband of eleven years.

"Alyssa. We've been together for almost three years now. Luke was a surprise, but we love him...and now we're expecting another one. A little girl. I haven't been sure what to do because I know this is all going to be a shock to you, but I think I need to just focus on my family."

In all of this, Jason never looked away from the road, and now he was pulling easily into a parking space in front of the store...as though I would just get out and grab a buggy and start shopping for dinner. Sure, I'll go buy carrots while you focus on your family.

His family. For eleven years, I thought *I* was his family.

"Alyssa thought I should wait to tell you until after Sarah is born, but since you found Luke's pacie, I guess this is a good a time as any. Are you OK, Trista?"

Oddly, until that moment, I think I had been OK. I was shocked, obviously, but I guess the shock numbed me and I was somehow taking it all in, filling in the blanks of this story, and not feeling particularly overwhelmed. It felt like Jason had been living an alternate life in the time that he wasn't with me, and this must have been hard for him. In that moment, I felt sorry for how hard this must have been for him.

But suddenly, with "Alyssa thought I should wait to tell you..." I realized that Jason wasn't living an alternate life. *I was.* Jason had this whole *real* life with Alyssa and Luke and unborn Sarah, where they worked together to wean Luke from his pacie, and they talked about me and my feelings and how I would handle this, and they made real plans for a real future, and they saw themselves as a family...and I was the pitiable one, the one living in the sad, confusing alternate universe.

"I guess you'll want a divorce then," I said, stupidly, looking at my hands in my lap.

"I guess so."

It turns out there was no Chapstick in the glove box after all.

Chapter Two

April 27, 1859

My Dearest,

I have written those first two words, that expression of endearment, and then I have sat here quietly beholding them on the otherwise empty page, and I am unable to find the words to further express what those first two simple words mean to me.

The second word, "dearest" seems unequal to the place that you already hold in my heart, in my life, in my every hope for the future. I have, in the course of my twenty-seven years, held dear many other people and things and endeavors. I have deeply loved my family, which will shortly become your family, and I have devoted myself both to my family's business as well as to my own studies as I have decided upon a life spent in the healing arts. I have held dear many of the books in my father's library, books that I felt connected me to the wider world and to the people who lived and dreamed over the centuries past. I have dearly loved an old dog who colored my youth and whose quiet death, his muzzle grey and his warm eyes clouded with age, will always bring a tear when his still-young image gallops across the fields of my memory.

I hope that you will find me to be the sort of man who always seeks new opportunities to find the elements of life that can be held dear, the moments to cherish, the gifts to share and treasure. But on the whole, My Dearest, I hope that you will fully understand that when I refer to you as "My Dearest" you know that I mean with all sincerity that I have never known any person, any moment, any experience that rivals the precious regard with which I hold you.

The first word of the expression, however, is the one that gives me the greatest pause. My. My dearest. What kind of man am I that I have earned the ability to call you mine? It feels pretentious of me; I am wholly undeserving of this honor. And yet, by agreeing to be my wife, to share this life with me in all of its splendor and wonder and fleeting fragility, you have freely gifted me the right to call you mine. My Dearest.

On the day of our marriage, we will be instructed to share the time-honored vows that have bound countless men and women into holy matrimony, but on that day, I want you to hold in your heart this further vow from the depths of my being: I vow eternally to stand awestricken that you have chosen me from all the world of men who would be honored to share a single moment with you let alone their whole lives, and whatever the future holds, however the winds may blow us to and fro, I will never forget the invaluable treasure that I hold in the simple ability to call you My Dearest.

Chapter Three

Waiting for a call back from either Linda at Maine Federal or Kelly at Pillar Loans made the day seem interminable. I tried to distract myself with work, focusing on the day to day details of my little company, noting all the ways I can be professional while sitting in my recliner in my living room, wearing sweats, and with my little dog, Margaret Mary, on my lap.

But the waiting was miserable. My brain kept trying to sound an alarm, to jar me into obsessing over how bad this was, to put me in a position of shedding tears, or calling someone to complain about it...but I refused. Instead, while I waited, I went to Lisa's real estate web page and started looking at all the other listings she had in the area. There were hundreds of homes and properties for sale in Downeast Maine, and I think I must have looked at all of them.

There were big old homes on large rolling properties, cute little lake-houses, modern townhomes with tiny gardens, ramshackle "fixer-uppers," mansions I could never afford. There were lovely parcels of acreage where someone might build something brand new, tailor made for them. There were properties that I could have bought outright with the money in my bank account, and others that I could have made a hefty down payment on and Pillar would have happily provided the rest because...they weren't islands. I took the virtual tour of scores of these homes, looking at the interiors, reading the details, wondering about the people who lived there and why they were leaving.

I tried to imagine myself choosing one of these on the heels of losing Simple Island. I thought about what I would say when Kelly called back to tell me there was nothing she could do...this was a total loss...and I could say, "OK...but wait! I've chosen another property, and you already have all of my information. How quickly can we get approval on this one?" I thought, if I lost Simple Island, the quick replacement with another piece of property—one that better fit Pillar's idea of an approvable home—would make me feel better, and I could still fly to Maine in a couple days to see the house, to bond with it, to bask in the power of home ownership.

But it didn't work. I couldn't do it. I couldn't manufacture for any of these properties the kind of instantaneous "rightness" that I felt when I found Simple.

⋆ ⋆ ⋆

I had first learned of Simple Island two days after Jason had told me his particular truth (and had subsequently moved out), and I had been trying really hard to stay numb. Anything outside of numb was too painful to think about. But later that week, I had a meeting with a client...an in-person meeting, which happened rarely for me, and I needed to look like...well, like someone who doesn't do most of her work in sweats, in a recliner, with a dog on her lap.

So, I went to a nail salon. Having my nails and eyebrows done was generally my "go to" effort when I needed my appearance of professionalism to match the level of service I offered my clients. The chipper Korean lady who greeted me at the salon ushered me to the chair of a young man who was pretty rough on my nails, and not interested in talking. Which was fine. Me either.

I've always been the kind of person who doesn't complain to anyone who is providing a service. Not only that, I'm compulsive and practiced in the art of the unnecessary apology. Once, when I was sitting in a restaurant having dinner with Jason, a fellow from another table jumped up, realizing he was about to be sick. He rushed to the bathroom with his hand over his mouth, but as he passed our booth, he "coughed" and a spray of what I have to imagine was vomit spewed out from behind his hand and splattered me, the table, my twelve-dollar salad.

He ran on to the bathroom, but when he came back, he showered us with his apology...and I matched him sorry for sorry. I was literally apologizing for, I guess, being in the way when he needed to vomit. I was apologizing for making him feel bad by being the person he threw up on. If I'd had time, right there in that booth, I would have baked him cookies in an attempt to make amends for my role in his difficulty.

This fellow in the nail salon was really kind of hurting me...he was much too harsh in his treatment of my cuticles, and when, on three occasions, he drew blood, he would curse under his breath, and I'd find myself apologizing to him for...what? For having sensitive cuticles? For wasting his time that he could be working with someone less problematic? For being the difficult client who ruined his perfect record for the week by having the audacity to bleed not once, but *three* times? For only paying him $65 plus tip for this hour of his life that he could never get back? Where was an E-Z Bake oven when I needed one?

Maybe the pain he was inflicting on my fingers helped to temporarily distract me from the other pain in my life. In any case, I turned my focus away from my bleeding digits and toward the television on the other side of the salon.

The show on the TV was a real estate show, where a blonde agent in a trim navy suit and high heels was showing an older gentleman and his much younger wife a number of properties—within their modest budget of three million dollars—for them to choose from. The young woman, whom I felt confident had not been overly involved in the *earning* of the three million dollars they were seeking to spend, was exhibiting the kind of whiny pickiness about the properties they were being shown that I assumed probably got them on this show. Nice people don't get picked for reality shows. *Nice* doesn't sell advertising.

When I first began paying attention to the show, the couple were on a wooded plot of land, looking at the grounds with the big house behind them. It was glorious. Old Money. The young woman didn't like it...the ground was uneven, the house needed remodeling, the bedroom carpet didn't match her toenail polish. So, they left that property and went to another...and it was at this point that I realized this couple was specifically looking to purchase an island. A private island.

This was rather a revelation to me. I'd never thought about regular people (not that people with three million dollars to spend are "regular" in my world) could just say, "Let's buy a private island" ...and then call a real estate agent. But here they were, doing just that. There was something more though; if you had asked me just moments before, before this cursing young man was mangling my manicure, to describe my idea of a "private island" I would have closed my eyes and given you a description of something tropical with sandy beaches and colorful umbrellas, teal-blue water lapping the diamond-white shore. Palm trees swaying overhead.

But these people were strictly looking at islands off the coast of the Eastern United States: New York, North Carolina. This was an entirely new concept to me. I knew, of course, that there were islands off the coast of the US...living in Texas, I had many times made the trip down to Galveston for a beach weekend. Galveston Island. I'd attended a surrogacy conference on Navarre Island in Florida, which is connected to Pensacola by a long bridge. I'd been in Manhattan, of course. Sure, there were islands...I just hadn't thought about real people owning any of them all for themselves.

But here they were, Mister Money and his whiny young wife, visiting at least four different islands in two states while I had what was supposed to be a professional manicure, but was instead spiraling into one long apology on my part.

I never saw which one they chose. That wasn't important. My manicure was finished, with three of my fingers showing tiny streaks of blood at the cuticle, now permanently encased in clear-coat shellac. Nice. I tipped the fellow more than usual because I could tell he didn't like me and my wimpy fingers.

But when I got home to my empty house, I filled my evening with Googling about private islands. It turns out there are many, many islands for sale around the United States (and Canada) ...some of them are in lakes or rivers, but most of them are proper islands, in the ocean. Some of these islands are absolute wilderness, completely undeveloped. Some are *almost* completely wilderness, with maybe a hunting cabin and—in the fancier places— an outhouse. Some, on the other end of the spectrum, are what I would think of as *over*-developed...with a giant house and a retaining wall and an acre of decking...and no trees. I looked at some of those islands and wondered...how did they do that? How did they transport all the material for that house and outbuildings across the water and to the building site? How do they have running water? Electricity?

In my searching, I came across Vladi.com, a website that was a clearinghouse of sorts for private islands for sale. From the outset, it appeared to be focused on the kind of island I would have described before the nail salon TV show: five acres in Belize for 9.9 million dollars. But then I played around and discovered that I could narrow my search to the United States, and once I did that, I didn't even have to scroll. I saw it. Simple Island, off the coast of Downeast Maine.

The initial listing said that it was a single acre with a "nicely finished" cabin, for $120,000. That didn't even look right to me. There must have been a zero missing. But I clicked on the little camera icon, and, after a few seconds of loading, was treated to 33 photos of the island and existing structure. It was a rocky shoreline island, as you would expect in Maine, heavily wooded like many of the other Northeastern islands I had looked at, but in the center of the island, perched on the highest point like Noah's Ark grounded on Mount Ararat, was a 640 square foot cabin.

On the outside, the cabin could not have been plainer. Definitely "simple." Stark and narrow, it was 40 feet by 16 feet. At first blush, it might have been mistaken for a single-wide mobile home...only not as long. The outside walls of the house were covered in hundreds (thousands) of ragged and uneven looking little pieces of wood. I instinctively knew to call them wooden shingles, but I didn't think I'd ever seen them before. They were ugly— weathered gray and bereft of any homey charm. The cabin had nothing that could be called a porch...just a small square platform no wider than the door, and several steps down to the ground, with no railing. The front door was just a flat rectangle in the flat face of the front of the house. On the back end there was a deck of sorts, also with no railing around it, nor any rails down the steps that led to the ground. Even so, the deck was the one part of the cabin's exterior that had any life about it...it had two evenly spaced holes through which two tall pines grew up from the island's floor and reached for the sky. I don't know why this appealed to me so much. Clearly a house had to be built if anyone was going to inhabit Simple Island, and clearly trees would have to be cut in order to make space for the house, but it satisfied something deep inside me that great effort had been made to preserve these two trees growing through the deck.

Other than that, though, the outside visual of the cabin was plain as paper. Like something a first grader would draw if you asked him to draw a house. Just a box with a basic triangular roof, and a centered front door with a window beside it. But the inside...

The current owners (and apparently motivated sellers) of Simple Island obviously knew that the inside of the cabin was their selling point, because where they had included four pictures, at different angles, of the exterior, there were at least twenty photos of the inside. The interior walls were warm with golden pine planking that extended all the way to and across the ceiling. New-ish carpet covered almost all of the floor except the kitchen and bathroom which were done in laminate tile. The kitchen was small, with a bar that separated the food preparation area from the living room area. The bathroom, despite the squatty awkwardness of the composting toilet, was charming, with white fixtures and a rack hung with matching towels. There was one bedroom, just big enough for the queen-sized bed it held.

The cabin décor had a bit of a "personality disorder" ...I could tell the owners had put a lot of effort into making it look like a classic beach house, like on a South Carolina island. Lots of white and watery blues, and artwork with seashells and phrases like "life is good at the beach." Not only did this contrast almost painfully with the warm pine walls, but it was just all wrong. This was a tiny lodge in the middle of a forest which just *happened* to be surrounded by water. This was not a beach house.

The listing repeatedly tagged photos with the words "Everything Conveys." I had to think hard about what that meant in this context. When I think of the word "convey" I think of, I suppose, a conveyor belt carrying my groceries to the check-out girl. Or just simply the definition that means I am, personally, carrying an item or items from one place to another. Or, sometimes, I might use the word *convey* in terms of communicating an idea: "What I'm trying to convey, here, is that my husband has an entirely other family, and now I must convey myself and all of my belongings to another domicile."

But, based on the context, I assumed this meant that everything I was seeing in these pictures...the furniture, the appliances, the cabinets full of supplies—even the little bottle of Crest mouthwash that I could see sitting on the floor in the photo of the bathroom...all of these things came along with the sale of the island. That's good. I'd been meaning to get some mouthwash.

I was immediately drawn into the listing for Simple Island. As I perused, again and again, the 33 pictures, I could see myself in that cabin, walking that rocky shoreline, sitting on that deck. I pictured it without even trying. Over the past couple of days, ever since Jason's

Truth, I had half-heartedly looked at other real estate listings. Mostly I'd been looking in the Dallas area, maybe as far north as Oklahoma. My subconscious paradigms kept me thinking local. But upon finding and studying the listing for Simple, I realized, all in a rush, that there was literally *no* good reason for me to stay in this area. My mother is in Dallas, and my best friend is in Dallas, but I really only see either of them if we've made an appointment—sometimes weeks out—to get together. Why couldn't we still do it that way, but just add airfare?

Suddenly, I thought of one imminently important reason why I needed to get out of Dallas. Did I *really* want to bump into Jason, out and about with his kids? Did I want to run into Alyssa in the grocery store? Did I want to run into people who had, themselves, run into Alyssa in the grocery store? How many of Jason's friends—of *my* friends—had known about Alyssa and Luke and Sarah for weeks, months, years already? How many people that I saw every day were already looking at me with pity, wondering how I would take the news they already knew. The thought twisted my stomach. The humiliation was beginning to feel worse than the dissolution of my marriage.

In that moment I knew that Simple Island was exactly what I needed. I needed my own little kingdom, where I could focus entirely on myself, where I could reinvent the parts of me that I had grown indifferent to. For the first time in days, I felt a little finger of excitement beckoning to me...look, here's a chance to just *start over*.

It was time to call Jennifer. I hadn't told her anything yet...hadn't told her about Jason's Truth. Jennifer and I had been best friends since pre-school; she was the one person who, over the years, had evolved so very much in tandem with my own evolution that we still had the whole world in common. That's rare, I know, and so I take every opportunity to deeply appreciate it.

Though Jennifer and I are very much alike—in appearance as well as temperament—we are also very different, in ways that complement each other. Jennifer is much more spiritual than I am. I tend to think in logic, in verbal answers and utilitarian reasoning. That sounds kind of bland when I put it that way...I see myself as a creative person, and when I have an idea, I focus on the end goal and then logic my way through all the possible paths to get there, choosing the one that makes the most sense. I'm the same way with problem-solving, and I think that's why I hadn't allowed myself to just go to bed with a case of wine after Jason told me his story and moved out. This was a problem that, I knew, had a series of solutions, and focusing on the solutions kept me from just crumbling.

I knew Jennifer was going to make me walk through the valley of the shadow of death, and I knew why she would think that was important...and I knew she was right. The emotional impact of this major shift in my life was going to have to be felt. This piper would have to be paid before I could move on.

I'd resisted the initial urges to call Jennifer, or my Mom, because I guess I thought if I didn't tell them, then maybe it wouldn't be real. Maybe Jason would come back and say it was all a mistake, or some kind of test...of course when I allowed that possibility to play out, I knew how ridiculous it sounded. In the first 24 hours, I guess I didn't call them because I knew they would both jump in and try to "help" me and I wasn't ready for that. After 48 hours, I didn't call them because I knew that when I did, they would immediately want to know why I had waited so long to call.

When Jennifer picked up the phone, she didn't even say hello. She jumped right in, with a worried tone, "Are you all right?"

If it was anyone else, I would have reacted in two ways. First, I would have wondered why they thought I wasn't OK, and second, I would have lied and said that I *was* OK. But not with Jennifer.

"No...I'm not. But I will be."

"Oh, Trista...what's going on? I've had you on my mind for two days, and I kept thinking you would call and tell me what's happening. Do you need me to come over?"

I thought about this for a minute. The house was a mess. I was a mess. But this was Jennifer.

"Yeah...can you?"

An hour later, at 9 pm, Jennifer pulled into my driveway. She shut off her engine and fairly jumped out of the car to come and hug me. "It's cold out here!" she exclaimed and led me back into the warmth of my own house. Once inside, before I could say a word, she reached into her bag and produced a full bottle of Southern Comfort. "Whatever it is," she said with her signature crooked grin, "this will help."

Like ripping off a Band-Aid, I just plunged in and told her Jason's Truth, and, not allowing her the opportunity to cluck over me in concern, I opened my laptop and showed her the listing for Simple Island. Jennifer's hand shot out to touch the picture of the island on my screen. "That's in Maine?" she asked, incredulously.

"It is," I said, "And I know that sounds really far away, but it's still the USA...like you wouldn't need a passport to visit me." I knew this was where I would have to justify why I wanted to go so far away without sounding like I was simply *running* away. So, I tried to put it in terms I felt Jennifer would understand.

"Jen, you know me. My whole life, I've basically done what I was told to do. My comfort zone has been like a small square playpen, and my fears and my sense of obligation have always put me back in the playpen every time I thought I would climb out."

"That's not even true!" she protested. "Don't talk about my best friend like that! Look at you! You saw people that you cared about who wanted a baby, and you volunteered to carry the baby for them...two babies! And when it turned out, then, that you couldn't have a baby of your own, you built a business out of helping other people have babies. This is huge! Look how many lives you've impacted! How many babies have you helped come into the world now...a hundred?"

"A hundred and sixteen," I said, "But, Jen...I've done most of that from my playpen. I always used my responsibilities and my mother and my husband and...whatever...as excuses to just stay put. I'm all powerful behind my keyboard, but when it comes to actually going out into the world and *living*...I wimp out every time."

Jennifer's eyes softened and I knew she knew what I meant. She put her hand on my arm and said nothing.

"This is my time, Jennifer. You're always telling me to listen to the Universe, to hear what it's trying to tell me...and maybe I've been selectively deaf for a long time, because I've pointedly ignored the staleness of my marriage for—well, for at least three years, obviously— and now the Universe is booming so loudly at me that I can't ignore it. It's time for me to actually do something, something big. I mean, sure...I could buy a little house in that new subdivision where all the houses look the same.

It would be clean and pretty, and the neighbors would be nice, and I could shop in the same stores and see the same people and breathe the same air...or I could take this booming message and really *go* with it. I could start over." I paused for a moment, deciding how I felt about this as I went along. "I'm thirty-three...I'm not old. Thirty is the new twenty, right?" Jennifer giggled and rolled her eyes. "I'm unencumbered in the way most thirty-three-year-olds are not. I don't have kids, I can work from literally anywhere there's internet, and I've got about fifty thousand dollars in my savings account."

Jennifer's eyes lit up. "Fifty thousand?? Girl, you've been holding out on me!"

"Yeah, well, I don't have fifty yet, but I will when Jason gives me thirty-five for my half of the equity in this house...this *playpen*." I looked around at my comfortable home, full of comfortable stuff, none of which I felt any particular sadness about leaving. Every piece of it was a representation of a life that hadn't really existed.

"So, you'll just pack up and go to *Maine*?" Jennifer asked, still sounding incredulous when she said the name of the state so far away.

"Well, I haven't even contacted the real estate agent yet...and I'm sure there are quite a few steps between here and there—paperwork and loan approvals and...I don't even know it all. I'll figure it out as I go. People do it every day."

"But how will you...get there? Will you hire movers, drive one of those monstrous trucks? These are the kinds of things I think of as hard to do without a...man." Even as she said the word, Jennifer winced, partly because she hated bringing up the reminder that "my man" had gone to be someone else's man, and partly because she hated to admit that anything in life required the help of a man.

"I don't imagine I'll need more than I can take in my car...just my personal stuff—clothes mostly. And Margaret Mary."

At the sound of her name, Margaret Mary came running from whatever dark corner she'd been sleeping in and took up residence on the sofa between us.

There's something about a dog that makes any difficult situation seem more acceptable. When Margaret Mary jumped on the couch, Jennifer and I both instinctively placed a hand on her, as though to soak up her innate confidence that life was good, and everything would turn out for the best. It must have worked, because, with her other hand, Jennifer reached for the bottle of Southern Comfort and, after taking a long drink and then passing the bottle to me, she said, "Show me those pictures again...how does the tide thing work?"

✭ ✭ ✭

Jennifer's Southern-Comfort-infused approval gave me the confidence I needed to click the "contact the realtor" button on the webpage for Simple Island. I wrote something cheery about being interested in seeing it, and how soon could I come up. I resisted any temptation to add a note of urgency due to my soon-to-be ex-husband needing me to vacate my current home so that he could ensconce his previously unmentioned family.

Her answer, which came the next morning, was my first moment of culture shock...she told me that, at the moment, the island was winterized and snowed in, and that I should wait until at least early April, and even then, make "soft" plans in case there was a late snowfall.

Growing up in Texas, I'd never had to consider any area being so affected by winter that you couldn't get there for weeks or months. When we had "snow" the kids got excited to be out of school, and they hurried outside to make snowmen out of the dusting of powder: snowmen that were mostly held together by mud. Of course, I knew that Maine got *real* winter, but this was my first moment of being faced with it.

It was mid-February, and in Dallas, that meant Spring rains were already beginning to make the world soggy. We still had occasional cold days, but Texas was always in a hurry to get back to being hot and humid. All other seasons got to take a turn...but only a short one. Within another email exchange with the real estate agent, Lisa (who I would come to know very well), I learned that, even though I hadn't seen the property yet, I could go ahead and make an offer, sign a contract, get my loan in order...all the things that would have to happen anyway. That way, if I wanted to move forward after being on the island, I could literally sign the closing papers the next day.

The impetuous, intuitive part of me wanted to leap forward, but there was also a reasonable element that weighed in...what if I did all of this, including paying earnest money and paying for inspections, an appraisal...and then I didn't like it after all...was that risky? Lisa said no...we could build a safety net into the contract that said it was all pending my final approval. In that case, the only thing I would lose would be the cost of the inspections, which might be seven hundred dollars.

Lisa told me, though, that with a safety clause like that, there would also need to be what she called a "kick-out clause" for the benefit of the seller. This would be a statement allowing the seller to cancel the whole deal if he got a better offer before I came and gave my final approval.

"How likely is that to happen?" I asked, horrified at the idea of losing the island because the snow prevented me from coming up just yet.

"Not very," Lisa said, reassuringly. "Simple Island has been on the market for two years, and there has only been one other contract on it...that was an elderly couple who realized, when they got here, that climbing the rocks to actually get down from the mainland and up onto the island was too treacherous for them at their age and fitness. Other than that, there's one fellow who came to see it...came several times, actually...and made three different low-ball offers that the sellers rejected."

Making a low-ball offer on a private island with an asking price of a hundred twenty grand had never occurred to me. "So," I conjectured, "Since I'm offering the price they're asking, it's not likely that someone is going to come in the next 6 weeks and offer *more* than they're asking...right?"

"Right. That's highly unlikely."

I told Lisa to go ahead and start the contract process, and as soon as I hung up, I went online and looked up the website for Pillar Loans. Of course, within five minutes of entering my information, my phone rang with a friendly person who was ready to walk me through my home-loan needs.

This flurry of activity, between the contract and the loan process, was cathartic. It was much healthier to be doing something, a whole lot of something, than sitting on the sofa wondering where my life went wrong. Wondering what Jason was doing now and if he thought about me at all. My focus on Simple Island also helped me move relatively smoothly through the divorce process. In Texas, a do-it-yourself divorce, where there are no children involved, and nothing being argued by either party, is unnervingly effortless. My marriage was officially dissolved by the last week of March. It seemed almost insulting that an eleven-year commitment didn't even cost five hundred dollars in paperwork to untie...but there it was.

In my effort to keep myself positively focused, I had begun looking up articles all over the internet using search parameters like "I bought a private island" and "owning a private island" ...I learned a lot from these, but most of them were talking about the kind of vacation property that you would then rent out when you were not staying there, and many people wanted to caution me about unruly or destructive guests. Other articles wanted to tell me how accessibility to a private island can be a real problem; one real estate agent wrote about how he took a couple, by boat, out to an island they had come to see, but the boat trip was 14 hours, and by hour 5, he knew he had lost them.

None of this applied to me. If anything, reading the things these people were discouraging me about made me feel more confident in my decision and my own perfect Simple Island. One writer spent his whole article talking about how buying an island was only for the wealthy, as banks wouldn't loan you money for a private island. "How funny," I thought, "I'm having no problem getting the loan."

...until I did.

Chapter Four

May 5, 1859

My Darling,

Your letter has so deeply touched my heart that I find myself paralyzed by my desire to respond in kind, and I don't know that I will succeed, but my pen upon this paper is my promise to try. Like yourself, I am perpetually overcome with the full astonishment that we have found each other in all the world and that, seemingly without obstacle or opposition, we are hurtling toward the day when we will be man and wife.

You touched for only a moment on something I've contemplated in quiet moments, the idea that your family will become mine. It is a thought that causes more than slight trepidation, but not because I fear they are unpleasant or unwelcoming people. How could they be when they have created and nurtured a man such as you? No, the trepidation is due to my own feelings of inadequacy, and the secret, stalking fear that I will not find myself acceptable to the other people that you love most. I have passed, on the whole, a very quiet life, almost entirely at home. The visit to New York with my brother was the first time I have traveled so far away from home, and I know that to you that must seem pitiable as there is such a very large world and I've seen none of it.

Still, even if later I should travel the wide world, no other city or adventure will equal the visit to New York, as that is where we found each other, my darling, and every other element of my life henceforth will gravitate around that singular lynchpin which is you.

I am pleased to hear you mention your affection for your father's library, as my own father also has a library and I have spent many happy hours curled up reading books that were perhaps not what my governess would have wanted me to read, but alas I have never been one to pay heed to the people who would say what is proper for a young lady and what is not. I hope that this is not shocking or off-putting to you. Certainly I have learned the various arts that are required of a woman, and as your wife I will serve the duties that the world would expect of me, but in between the lessons on meal preparation and embroidery and dancing and penmanship and all the other arts that are considered essential for a woman to learn if not master, I have found myself always drawn to the library, where I can surrender myself to the countryside of Jane Austen, or the dirty city where Charles Dickens can always find the most valuable characters. I have repeatedly traveled to Canterbury with Chaucer and have shed my tears for the star-crossed lovers of Shakespeare. How many books have we shared over the years without knowing that we did so? How many more books will we share after our two separate paths become one?

And so, I close this letter in hopes that you will find it to be a glimpse into my deeper self, the self that you, and only you my darling, will truly come to know. I send you, along with these careful pages, all of my hopes, and all of my love.

Chapter Five

Ultimately, I was glad I spent the whole day looking at other properties, because it helped to really reinforce my determination about Simple Island. There just wasn't anything else that I wanted...and this led me back down the path to my usual state of optimism...my general belief that things have a way of working out for themselves. Maybe Jennifer was right. Maybe the Universe was trying to tell me something, and this little detour of uncertainty was the trick to help me feel that sense of solid footing that I needed.

Whether it was the Universe, or just dumb luck, my phone rang at 4:00 that afternoon, and I recognized the number as Maine Federal. I took a deep breath, prepared for bad news, but expecting something better.

"I've got good news for you!" Linda jumped right in. "It took me a while to get an answer about using your appraisal, but the final answer is yes, since it is so very recent."

"Great," I exhaled the word in a whoosh of relief.

"Everything looks good, we have all that we need, and we are willing to offer you a loan at 6.49% interest for fifteen years."

Suddenly, to me, everything did *not* look so good. The other loan had been 4.75% for thirty years...these new terms meant a much larger payment. Sounding cooler than I felt, I asked Linda to tell me what that monthly payment would be, and she rattled off a number nearly twice what I'd been expecting.

This was a stumbling block, because, while I had hoped to be able to pay the property off much faster than the thirty-year mortgage, I didn't want to be bound to the larger payment...and the larger interest rate. I mean, even without any unforeseen emergencies, sometimes a girl just wants to be able to buy Christmas presents.

But, after this long day, I knew that if this was the only path to Simple Island, I would take it, no question. Things have a way of working out for themselves, right?

I thanked Linda profusely, and she told me to watch my email for some documents that needed to be signed and returned. I think I thanked her profusely again...and then she said goodbye. I immediately sat down to my computer to log in to my email to await Linda's documents, but before I could even input my password, my phone rang again.

"Miss Maybrey? This is Kelly at Pillar Loans."

"Hello, Kelly," I said, feeling quite indifferent about whatever she was about to tell me. I felt positively haughty with the power of the Maine Federal loan in my back pocket. My mood could have been personified with a photo of Maleficent from Disney's cartoon *Sleeping Beauty*.

"Hello again! I've spoken with the Executive Leadership, and they understand that you can walk to the island at low tide, but I guess they are concerned that you can't...drive there?"

"No, no, that's right," I said, in full Maleficent. "You can't drive to an island." Then I thought better of my haughtiness, and I added, "But the title includes deeded access to park on the mainland and cross over. It's about a hundred yards to walk from the parking spot...I walk that far from my carport to my front door every day."

"I understand about being able to walk at low tide...but does that change in the winter?"

I tried not to roll my eyes in any way that Kelly could hear over the phone. "No," I answered, "The ocean tides do not change in the winter. In fact, it's winter now, and the appraisal from last week has pictures that the appraiser took of the path she walked to cross at low tide."

"And you can park your car on the mainland?"

"Yes...the title includes deeded access to park."

Kelly fumbled for a moment as she got a paper and pen, and I could tell she was writing this down. "OK," she said, "I want to make sure I get this wording right...so you have...deeded...access..."

"Kelly," I said, in a soft motherly tone that can't help but be condescending, "I got that verbiage from the appraisal. The appraisal which *you* have. The appraisal you used to reject me for this loan. There's a whole page that is a photocopy of the original quitclaim deed which talks about the island including deeded access to park on the mainland."

Kelly suddenly brightened: "OK! I'll call you back!" and she hung up.

Shrugging my shoulders, I entered my password to find that Linda's Maine Federal loan documents were indeed in my email inbox, and I began saving them to my documents so that I could print them...when my phone rang again.

"Hello, Kelly," I sighed, without letting her greet me this time.

"Hello, Miss Maybrey; everything is good. They are approving your loan!"

I was flabbergasted. "Are you serious??"

"Yes, ma'am! I've got all the paperwork here and we're ready to go. I'm going to connect you back to Megan and she will walk you through the final details."

I was too shocked to say anything more than "goodbye" before I hung up. The computer on my lap dinged with a new email from Lisa, the real estate agent, and she was forwarding me the newest email from Megan telling her that Pillar was ready to move forward with the loan. All she wrote to me to accompany the forwarded message was, "What are you going to do? Personally, I would kick 'em to the curb!"

Oh, how I would have loved to let Maleficent rule the day. "Take your sad little loan and offer it to someone else; someone who hasn't already seen your slimy backbone. Go back to school, you peasant, and learn what an island is and how the tides work and learn to read an entire document before you wield it against your better-prepared adversaries!"

But I couldn't. I needed the thirty-year loan at 4.75% interest. I needed the breathing room in my payment plan. I needed the big corporate loan, and I knew they didn't need me at all. If I stood on principle, they would hang up and never think of me again...and I would think of them every time I made that overly large payment for the next fifteen years.

But, oh my god, Linda at Maine Federal. She was a real person who had spent her entire real day pushing this through for me, and she had succeeded...and I was about to ditch her. I felt rotten about that.

The truth is, when I'm not feeling my Maleficent, I'm a total coward. I couldn't even call Linda to tell her what had happened. I took the chicken path and emailed. But it was a really good email.

"Linda, you're not going to believe this—I hardly believe it myself—but after all they put me through, Pillar came back to me and offered me the loan. I really wanted to tell them what they could do with it, after the day they've caused for me, but in the end...I just need the longer-term loan at the lower interest rate. But I do feel honestly terrible going back to them after how wonderful you have been for me. This has been a painfully difficult day, and I don't know how I would have managed if I hadn't had you holding my hand in the tunnel. I am eternally grateful for you. Trista."

I followed it up by going to the FTD website and ordering a fruit and cheese basket to be delivered to her office the following Tuesday. Linda never responded to my email or the gift...I can't say that I blame her. I would have been really pissed at me too.

About the time I clicked "confirm" on the FTD gift basket, my phone rang again, and Megan was there to round out my day. She began with pleasantries and congratulations as though nothing had happened out of the ordinary. Nothing at all. Just another sunshiny day in the land of King Mortgage.

I played along, until I realized she was telling me the closing would now have to be on Tuesday rather than Monday. I stopped her.

"Wait a minute...I'm flying Saturday, visiting the island Sunday, signing on Monday...flying home on Tuesday! Early morning! I can't do closing on Tuesday; I won't be there!"

There was no Maleficent in there. Now I was a teenage girl whining to her Mom about why she can't have the car to go to the party. I knew, it, but I couldn't help it.

"Unfortunately, Miss Maybrey, the closing rule is that there has to be three business days between the final documentation and the closing. Today is already over, so tomorrow is Friday, then Saturday, then Monday, so we can't close until Tuesday. There's no way around that."

"But...but..." I stammered, in full teenage girl mode, "But...you did this to me! If you guys hadn't stumbled over what to do about an island, this day wouldn't be lost, and I could close on Monday...but now, what, I'll have to extend my trip? Take off more work time? Pay the change fee for my flight?"

"No, no," she reassured me, "You could have a mail-away closing. The title company can send you the documents and you can sign them and send them back. It's done all the time."

I don't know why it bothered me so much, but it did. The idea of doing this enormous thing in my life...and not even getting to be there in person for the final closing. I wanted a moment to document, to celebrate...and this new path was going to mean wondering if the title company had received my package yet, and if it was sitting in someone's inbox, unopened until tomorrow or the next day...do I call them, or will they call me? There was nothing I could celebrate in that.

But what could I do? If this was the rule, then Linda wouldn't have been able to let me close on Monday either...we just hadn't gotten that far in the discussion. It was what it was, and I allowed myself a big sigh of closure.

But Lisa, ever my champion, was already working things out. While I was whining to Megan, she had been talking with the title company and they had agreed to have someone meet me in New Hampshire on Tuesday morning before my flight out of Boston. I just had to change my hotel reservations for Monday night, and I *would* get to be there for my closing.

Things have a way of working themselves out.

Friday was a day of packing, between answering calls and emails for work. I realized that I was packing like an actress preparing for a part. Does this jacket say, "I totally know what I'm doing in New England"? Should I smear a little mud on these boots, so they don't look brand new? What color eye shadow goes with "my private island"?

The answer, of course, was to pack it all...pack for cold weather, pack for warm weather, pack enough pajamas and underwear for a week-long vacation, and hope that's enough for three nights in two different hotels. Will I need a blow dryer? Bring it! Will I need an extra phone charger? Possibly. Will there be snacks on the plane? Better bring a bag big enough for a first-grade class birthday party. Bring it all.

I was giddy, and overdoing everything, and didn't even care...and then Jennifer called, which made me even giddier.

Now that it was over, I was able to tell Jennifer the harrowing story of Thursday's mortgage hiccup, and it sounded so much more comical now that I was telling it from my Place of Safety. I told it with gusto, happily defining myself as the hero in my own story. I singlehandedly took down the mighty Pillar Loans with my indefatigable expertise in the tidal patterns of Downeast Maine!

Jennifer listened, laughed at all the right places, but when I was finished, she said, "But, why Maine?"

I didn't understand the question. "Maine is where the island is..." I answered.

"Right, but I mean...when you thought you were going to lose the island, why did you spend a whole day looking at other properties in Maine? It's a big world, and as you said, you can go anywhere. I'm just wondering why you didn't look at properties in Seattle, in California, in Nebraska...Ireland."

"I...I guess I don't know. I felt like I wanted to be in Maine. I honestly didn't even think about looking elsewhere." This had not occurred to me.

"You know what I think," Jennifer said, and I could *hear* the twinkle in her eye, "I think something's calling you."

"Calling me?"

"Calling you home," she said.

I have spent a lifetime growing accustomed to Jennifer's quirkiness, her perpetual state of being "tuned in" to the cosmos. On the one hand, I deeply appreciate it; she has a way of making me feel like there's truly a ribbon of purpose snaking through my life and tying everything together. On the other hand, I've learned to pat her on the head and disregard it.

"I don't have a home in Maine," I said, choosing the patting-her-on-the-head method this time. "Not until Tuesday morning, at least!"

✳ ✳ ✳

The flight from Dallas to Boston had me seated in the middle between an elderly man who had the aisle seat, and a young college-aged fellow who sat by the window. I don't mind the middle seat so much; I had my laptop and headphones. I was prepared to tune out the world for four hours no matter which seat I was awarded. Both of the men took the obligatory moment to be friendly, to ask if I was leaving home or going home, and it was interesting to explain that I fell into both categories.

I worked for a little while, but my mind wasn't on it. When the flight attendant came around with drinks and snacks, I put my laptop away to make room for the cup of seltzer and Barbie-doll sized bag of pretzels she brought me. Even such a small number of pretzels was more salt than could be assuaged by the four ounces of seltzer...but of course they don't offer more.

I decided to listen to some music while I waited for the ice to melt, so I leaned my seat back the extra three inches allowable, put on my headphones, and closed my eyes. Elton's *Yellow Brick Road* album can always take me away from any circumstances where I may find myself, and this time was no different. When I was a teenager, I had the album on the big 2-record gatefold LP with the lyrics and pictures in the middle, and I would do my afternoon homework day after day to the sounds of "*Sweet Painted Lady*," which I knew was a naughty song about prostitution, and that made it all the more a favorite, knowing how shocked my mother would be if she ever listened to the lyrics.

Without even an intro note, Elton began, "I'm back on...dry land once again..." and I closed my eyes to let it wash me away.

I didn't even realize I had fallen asleep until I was startled awake by the most vivid dream. I dreamt I was falling, falling, and then landed in ice cold water. I could hear a man shouting something at me, but I couldn't understand him over the noise of the water. The dream must've spanned less than a full second of real time, and I jumped awake in my middle seat...to discover that the elderly gentleman on the aisle had tried to get up and had bumped my tray, toppling my partially melted ice into my lap.

Thus, the dream, I supposed.

I immediately began apologizing to him, for falling asleep, for leaving my tray in his way, for leaving my cup of ice on the tray. How thoughtless of me to leave my lap right where it could get spilled on. The cup had originally come accompanied with a tiny napkin, and I used this to pretend to mop the ice water off of my jeans. The man finally left his seat, wearied no doubt by my pleas for forgiveness, and headed toward the bathroom in the back. I settled back in with Elton but found myself preoccupied by the brilliance of the fragment of a dream, the icy water, the unintelligible voice over the din.

I finally gave up trying to sleep again, and instead pulled up a simple crossword puzzle app on my phone. Anything to pass the time.

The young man next to the window was asleep. Really asleep. The kind of sleep that includes drool. I couldn't help watching him for a second, maybe a little jealous. I could never sleep that soundly unless I was in my bed. As I turned away to refocus on my crossword, he startled in his sleep like a baby, arms and legs jerking outward in a single, sudden movement...spilling his own glass of melting ice on the other side of my lap. Immediately, he was awake, and matching my apologies with his own. Without thinking, he tried to wipe the water off my leg with his own scrap of napkin, but then realized the awkwardness of that gesture, and let me handle it myself.

That was my breaking point. I burst into laughter, laughing uncontrollably until I could hardly breathe. I gasped and laughed, and snorted, and laughed, tears streaming down my face. I couldn't stop. The elderly gentleman returned to his seat and stood over me for a moment, looking from me to the young man and back again. I tried to indicate by waving my hand and shaking my head that everything was OK, but I'm not sure I got the message across. I had quickly become the unstable woman no one wanted to sit beside. I fought to regain my dignity, taking long, cleansing breaths until the laughter subsided, and then dabbing my eyes on my sleeves. I finally let out one long loud sigh, "Whoooooo!" and ducked back into my headphones, where Elton was waiting to sing me the *Ballad of Danny Bailey*. Apparently, some punk with a shotgun killed him.

Anyone who knew me understood why I chose to fly into Boston and drive all the way up to Maine rather than just flying into Bangor or Bar Harbor. Within five miles of the Logan airport, along the main street in Cambridge, is the world's greatest vegan restaurant. By the time I got there, the large wet spot on my jeans had almost completely dried, and it was just lovely to come out of the cold night into the welcoming warmth of the crowded place. I ordered my favorite: chicken and waffles...fried chicken made from something plant based but tasting like childhood comfort food. There are a couple of vegan restaurants in Dallas, but nothing like this.

I also ordered a milkshake and a dessert to take with me. It was going to be a long drive.

More than four hours later, I passed the sign that said "Welcome to Maine" ...it was nearly two A.M. by then, and my eyes were starting to cross a little. Less than an hour later, I pulled into the snowy parking lot of the little inn where I had reserved a room for the night...the night which was already well into morning.

My room key was waiting in an envelope with my name on it, left on the desk by the owners who had been warned I would be "late." I dragged my suitcase up the rustic wood stairs, and found my room, one of only eight guest rooms at the inn. Tempted to just fall into bed in my clothes, I thought better of it and put on my pajamas. When I was in my twenties, I mostly just slept in junk— baggy shorts and a tank top. But as I've gotten older, and sleep has become more like high priced real estate I'm eternally trying to make payments on, I've become very particular about sleeping attire: loose, cool pajamas, preferably matching. How can I tell, in my sleep, if my pajamas match? I don't know, but apparently, I can.

I was awake by nine but forced myself to stay in bed with my eyes shut until ten. My bladder knocked softly, at first, on the door of my consciousness, but ultimately it began screaming to be acknowledged, so I dragged myself up. As I was pulling on my jeans, which were now completely dry (next time, maybe I can get someone to spill just a touch of fabric softener with their ice water), I pulled open the curtain of my little room, and then gasped.

I had not been prepared for the view. It was so late when I pulled into the parking lot, and so dark and cold, I hadn't realized that this inn was sitting right on the water, and I was looking across at several little islands. None were *my* island, of course, as that was still about 20 miles away, but even so, this was an exciting moment for me.

I'd read that there are more than four thousand islands off the coast of Maine alone. Some, like mine, are just big enough for one little cabin. Others are lively communities of people who owned homes there. Others were too small to be inhabited, or even to be properly named, simply referred to by a code number in the Maine Island Registry.

The innkeepers were waiting for me downstairs. They had kept breakfast overly long for me, because they hadn't realized how very late I had gotten in. I apologized for their extra trouble, and just grabbed a banana on my way out the door.

Now that I was awake, I was anxious to explore. I wasn't supposed to meet Lisa until 5:00, because low tide was at 6:45, and at 5, it should be low enough to cross...but I wanted to go out by myself and see it first. I wanted time alone to look across at the island that was going to be my home.

Chapter Six

May 23, 1859

My Dearest,

I have taken great joy in your last letter, finding all the while more and more parts of yourself which will meld comfortably with the various parts of me. Rather than being shocked or off-put by your proclivity and taste for literature, I am instead eager for long hours of discussion upon various points of interest and character traits we would incorporate from our favorite fictional people. I often attempt to think of my own life as a book in which I am both the author and the principle player; I'd like to turn back to certain pages and experience them afresh, as though for the first time. Unfortunately, the human mind does not work in the same way, and though I may turn back to a savory moment in my story, I can only experience it in hindsight, no matter how I might try to see it newly again. The beautiful moment when Lucie Manette finds her father alive and holds him, comforting him with the words, "Weep for it, weep for it," – this moment is new and painful and beautiful every time, for no matter how often the reader has chosen A Tale of Two Cities from the shelf, the experience is eternally fresh for Lucy, and therefore the reader can have that new moment over and over by sharing it with her.

Would that I could turn the pages back to that night in New York when I first beheld you across the room, My Dearest. To have again, just for returning to that chapter, the feeling of catching your eye for the first time, the blush on your cheek, the glow of the candlelight flickering on the walls as I made my way through the crowd to your side. The soft lilt of your laughter, the touch of your hand upon my arm, The way the lace of your gown brushed against your elegant throat as you bowed your head in greeting. These are the paragraphs etched into the pages of my autobiography, and yet I know, with the full sadness of maturity, that even now they are fading into a comfortable collection of happenings that I can never fully recapture no matter how devotedly I re-read this novel.

I fear the only solution is to commit my life to the creation of countless more words and pictures and to strive always to drink them in fully in the first moment of their happening. This is my promise to you, My Dearest, that I will be ever creating the memories that bind together our stories.

Upon the other side of this topic, I suppose that, even if I am not shocked that you have "traveled to Canterbury with Chaucer," I can understand why you would not wish for your governess or your parents to know that you have undertaken that particular journey. I think that Geoffrey Chaucer is an excellent test of someone who likes to claim to be well-read. If a man says he has read Chaucer, and he says it without that peculiar glint in his eye which truly belies an understanding of the spicy content within those pages, then I believe he is simply attempting to blend in with others he feels are well-read.

I do not feel that we know each other well enough yet to openly discuss the scandalous tales of Chaucer, but I do believe that marriage will afford us that level of familiarity. I promise you that this is a discussion that we will hold, and I will hear again the lilt of your beautiful laughter, a sound which I expect to recall with warmth and love even at the very end of my life.

In the interest of sharing literary proclivities which might tend to shock the senses, I will relay to you that, of late, I have been indulging myself heavily in the works of Thomas Paine. While I believe that Common Sense is one of the most impactful uses of the written word in all of human history, it is The Age of Reason that I have been most enamored with of late.

Does this shock or repel you, My Dearest? Please say no, as this is a subject I would most like to share and explore with you as our two lives become one.

Chapter Seven

There was a time in my life when I would have been overwhelmingly afraid to just start my car and drive somewhere new. I spent many years perfecting my excuse-mechanism so that people wouldn't find out right away, but I have an extreme fear of being lost. Back before it was common to have a GPS in my car—and then, more simply, on my phone—if I was just driving by directions someone had given me or, god forbid, with a paper map, I would often have to just pull off onto the shoulder somewhere and cry. Literally, I would shed tears in order to help the panic subside if I had missed an exit or taken a wrong turn, or if the traffic was just really heavy and I was terrified I'd miss a road sign I needed.

I realize that this is an unreasonable fear but paying lip service to its unreasonableness doesn't make it any less real.

They say that the earliest dreams we can remember are not remembered because they are in some way indicative of how far back our memory goes, but instead they are the dreams we remember because they are most indicative of who we are as individuals.

All of my earliest dreams are nightmares of being lost, separated from my mother, terrified and sobbing. The one time in reality that I remember being lost from my mother was in a grocery store. I was about three, I guess. I stopped to look at something and when I turned to follow her again, she was gone. I realize now that she had just turned the corner to the next aisle, but at the time, I was so immediately ripped with panic that I couldn't see straight. I ran in abject terror, screaming for her. Other patrons tried to stop me, to help me, but I tore away from them in my desperate, sobbing, hyperventilating quest to find her. When I did finally find her, she was, of course, looking for me as well, and she tried to soothe me with the promise that she would never just leave me behind; she would always find me...but that was little comfort.

As I got older, my greatest anxiety was school field trips. Getting on a bus with a hundred other kids, knowing that there was not a soul among them who would go out of their way to make sure I was with the group. How easy it would be to be left behind, or to get out to the parking lot and see twenty field trip school buses lined up and maybe not remember which one was the right one for me. What if I got on the wrong bus and didn't discover it until the right bus was already gone? The only way to ensure my safety was to stay so close and so attentive to every movement of every one of my classmates that there was absolutely no way to enjoy whatever it was the field trip was to offer us.

In high school, I earned my learner's permit, and then my driver's license, along with my classmates, but I rarely drove myself anywhere. The entire city of Dallas seems to be an afterthought...in 1841, the city founders ostensibly had no idea people would actually want to live there, and in the century and a half since then, Dallas has been attempting to accommodate with a tangled sprawl of overpasses and cloverleafs, ever widening, ever expanding, ever adding more toll stops. Unless I was driving from my house to the store three blocks away, I wanted nothing to do with trying to find my way around Dallas. If a friend was having a party and I had no one to drive me there, I would have a solid, unimpeachable excuse why I couldn't attend. I missed a Huey Lewis concert because my ride fell through. I had a car, but I wasn't going to drive it. I'm sure Huey would have understood.

Looking back, this was all probably a great relief to my mother. When my friends were getting in trouble in the first part of the new century, I was at home with her. We played a lot of Scrabble. I play Scrabble to the death.

When Jason and I married, he easily stepped into the role of designated driver. He came to understand my anxiety, but it really was just the natural order for him to drive. I had my own car, always sitting in the driveway, but because I worked from home, it was rarely on the road. Even with GPS readily available these days, I had carefully built a life where I didn't need to go anywhere. If I'm always at home, I can never be lost.

Which is ironic, when I think about how completely lost I was at home, I simply didn't recognize it.

But on that first day in Maine, I didn't feel the anxiety. It was a small town: no exit numbers to watch for, no right lanes that became turn-only nightmares, no obsessively checking in with Siri to make sure I hadn't missed my landmark.

I knew how to tell my GPS to take me to Parson Point. Thanks to Google Maps, I had a thorough grasp of what I was looking for, at least from an aerial satellite perspective. Simple Island was shaped like a long triangle, with the top tip pointing to the end of Parson Point, which was someone's private property. Whoever these people were, they had a circular drive that was heavily covered with blue-gray gravel, and this stood out in the satellite picture. It looked like a blue stream that wound out of the woods, then curled back in on itself. The rest of Parson Point, however, was a dirt road that simply didn't show up on the satellite. It was this dirt road, and its possible conditions during the snowy season, that had held up my trip for six weeks.

In those six weeks, when I had tried to look up Simple Island on any map, I could always find it by first finding a much larger neighboring island called Pinkley. Pinkley Island was about a hundred times the size of Simple Island. A little research had taught me that Pinkley was privately owned, but it appeared to be undeveloped. I could always find it on a map of Black Bay, though, because it was shaped like the little transmission symbol for a standard "check engine" light on the dashboard of every car I'd ever known. I'd seen lots of maps in the past six weeks that were too small to show Simple Island, but I could always find Pinkley's check-engine light, and then point to the general spot northeast of Pinkley where Simple would be.

I told my GPS to take me to Parson Point, but as I drove through the little town of Milton, I began realizing how very long ago was my last meal, and how small that banana had been. I decided a quick stop at a local diner might be the perfect combination of sustenance and culture.

Of course, I didn't expect this little town to have a vegan restaurant, or even a restaurant that specifically offered vegan items, but I never want to be that one in any gathering who makes the meal or outing difficult for anyone else because of my own preferences, so I have become quite adept at finding food anywhere I go. Most places either have things that just happen to not include any animal products, or they have items that I can easily alter. "No cheese" is a phrase I say quite often.

This little diner was charming. Cozy and friendly. I was shown to a booth and offered a menu where I had no difficulty finding what I wanted. *Julienne Rosemary Fries with Blueberry Sauce.* I'd never seen anything like this at a diner in Dallas. When the waitress brought me my order, it was an enormous pile of very tiny, crispy, flavorful fries...and a big bowl of what seemed like the kind of blueberry sauce you might put on pancakes. An odd pairing, and yet it was fantastic, and I tried not to groan audibly with the first few bites.

I checked my email while I sat there. Jennifer had written just to wish me well on what she knew was an important day. Mom emailed to ask if I made it safely to Maine, and to let me know that Margaret Mary missed me, but she was doing fine. Several clients had questions that could probably wait until Monday, but I answered anyway. It's always good to look busy when you're sitting alone in a restaurant; that way, the people around you think that eating alone was a choice, so that you could have the space to get some work done. That's better than having anyone look at you with pity and wonder how much longer your husband's other life would have gone unnoticed if he hadn't finally told you. I felt like people were wondering that about me a lot.

On the main roads I had noticed the occasional pile of muddy snow that had been swept to the side by the traffic, but when I left the diner and headed at last down the long road of Parson Point, I began to more fully understand Lisa's encouraged delay. The further I got out of town, the more snow still lay on the roads themselves, and as the asphalt sighed softly and became a dirt road, the impassibility became a real issue, even on April first. Perhaps I hadn't waited long enough.

I bumped along carefully for what seemed like twenty miles but was in actuality only five. Suddenly, the road ended and a padlocked chain between two boulders blocked my going any further. The glaring orange "No Trespassing" signs would have been discouraging, had I not also seen the blue-gray gravel circular drive that I knew was the path to Simple Island.

I pulled over as far as I could between the road and the fir trees which lined it heavily on both sides. I took a moment to change from my every-day sneakers into my knee-high red rubber boots. That felt official.

From my parking spot, I could see the big house on the point, and I could see a heavy tree line, but I couldn't yet see far enough to behold my island. Feeling the confidence of my new boots, I stepped gingerly over the chain and crunched my way down the gravelly path toward the very point of the Point.

And there it was. In the overcast haze of the Maine morning, the island looked like it was a superimposed painting. Like everything I was seeing between the trees on this Parson Point property was projected on a greenscreen backdrop; beautiful, but unreal. I was Dorothy looking at the Emerald City for the first time. Scarlett looking at Tara. There was the island I had seen a million times in pictures, only this time, the trees were blowing in the wind, and the water was lapping noisily against the rocky shore.

This was clearly the perspective from which all of the photographs of the island had been taken. It was perfectly framed between the fir trees on the Point. I'd not seen the whole island from any other angle other than the satellite view on Google Maps. But something none of the maps or photographs I'd seen could show me was...how do I get down to the shore in order to cross? In fact, Lisa's real estate listing offered directions that said, "Drive to the end of Parson Point, park your car and just walk over!"

Except...there was at least a twelve-foot drop from where I stood, down to the rocky shore. At the moment, the tide was still too high to walk over, but in a few hours when it was low, how would I get down there? How does anyone get down there?

I began exploring all up and down the edge of Parson Point, discovering that there were several places where the drop was not as dramatic. Four feet. Three feet maybe. But even where there was a three-foot drop, I could confidently get down... how would I get back up? And everything was muddy or snowy. I felt so discouraged. Just crushed. I had this picture of myself in my new red boots, confidently striding across the ocean floor like Moses fleeing the Egyptian army, fully secure in my own ability to take possession of and live on a private island.

I couldn't do any of that. I couldn't even get down to the shore.

I remembered what Lisa had told me about the elderly couple who had taken a contract on Simple Island but had backed out at the last minute because getting to it from the mainland was too difficult for them. What if Lisa had been doing that thing real estate agents do where they downplay major issues and couch them in language that sounds more acceptable but isn't actually a lie? Like calling a home "quaint" instead of "mildly dilapidated." Using the word "cozy" instead of "impossibly small."

Suddenly, I felt absolutely deflated. I stood there, looking at my island on greenscreen, and I was the total fool. I'd focused every milligram of my survival instinct on this tiny piece of the world, and now I couldn't even find my way over there. I'd come more than 1900 miles, but I couldn't manage the last 100 yards.

I huddled in my jacket, feeling the cold for the first time. My weather app told me it was 47 degrees in Milton today, but the temperature in my world just dropped below freezing. What a fool I was. What had I been thinking?

In a humiliated daze, I drove bleakly back to the inn, made my way up the stairs and flopped onto my bed. I set an alarm to wake me in a couple of hours and allowed sleep to numb the disappointment and anxiety.

I dreamed I was standing there again, at the end of Parson Point, looking out at Simple Island, only this time, Margaret Mary was with me, running up and down excitedly, barking at gulls or squirrels, or something. I watched her, just a little white puff ball, running further and further into the woods of heavy firs which had replaced the big house that stood there in reality. Then I realized I couldn't see or hear her anymore, and this made me feel panicked. I began running toward the last place I had seen her, calling her name over and over, and suddenly, I was in the trees, and they were so thick it was pitch dark. I kept calling her name, but now there was smoke, heavy smoke, and I was choking. I heard a man's voice calling, "Em! Em! We are lost!" and then the woods exploded into fire and the explosion threw me high into the air and I was falling, falling toward the cold, cold sea below, and I could see Simple Island as I was falling, but there was no way to get there. I was going to hit the water.

And I jerked awake, my heart racing, shivering cold even though I was warm under the covers of my bed in my room. Margaret Mary was safe with my mother, and Lisa was going to meet me in an hour to show me how to cross over to my island.

Chapter Eight

May 30, 1859

My Darling,

Rather than shocking or repelling me, your mention of the works of Thomas Paine quickens my pulse. Again, this is a topic upon which my governess or my parents would be notably non-plussed, and yet I find myself not surprised that you are intrigued by what Mr. Paine writes with such passion and conviction.

I am certain that, like myself, you have been born into and groomed for a life of traditional religious conviction, a casual relationship with a distant deity, and one who seems quite fickle in his affections and his decisions. I fear I was quite a naughty child, asking questions my mother insisted I should not have been asking, but I asked them because I truly sought an answer. Why did this God bless my family with so much when I could see other children in the marketplace who had so little?

As I grew older and became aware of the horrors of slavery in the world, I could not reconcile in my mind a God who created all people, but openly favored those of a particular faith and a particular color of skin. To me, this seemed as logical as if my parents, with three children, had chosen to love my sister the most, with her round cheeks and her bouncing curls, and my brother and I had been relegated to carrying her luggage, and sleeping on her floor, and licking the crumbs from her plate after dinner each night. Human parents who behaved thusly would be considered monstrous, and so they would be. What all-powerful God would treat his children in this manner?

But I was not to ask those questions. It was my brother who gifted me a copy of The Age of Reason, and he did so by exacting the same promise of silence that he required upon leading me to Canterbury Tales. I fear that, by some standards, my brother has been the most unwholesome influence upon my education, but also the most broadening. Within the first chapter of Mister Paine's book, I knew that I had found the answers to the questions I'd been forbidden to ask, at least I had found the beginning of the answers. I also believe that I had never laughed quite so heartily at any written words as I did for Paine. His early description of "Saul prophesying badly" still evokes the kind of laughter no one would consider ladylike. Your repeated reference to "the lilt of my laughter" would be a memory shattered were you able to go back to the first night I held that book in my hands and laughed aloud until I thought I might choke, and my sister—my very good, very devout sister—banished me from the room where she was trying to sleep.

Perhaps this is why parents keep their betrothed children apart until the day of the wedding, so that they do not come to know each other so well that they decide not to marry at all.

Perhaps, one day, you too will banish me from the room for my laughter which prevents your sleeping.

I welcome a time where we share a level of intimacy where my laughter disturbs your rest...or perhaps you will simply laugh with me.

Chapter Nine

As I picked my way back down through the roots and ruts of the dirt road at Parson Point, I realized I was being followed, bump for bump, by a red Jeep Cherokee. Moving further and further into land where no one else would be going, I realized this must be Lisa, right on time.

I pulled off and parked in the same spot as before and got out of my rental. Lisa greeted me warmly, and introduced her husband who had joined her because, he said, he had never seen one of these islands so close to land that you could walk at low tide.

Lisa and her husband had brought their boots, but weren't yet wearing them, and I felt a nagging impatience as they leaned against the back of the Jeep to change into them. On the drive over, I had reminded myself that, in the past couple of weeks, two inspectors (building and septic), and one appraiser had crossed over to Simple Island from the mainland, and none of them had mentioned particular difficulty. Since they were not working for the real estate agency, and in no way invested in my purchasing the property, there must be a reasonable way to cross, or they would have said something.

Appropriately shod at last, Lisa began leading us to the tiny storage shed across the driveway from the main house on the Point. Ducking under the low limbs of a large fir behind the shed, she indicated an overgrown, but obvious, trail snaking into the forest. We followed Lisa down the trail, and it began to widen, showing the obvious signs that someone, years ago, had carefully marked the path by lining it with birch logs, most of which were still in place.

Many parts of the trail required ducking under low branches or, in one spot, a partially fallen tree. Lisa's husband commented that before long, I would be stepping over that tree rather than ducking under it. Shortly thereafter, the trail curved toward the sea, and in a moment, we were standing at the place where we would cross.

This was much farther down the shore than I had come before, and now I could see that there was a natural progression of rocks that served as steps from the upper shore down to the lower one.

"Well, this is convenient," I commented as I stepped down, sounding as though I had, all along, assumed there would be something like this to allow passage.

"It really is," Lisa said as we stepped down onto the lower shore. "There used to be a long set of stairs there at the very center of the point, because the island used to belong to this property...but years ago the owner sold the island as a separate property and the new owners at the Point tore down the stairs."

"Do you know the people who live in that house now?" I asked.

Lisa laughed and said, "Not really, and I don't want to. I've been warned repeatedly by neighbors who saw me coming and going out here that the Beardens are not exactly congenial."

"Uh oh..." I said, skeptical.

"Oh, you don't have to worry about them...They're only here for the odd vacation weekend. Just keep to yourself, park all the way off the road, and cross their property as close to the left side as possible. They're both lawyers, and they love making legal threats, but it's all bluster. Someone told me they just think they're better than everyone else because they own this property at the end of the point."

"That's funny," I said, wryly. "I thought I would be better than everyone else because I'll own the island."

Lisa's husband guffawed and clapped me on the back. I wasn't sure if he agreed with me or just liked my attitude.

"Now here's the tricky part about crossing," Lisa continued. "We need to walk across this grass and then down that long grassy point. All of this is underwater during high tide, but at low tide you can clearly see where we have to go."

I followed her down the long grassy point she had indicated, stepping over crunchy wads of seaweed that had washed up during high tide and dried in the sun. Tiny dead crabs and piles of clam shells were tangled here and there in the seaweed.

When we reached what I thought was the end of the point, Lisa was still going. She anticipated my question.

"You really have to come all the way out to where the very last little clump of grass is growing. When we cross down here, you'll hardly get your boots muddy...but if you turn any sooner, it's really squishy ground and it's easy to get bogged down."

Her husband and I followed her to the very last sprig of grass, then she turned sharply to the right and headed for the island. As I followed her, I could hardly watch my footing as I was just so excited to see Simple Island looming larger with every step. It was about the length of a football field that we crossed before we began mounting the grassy slope up the east side of the island.

I did my best to hide the wave of emotion that ploughed into my chest when I first put my foot onto the island soil. This was it. This was home. This was my moment to actually be here after weeks of studying it, memorizing every angle of every picture that I could find. This was real.

Lisa was, of course, an old hand at this traversal, so she didn't pause to savor the moment...and I didn't want her husband to bump into me, so I kept walking. But I was surprised by the tears that forced their way into my eyes, and I batted them away quickly. This had been such a long, emotional journey for me, and being here in person was a moment that wanted to be accentuated. My new life beginning.

The grassy slope gave way to a series of big rocks to step across. I was thankful for my new red boots, which were turning out to be as utilitarian as they were fashionable. I wondered about the older couple who had passed on Simple Island at this point. What kind of shoes had they been wearing?

The series of rocks gave way to the soil of the island, soft from centuries of pine straw and mulch that gathered under the thick trees. We were now on another well-used trail, headed up to the center of the island. On either side of the trail there was evidence of the snow, though not much had made it down through the tree cover. Seashells, bleached by the sun, showed a history of gulls bringing their treasures to the island to feast.

And then I saw the roof of the cabin, and each step brought more of it into view. I'm not even sure what Lisa was saying to me at that moment, but I interrupted her. "Oh! There's my house!" I exclaimed, and this time I didn't even try to keep the emotion out of my voice.

As we approached the cabin, I became aware of the care that had been taken in the photographs I'd seen. None of them had been wide enough to show all the *junk* that was lying around. Buckets and barrels of all colors and sizes, various plastic tarps that had, probably at one point, been for keeping piles of firewood dry. A scatter of cinderblocks indicated where a firepit had been. Everywhere were abandoned foam buoys, the kind fishermen attach to lobster traps so they can remember where they are. The idyllic dream of Simple Island was somewhat marred by all the garbage, and yet the practical side of me was able to acknowledge that it could all be cleared away. And would be.

As I looked around carefully, making mental note of the work that needed to be done out there, Lisa was fumbling with the lock box on the front door. I stood at the bottom of the steps until she had the door open and welcomed me inside.

"Here it is!" she announced, and I passed her at the threshold to step, for the first time, into my cabin. I almost laughed out loud. Everything conveys, indeed! It was exactly as it had been in every photo I had seen. Every piece of furniture, every dish on the shelf, even an old raincoat hanging by the door. I laughed again when I spotted the little bottle of Crest mouthwash on the bathroom floor.

Lisa and her husband were chatting, and I was free to roam—not that there was far to roam. It was only 640 square feet, but it was perfect. It wasn't perfect as it was, of course—it had that personality disorder I mentioned— but it was perfect for *me*. I took a moment to walk to each window and look out, seeing the view of the water from every angle, easily imagining myself cozy in this cabin with Margaret Mary and a good book.

When I looked out the sliding glass doors that led to the little deck, I had a sudden thought that hadn't occurred to me before.

"This isn't the original house, is it?" I asked, interrupting Lisa's chatter.

She looked confused for a moment, then realized what I was asking. "No...no it isn't," she said. "This cabin was built in '96, but there was a little house here, oh, way back. Like in the early twentieth century. If you go out there and look close to the shore, you can see the remnants of their fireplace. That's all that's left. The state doesn't allow you to build that close to the water anymore, but the original house was just almost right on the rocks. I don't even think it was as big as this house."

Before she finished her sentence, I was already out the door and down the deck stairs. I knew exactly where I would find the crumble of bricks that had been the original house. Before I could even see it, I was sweeping away the pine straw where I knew it would be...and there it was. A flat layer of bricks about six square feet, and a few remaining random bricks that would have made the first and second rows of the rising chimney.

Again, that wave of emotion crashed against my ribcage, and I caught my breath. Somehow, this made Simple Island so much more valuable to me, this connection to the past, to the people who had lived here. Real people with real lives and hopes and dreams and sorrows just like mine. I squatted there, with my hand on the exposed bricks, just feeling my feeling.

Lisa stood over me. "It wouldn't be that big of a deal to have that removed," she was saying. "It's probably several layers deep, but if you got some grunt-work guys out here, they could dig it up and fill it in."

"I bet Troy out at Vincent Lumber could help," her husband chimed in. "Troy seems to be connected to everyone."

Lisa agreed enthusiastically; I realized she was still trying to anticipate any element of this property that might turn me off to the sale. "No," I said, without looking up. "I love the history. I'm glad it's here."

I appreciated that Lisa didn't try to tell me that she had another buyer interested in the place. I've heard that ruse so many times, and I never believe it. It just makes me disrespect the agent. Makes me wonder what other lies they've told me. Lisa already felt like an old friend; we'd been through a lot together since that first email exchange. She didn't even ask me if I was going to go through with the purchase. She could tell.

★ ★ ★

My original plan, before the unfortunate intervention of Pillar's Executive Leadership, had been to sign the papers on Monday and then spend my first night on the island that night before heading to the airport Tuesday morning. I wanted quiet time to bond with my new home, to start making it mine by rearranging furniture and taking measurements, making plans. But now, I knew Lisa couldn't let me do that; no matter how close we were to making it official...it wasn't official, and she couldn't let me be alone in the cabin until after the closing...which meant not until my final trip to Maine when I would be moving in. But I decided to take a chance on something else.

"Lisa," I began, looking up from where I was squatting by the remains of the old fireplace, "I know I can't take possession of the cabin before the closing, but do you think I could have a little time to myself today just to walk the perimeter of the island, kind of get to know it a little on my own?"

Lisa looked at her watch, no doubt thinking about the tide. She scowled as she did the mental calculation, then smiled at me. "That's fine," she said, "It's not even low tide yet; that's at 6:45. You should have at least an hour and a half after that too. If you're ready, I can go ahead and lock everything up. Do you want to look around the house one more time?"

"No. I feel like I could walk that cabin blindfolded." I stood up, smiling, and brushed the debris off my hands. "But thank you. I'll enjoy quiet time just to scramble over the rocks a bit."

Lisa walked back up the deck and locked the sliding doors from the inside. I walked around the cabin to meet her on the front steps as she was returning the key to the lockbox.

"I don't suppose I'll get a key at the closing..." I mused.

"No," Lisa said, "but as soon as it's officially yours, I'll give you the code for the lock box, so when you come back for good you can get the key out of there. Just drop off the box to me whenever you're in Elmore. Everyone comes to Elmore sooner or later...that's where Walmart is!"

I laughed at her joke, knowing it was probably only funny because it was true, and I followed Lisa and her husband back toward the northern tip of the island where they would cross back over. I waved goodbye but stood there watching carefully as they walked across the dry ocean bed to the tip of the long grassy point, then followed their progress up the path back to the place where they climbed the rocks and disappeared onto the forest trail. I took a mental photo of the spot where they disappeared so I would be sure to find it again when I went back alone.

Alone. I realized that's what I was. I was well and truly alone now. This moment seemed like a metaphor for my whole life. Sure, I had people who loved me, who would always be there, but ultimately, it was all me. I could see it like the cover of a knock-off Nancy Drew novel: *Trista Maybrey and the Mysterious Island*.

I took a moment to reach inside and see if I felt any of the old familiar fear. But no. I think by that time I had come to realize that it had *always* been all me. My parents and my friends, and then Jason, had been more of a crutch than a necessary support...I had done so much on my own, but I'd always believed I was helpless alone. Without my Mom or Jennifer or Jason, I must surely be as lost as I was in that grocery store at three years old, just screaming and running aimlessly.

But the current evidence proved something different. I was standing alone on a private island which would be legally mine in a day and a half. I wasn't screaming. I wasn't running. I wasn't leaning on any other person. I felt like this had always been me. *Trista Maybrey and the Mysterious Island*: In this chapter, Trista grows up a little.

I turned and ducked back into the trees, making my way up the path to the cabin. Once I reached the spot where I could see the roof through the trees, I turned right, to the west side of the island and walked out as far as I could go to the edge. I walked along the upper rim of the island, circling the entire acre within the tree line, and realized there simply was no place to get down to the shore. Just as I had found on the mainland, everywhere I looked was a steep drop from the forest down to the rocks.

Undaunted, I went back to the northern point where we had first entered Simple Island. Stepping out of the trees, down the rocks, and then back down the grassy slope where I had so recently waved goodbye to Lisa and her husband, I turned left and began stepping on and around the rocks down the eastern side of the island.

The tide was still out, and I could have simply walked a path through the mud around the island, but I wanted this rocky experience. These were *my* rocks, the border of *my* island, and I wanted to really feel them. I kept my phone in my right jacket pocket where I could reach it easily to take pictures. Everything seemed photo-worthy, and what I really wished was that someone, hidden somewhere, was taking pictures of me, clambering on these rocks in my new red boots.

At the south end of the island—the widest point of the long triangle—was an actual sandy beach. Not a big beach, mind you, but big enough for a couple of umbrellas and a cooler. Even standing there on that 47-degree April day, I could see how lovely this spot would be in the summer. The beach was lined with enormous boulders which were probably all underwater at high tide. Turning the corner to travel back up the west side of the island to the point, I saw what the trees had been hiding: a magnificent sunset.

On the west side of Simple Island, it was a broad expanse of ocean all the way to the shore of Pinkley Island. At that moment, as if welcoming me home, the golden sun winked down through pink and blue clouds and the whole world was a paint-by-number masterpiece.

I surprised myself by how well my iPhone captured the colors and the expansiveness of the scene. My first sunset on Simple Island.

Chapter Ten

June 10, 1859

My Dearest,

With every letter from you I am more convinced that we were brought together for more than the purposes of human coupling or the melding of our family fortunes. You surprise and enthrall me with every word.

I confess I did not recall the passage you mentioned in Paine's book, and so upon receipt and study of your last letter, I sought it out, and perhaps you heard me laughing. I hope so. I am uncertain how I missed the passage previously. I believe I have devoured the work so hungrily, making notes and memorizing passages of import that I had somehow merely passed over that page without allowing myself to appreciate the overt humor. I eagerly anticipate sitting with you in the quiet of our own home and reading the whole book with your eyes. What else have I overlooked—not just within this book, but in all of the folds and features of this life—that you will reveal to me?

Has your brother's unwholesome influence upon your education included any works of Eastern Mysticism? These are probably not books that are included in your father's standard library of matching leather-bound tomes, and so I would not be disappointed if you have not had any opportunity to study the ideas of the Buddha. We will include these books in our own library, My Dearest, and we will study them together.

In my travels and studies within this part of the world, I have generally found there to be two camps of belief: the one camp of people who believe in the distant, fickle deity you questioned in your childhood, the one who is harshly judging our brief lives in order to decide whether we may spend eternity in blissful reward or horrific punishment, and the other camp of people who believe there is nothing beyond this human life, that we are like all other animals in that we are born organically, we live our lives, creating what meaning we can, and then we die and become the dust from which another life will eventually rise.

The belief of this second camp can seem discouraging, I know, and this is why—I believe—the first camp is so much larger. Humans crave meaning to the point that they will fabricate it for themselves rather than even glance at the possibility that there is none.

But Eastern Mysticism offers another possibility, an in-between those two extremes, and the closer I feel to you, the more deeply their ideas resonate with me.

What if we have lived, already, countless lives? What if you and I have been seeking one another throughout each of these lives, sometimes finding each other, sometimes not? What if each life we live is an opportunity to learn more, to grow wiser, to better define the sort of people we wish to be? What if, beyond amassing financial fortune or building a family *dynasty within a single life, we are moving through life after life, building slowly our ability to overcome fear, to grow in acceptance of circumstances, and to love most of all?*

Until the night I met you, these concepts were merely interesting ideas to illustrate the vast differences between cultures on this planet. But on that night, and in the days since, I feel more certain that these are the ideas that hold the most truth for me. How can it be chance that you and I, living so far apart in our separate worlds, came to be in that same moment in a city far from each of our homes, sharing a room with blustering businessmen, and finding one another in the candlelight? It wasn't as though I was meeting you at that gathering; it was as though I was finding again someone I had always known and had been desperately missing, though I didn't know it until that moment.

I saw in your eyes the same astonishment at finding me.

Chapter Eleven

And so, the packing began.

The problem wasn't that I needed to take so much, but that there was so much to go through to decide what I *was* going to take. I had a closet full of clothes that were almost all going to the Goodwill, but some things were coming with me.

My closet in Jason's house was bigger than my kitchen in the cabin, and in the bedroom of the cabin, there was simply one small shelf hanging on the wall with a two-foot bar for hanging clothes. My mother had made several helpful suggestions about how to increase my storage space, but I had decided on minimalism. This was a new life, and I was going to live it in a whole new way.

Just going through clothes, I had to really steel myself. I found my heart reacting sentimentally to things I literally hadn't worn in years, couldn't ever see myself wearing again. I had to shut off that part of me and be ruthless. In my new life, all I would need were jeans and t-shirts, one or two nice blouses to wear when I Skype, underwear and socks...and pajamas. If I ever found myself needing a pantsuit or a dress, I could buy one in Elmore.

My bathroom was a menagerie of bottles and bags and partially used potions that had promised eternal youth. Hair treatments and makeup possibilities. A dozen bottles of fingernail polish in various states of separation. Every Christmas, someone would give me a set of pretty soaps or matching soap-and-lotion, and I kept it all dutifully...but what did I really need? Shampoo and conditioner, one tiny bag of makeup items, a facial cleanser, a blow dryer and a comb, toothbrush and toothpaste. Chapstick.

Everything else went in a giant black garbage bag. As I used my arm to rake it all off the counter and into the bag, Margaret Mary startled at the noise. She'd been watching me carefully, probably afraid that I was going to put her in a bag too.

I often wondered how much of her beginning Margaret Mary actually remembered. She was an accidental puppy for me. I hadn't meant to get a puppy that day, only to get my car inspected.

The inspection had been due by the end of April, but that year I let it slip by me and I was driving on May 6 when I noticed the sticker and panicked. I was on my way to a lunch meeting with one of my staff, and I immediately called to cancel the meeting and drove instead to the Pennzoil station where I usually got my inspections and oil changes.

When I entered the tiny waiting room at the station, I could immediately smell it: nasty puppies. Healthy puppies smell sweet, like fresh baked bread, but nasty puppies have a smell all their own—like sweaty feet and dysentery. I saw on the counter a black and white printout taped to their sign board; there was a blurry picture of puppies in a basket, and someone had written in Sharpie: FREE PUPPYS.

"What kind of puppies are they?" I asked, of no one in particular, squinting at the pixilated photo.

A fellow stood up from way back behind the counter and answered, "There's just this one left...you should take her home with you!"

As he spoke, he held up the saddest looking dog I had ever seen. She was eaten alive with sarcoptic mange, such that she was almost entirely bald but for a few white sprigs that stuck up from her wrinkled forehead. Her little belly was distended with worms, and her eyes fully expressed the misery of her sad six weeks of life.

"Ohh..." I groaned, rolling my eyes and knowing myself well enough to know what was about to happen. "I probably will," I answered him.

He brought the puppy to me and I held her and talked sweetly to her there in the Pennzoil station. When I put her on the floor at my feet, the sadness dwindled, and she began wagging and sniffing around. She was just a handful of a dog, tiny little feet, tiny little ears. Her playfulness made me think she was actually survivable, though obviously in need of a lot of treatment.

The Pennzoil fellow told me that, on his way to work that morning, he had passed a burlap sack on the highway that he could tell was moving. He stopped, cut it open, and found this puppy and her two siblings.

"You mean," I asked, incredulous, "Someone tied them in a sack and threw them on the highway?"

"It happens more than you'd think," he said. "The way I figure it, people don't want to be responsible for the dogs, but they don't want to be responsible for their deaths, so they leave 'em there, helpless, figuring someone will run over the sack, but they'll never have to know about it."

"That's terrible," I mused.

"Yeah," he agreed. "People suck."

He told me that the other two puppies had been bigger and healthier, though they would probably need to be treated for worms and mange as well. He'd had no trouble finding homes for them, but he'd been worried about this little one. He couldn't take her home and risk her making his own dogs sick, but he also knew if he took her to the shelter, she'd be put down.

Before I left the Pennzoil station, I had located the nearest veterinarian, and I called to let them know I was dropping in with a sick puppy. When I arrived, the elderly doctor, who turned out to be as kind as he was hard-of-hearing, took one look at the puppy in my hand and called loudly across the lobby, "THAT DOG'S GOT THE MANGE!!"

Embarrassed, I did my best to stumble through explaining that I *knew* that, and that I had only had the puppy for a few minutes. I didn't want anyone to think I had allowed this baby to get in this condition. The doctor quickly gave her a few drops of wormer and then whisked her away for the first of several mange treatments.

When she came back, she smelled of antiseptic, which was better than her previous perfume, and the nurse brought me three pages of instructions, which included keeping her quarantined from my other pets. I didn't have any other pets, but the note didn't say anything about keeping her quarantined from myself...maybe it should have.

About two days later, I begin itching incessantly on the side of my left breast. It took me half a day to realize that this was where I held the puppy tightly against me when I was carrying her. At night, the itching was unbearable, and in the morning, I could see what looked like little red tracks across my breast and going down my left side. A little bit of Googling told me that I had, indeed, contracted the mange from my puppy, but in humans it's called Scabies...an army of microscopic critters that were burrowing under my skin, mostly on the move at night. As bad as this was for me, I could only imagine what it had been like for such a tiny puppy.

My treatment, however, was a single tube of prescription cream and a couple of oatmeal baths. The puppy, whom I simply called "Baby" (or, often, "Poor Baby") at that point, had to have a series of five dip treatments, plus her puppy shots. No one could have gotten away with calling her worthless...she cost about six hundred bucks.

Even during the treatments, her hair had started growing back in, thick and soft and white. I decided to give her a strong Irish Catholic name to go with her pure white coat. I named her Margaret Mary and planned to call her Maggie...but that never happened. Margaret Mary just stuck, and I got used to using the whole name.

That was three years ago, and I couldn't imagine my life without her. She was always underfoot, wanted to be wherever I was, wanted to go wherever I went. Such a happy little soul. As she grew up, her hair became wiry and tended to stick out all over like a hundred cowlicks. She looked like a little albino Wookiee. I loved her so.

And now we were going on a whole new adventure, just the two of us. I tried to explain it all to her as I filled the garbage bags and the Goodwill boxes; she cocked her head from side to side, listening intently.

I had promised Jason I would be out of the house by the end of April, but now that I was in the process of packing, I realized I'd be out much sooner than that. No reason to delay. I hadn't spoken with him in weeks, and I was planning to just email him when I knew for sure what date I would be completely moved out.

That's why his phone call on the twelfth surprised me.

"Hello," I said, after seeing his name on my cell phone. I thought maybe he needed to come over and get something.

"What the hell are you doing?" he began gruffly, and I was completely taken aback.

"What do you mean?" I asked.

"I mean, what the hell are you doing? You're moving to Maine? You bought an *island*??"

"Well, yes—I bought an island property that has a little house. It's enough for me. How did you know?"

"I talked to your Mother. She thinks you've lost your mind too...are you trying to *prove* something? What the fuck is in Maine?"

I was broadsided by his tone, his anger. I was upset that he had talked to my mother, that maybe they'd discussed together this "crazy" thing I was doing. I found myself gearing up to an apology, but Jason started up again.

"You don't know a soul in Maine. You can't even drive yourself to Fort Worth! Who's going to help you live like a real person? You're gonna, what? Build a fire in that wood stove like a pioneer woman? You won't even strike a match to light a candle! I didn't give you thirty-five grand so that you could go blow it all on this insane goose chase!"

Honestly astonished by his hostility, several things happened in my head at once. Part of me wanted to explain things to him, talk to him like I used to, tell him about the island, about the cabin, the little town of Milton, about all the things I loved about it. But I was slammed with another part of me that realized his mentioning the wood stove meant that he had studied the real estate listing, seen all the pictures, passed judgement based on that. It was too late for me to explain. But before automatic explanation kicked in anyway, I then realized and held onto the last thing he had shouted at me...about not giving me thirty-five grand to blow.

"Wait a minute," I said, suddenly angry rather than apologetic. "You didn't *give* me thirty-five grand! That is *my* money. I put just as much of my weekly salary into the payments on this house as you did...and I made the payments by myself for the whole year you were starting up your business! When I was starting my business, I never missed a payment."

Feeling myself on a roll now, I just let it all spill out. "I didn't make this decision, Jason. You did. You made it a long time ago when you started cheating on me with Alyssa...or maybe there were other women before her. I don't know. I don't even care. I didn't fight you in the divorce. I didn't try to take anything from you. My half of the equity in this house was a settlement that was *way* in your favor. We're not a team anymore. You don't actually get a say in what I do from here on. If I want to take *my* thirty-five grand to Vegas and put it all down on one spin of the roulette wheel, that is my business."

I was almost panting by now, my heart pounding. I could hear the tears of frustration beginning to wobble in my voice, but I didn't care. Let it come. I was suddenly sick with myself for being so accommodating. This really had been years of mistreatment to me, whether I knew about it at the time or not, and I had taken it all quietly, just trying to be helpful, trying to make it easy for Jason. Why? And now he was trying to act like he should still be controlling me? Like he should still be in the driver's seat of my life?

Jason was apparently shocked, momentarily, into silence by my tirade, so I took a deep breath, and continued more calmly.

"I know this is hard for you to understand, Jason, but I'm building a new life for myself. My old one has ended, you know? You *know*. You ended it. I've been hurt, and humiliated, and scared, and confused; I've had to completely reassess the last decade of my existence. You didn't go through that. You knew what was happening. Your surprise right now is about decisions I've made over the past 2 months. I think you'll be able to get over it.

"This seems sudden to you because you just found out, but I've done a lot of study and preparation for this. I've been up there and learned my way around. Yes, this will be a lot of new experiences for me, but so would anything that I do. If I move next door, I'll have to learn things about the new house. But I don't want to be next door. I don't want to be where I have to watch you and your little Sunshine Family living the American Dream. I want something of my own. You've already found that. I honestly want you to be happy. I do. But now I've got to find my own happy. At the moment, that's a little cabin on a little island off the coast of Maine. This is *my* decision for *my* life."

I paused to let him respond. The pause seemed very long. Finally, Jason quietly said, "Whatever," and hung up.

I immediately dialed my Mother's number. More than Jason's hostile insults, I was bothered by that thing he said about her agreeing with him that I was out of my mind, or whatever he'd said. I didn't like the picture in my head of the two of them having a long, late-night phone call discussing how crazy Trista is acting.

I knew Mom didn't want me to move so far away, and I knew she worried about me starting all over in a whole new world, but I felt like she had come to accept it. She'd even texted me a couple of Amazon links for things she thought would be cute in my cabin: breezy curtains and some candlesticks that looked like fire logs.

The phone rang twice before she answered, and she was, as always, happy to hear from me.

"Trista! How's the packing going? Do you need any help? I heard once that if you go to Walmart late at night when they're stocking the shelves, they'll just give you boxes, however many you need."

"Oh, I don't really need any, thankfully," I tried to match her upbeat mood. In her mid-fifties, Mom was really "coming into herself" and she had spent a lot of time studying books on inner peace and happiness. She'd grown up in a hard situation, having lost her parents early on and being raised by a bitter and often abusive grandmother, but the last few years for her had been wonderful to watch, as she stretched her legs, tried new things. It's the main reason why I knew that, ultimately, she would be supportive of this big move for me.

"Well that's good to hear," she said, breezily, and I could tell she was a little out of breath, which meant she was probably taking a "power walk" on the wooded trail in her neighborhood.

"Mom," I started, tentatively, "I've just had a call from Jason, and he was really upset, like, he was yelling and cursing at me about moving to Maine. He said he talked to you about it and he said that you agreed with him that I've lost my mind..."

"Oh, dear," she said, and paused. I could picture her stopping on the trail and looking up at the sky as she gathered her thoughts. "I'm so sorry I didn't tell you; I should have anticipated something like that."

"What happened?"

"Well, I ran into Jason at Target. We made eye contact, so I couldn't exactly pretend I didn't see him."

"Oh." So, it wasn't a heart-to-heart phone call.

"I didn't know that you hadn't already told him your plans, though I probably should have guessed. It was all so awkward, and I found myself just wanting to show him that you're doing great."

"Did you actually show him the pictures of the island?"

"Yes—I'm sorry if I shouldn't have. I really just wanted to get away, but as long as he was standing there asking questions, I kept answering them. I pulled up the listing on my phone from that time you sent it to me, and I whisked through all the photos. I caught myself kind of bragging, actually. Then his girlfriend walked up, and that rather ended the conversation. Thankfully."

"So...you didn't tell him you think I've gone crazy or irresponsible or anything like that...?"

"Of course not, Trista! You know me better than that. Even if I felt that way—and I don't! —I wouldn't have stood there in Target and talked about it to Jason, of all people!"

"Thanks, Mom," I sighed, relieved. "I knew it probably wasn't the way he said it was. I think he's just annoyed that he doesn't get to help make any of my decisions anymore."

"Men are a caution," she said, and I could hear the smile in her voice. "And...Trista?"

"Yes?"

"I just want you to know...she's not as pretty as you are."

"Thanks, Mom."

I stood that night in front of my full-length mirror and thought about what Mom had said. Of course, she has to think I'm pretty because I'm her daughter, and all my life people have been telling her how much we look alike. How sad for her if she thought I wasn't pretty, but we look so much alike!

I know I'm not beautiful in the classical sense, but I can look at myself objectively and nod. I'm OK. I'm tall and long-waisted, so even when I put on a little weight, I carry it well. I have small hands and long fingers—piano fingers, my Mom calls them, though I utterly rejected her every effort to make me play. I have a pretty radical c-section scar ("from my navel to my nuts!" is how I described it to Jennifer from the hospital) and my thighs make me scowl, but my calves are shapely from power walking with Mom, and my ankles are trim. In the right outfit, I look pretty damn good.

I'm well aware that the most attractive thing about me is...Margaret Mary. No matter where I am, what I'm wearing, what I'm trying to accomplish, if Margaret Mary is with me, people of all ages and genders are immediately drawn to me, and I am the world's most arrestingly beautiful, most splendidly interesting woman. I always make sure Margaret Mary knows that I'm aware of this, so it doesn't go to my head.

That night, though, looking in the mirror, I felt suddenly old. Haggard. I know that thirty-three isn't old, but it's hard not to feel it sometimes in moments of weariness. And I was weary.

There was a night, about a year before, when Jason had stood watching me apply my various nightly potions and elixirs. I suppose he was waiting for me to get out of the bathroom, but at the time, I thought he was just watching me...like a husband. He finally said, "Well, this is quite an operation."

I replied that it took a lot of work being thirty-two and managing to still look thirty. That caught Jason off guard, and he laughed, which pleased me. I liked making him laugh. Of course, now, that was one of those moments I had to reassess. While I was standing there, pleased that I had made him laugh, he was probably thinking about how Alyssa was only twenty-three. Or eighteen. I honestly didn't know. Didn't want to know.

I've always liked my hair. It's very thick and naturally dark brown, almost black. When I was a child, it was, in my mother's estimation, "straight as a board," which pleased her, because she described her own curly hair as "steel wool" and constantly wrestled with it. As I entered my twenties, my hair started to curl, and over that decade it became what you could only call "curly hair" ...but not pretty bouncy curls, just unruly frizzy mess. So, if I take the time to blow dry my hair, I can make it behave, but if I don't, it goes in a vast number of aimless directions. Another one of the many things Margaret Mary and I have in common.

Standing there in front of the mirror that night, feeling weary, I made a decision. The best way for a woman to feel generally younger is to change her hair. I knew it was an unfortunate stereotype, and I hated being reduced to a stereotype, but the way things *become* stereotypes is by being true for a great many people belonging to a group. In this case, the group was women...and I was inescapably one of them.

The morning of April thirteenth, I went to my long-time stylist, Kristal, and told her to cut it all off. Make me a pixie. Kristal asked me if I was sure: "That's a lot of hair, honey...you've never been without your long thick hair!" I assured her I was sure, and she began performing what she called "major surgery." For about an hour, she worked on my hair, and all the while, she was catching me up on the trials and tribulations of her love life.

I could have written a redneck romance novel with the details of the past ten years of Kristal's love life, as well as that of her only son who had grown from an unruly teenager to a man with a child of his own during the time Kristal had been taking care of my hair. It seemed that every good-for-nothing man she'd wasted her paychecks on in that decade had all been met at the same bar. It was hard for me not to point out this obvious fault on her part...but I didn't. She was a miracle worker with my crazy hair, so I just listened and clucked my tongue in *shock* to discover that her latest boyfriend was just a repeat of the last one: unemployed, unempowered, and uninterested in changing. Kristal didn't seem to see the pattern.

When she was finished, I felt transformed. I'd never had my hair so short, and it was really cute. I must have left eight pounds of myself on the floor of her salon, and I waltzed out feeling brand new.

I spent the fourteenth finishing my packing, and on the fifteenth, Margaret Mary and I hit the road. I was more than ready to fashionably display the sprawl of Dallas in the eight-by-three-inch frame of my rearview mirror.

Chapter Twelve

June 19, 1859

My Darling,

I feel that I must tell you, warn you, that if my Mother has her way in all things, as she usually does, you will need not only an entire baggage car for my trousseau, but likely the entire train. It seems that every day there is another chest or trunk or case or basket or box or valise of something that she believes absolutely essential to my ability to fulfill my duties as your wife. She has hired six ladies to embroider fifty handkerchiefs with the initials "M.S." and while I do adore thinking of those as my initials, I cannot imagine enough occasions to need fifty embroidered handkerchiefs, even if I were to burn each one after a single use. When she is finished, I shall have a new dress for every day of the first five years of our marriage, god forbid styles should change over that time.

I have tried to temper her enthusiasm to no avail. Just last evening, as we sat at dinner, she lifted her fork to her mouth and then stopped, mouth open, to study the fork, and in that moment it was decided that this particular set of silver flatware should belong to me as we start our household. For your education, I will inform you, sir, that this is a set of silver designed to serve a party of one hundred, and—I have been assured—any less than that would be quite improper for any noble household to possess.

I tried to assure her that your family undoubtedly has plenty of fine flatware of their own, and that adding my initials to yours only increases their household by one individual. This seemed a logical argument, but I fear I carried it too far by suggesting that perhaps she might only gift me one set—one salad fork, one dinner fork, one knife, one soup spoon, one coffee spoon—and that I could simply carry these in my reticule to flourish when I sit at dinner with the rest of your family. Upon this suggestion, my mother removed the napkin from her lap, covered her untouched dinner, and excused herself from the table.

This morning, I discovered three of the housemaids polishing and packing the flatware to be added to the entire train I previously mentioned. On the whole, I know that it is because my mother loves me that she does these things. She wants to know that, when I am far away from her, I still have all of the good things that she has spent her life trying to provide. In accepting her love, I must also accept her forks.

And so, unfortunately, must you.

Chapter Thirteen

The goal for the first night was Lexington, Kentucky. Bluegrass. By the time we arrived, however, the grass was all black. It was after midnight. I was thankful that Hotels.com makes it easy to filter hotels for "pet friendly" so that Margaret Mary and I were able to just drag ourselves into our room at the Red Roof Inn and collapse with no difficulty.

The next day, I could see that the grass isn't blue, but it is really, really green. Driving past all the pastures of horses, and barns more beautiful than most of the houses in my Dallas neighborhood, I found myself singing the Everly Brothers' song *Bowling Green*.

"The fields down in Bowling Green (*ching!*) have the softest grass I've ever seen (*ching!*). A man in Kentucky SURE is lucky to lie down in Bowling Green!"

Margaret Mary gets very excited when I sing. Especially in the car, for some reason, and she tries to sing along. We make quite the duet.

The goal on the second day was Hagerstown, Maryland. Mom asked me "What's in Hagerstown?" and I said, "My pillow." Hagerstown was just a town that we would go through, and it looked like as far as I wanted to go that day. I started filling the drive time by listening to the John Case novel, *The Genesis Code*, on audiobook.

We arrived in Hagerstown about eight o'clock. This would have been early enough to relax and enjoy myself a little except that the hotel was really shabby. There was a TV on the wall, but it had no cord to plug it in. The carpet was wet, which I hoped meant it had been recently shampooed, not any of the other more distasteful reasons I could think of for wet carpet. The furnishings were all quite out of style and the bedspread was threadbare. The whole room smelled like 1982. Not that I would know.

The Middle Eastern man who had checked us in (and scowled at Margaret Mary, such that I thought we might not get to stay after all) did not seem to be the type that I could sweet-talk into a different room...nor did I feel it was likely he had a room better than this one.

I had stopped at a convenience store an hour before for "hotel snacks": a couple of sodas, a bag of chips, a granola bar so that I could pretend to have a healthy breakfast. I had intended to go out somewhere for dinner, but the way the clerk had looked at Margaret Mary, I was afraid to leave her alone. This is what the internet is for.

Half an hour later, I was eating pasta ("no cheese") from an aluminum container which had been delivered directly to my room at the Bates Motel, and listening to Stephen Colbert on YouTube. With my tummy full, I wriggled under the covers and lulled myself to sleep like I had been doing a lot lately, imagining myself walking on the rocks of Simple Island, climbing up to the tree level, walking the path to the cabin, taking the steps up to the front door, opening the front door, walking through the living room...before I got to the sliding back doors, I was asleep.

There was a woman in my dream. She was lovely. Old fashioned, and classy. Her long hair was piled up loosely on her head, but I knew that when she let it down, it was really beautiful. Her ivory colored dress had a lace collar that went all the way up her shapely throat. I felt like I knew her. *Really* knew her, though I'd never seen her before. She was standing in a field with her face turned away from me, but then she turned to look at me and she smiled. Then everything went black and I could hear the man's voice calling "Em! Em! We are lost!" And suddenly everything exploded, and fire was all around me, and I was flying through the air, terrified, knowing I was going to hit the water. I heard the man's voice again, calling, frantic, "Find me at the temple!" Then a man's face loomed in front of me, a man with red hair and freckles and a rough beard. His face came so close to mine that I could feel his breath, and he said it again, only much softer, pleading, "Find me at the temple." I knew I was about to hit the freezing, flaming water... I woke up with Margaret Mary licking my face.

I must have cried out and woken her. She was so sweet, trying to comfort me. I got up to go to the bathroom and to get a drink of water. She followed me closely, making sure I was all right. I wasn't.

Why did I keep having this same dream? Or at least, this same *kind* of dream. Who was the woman that had appeared for the first time in this one? Was she "Em"? was that Emma? Emily? Emmaline? The man's voice and face stayed with me, though it connected to no one that I knew. And now this part about the temple...what temple? And always the explosion, and the fire and the water.

I've always been a vivid dreamer. Even in childhood, I would entertain my Mom and Jennifer, and other friends and family, with my bizarre, detailed, colorful dreams. Long scenarios with celebrities such that when I woke up, I missed the friendship. Epic journeys into strange worlds that included various elements of whatever I'd been experiencing or thinking about at that point in my life. Once, as a teen, I dreamed I was having obligatory sex in a swimming pool with George Bush Jr.—except he turned into some kind of dog toy and I knew I still had to "finish the deed"...totally weird. I'm sure that dream had political underpinnings, but I never identified them.

But as much as I pride myself on my crazy dreams, I've never been one for *recurring* dreams. Certainly, starting a whole new life for myself could be cause for anxiety dreams, but I couldn't find any elements of these recent dreams that fit a recognizable pattern. They were so vivid, so frightening, and so disconnected from anything in my world...except for each other.

I was afraid of falling back asleep because I didn't want to find myself in the cold water again. Or the fire. I opened my phone app to listen to John Case again for a while, and after about two chapters, I drifted off again...and did not dream.

Margaret Mary and I took our time the next morning. I lazed a while, listened to the book, ate some granola bars, mused about my dreams. She napped. I figured that if I had to pay full price for this sucky room, I was going to stay till check out.

At about 10:30, I dragged my backpack past the front desk and dropped off the key. The same man was standing at the counter, and he grunted without looking up. I supposed if he had to be there night and day, perhaps his crabbiness was, at least a little bit, justified.

Except for last night's take-out pasta, I'd been living for two days on Taco Bell and convenience store snacks. I decided to actually go into a restaurant for lunch. I found a little diner that offered "sandwiches and more" and decided to take a chance. I parked, rolled down the windows to half-mast, and told Margaret Mary to "stay" ...she looked up from her little self-made nest in my dirty clothes and gave me a face that said, "I'm not goin' anywhere, Lady."

The diner was cute. They had just opened, and the chairs were all still up on the tables. I guessed I was their first customer of the day. A sign said "SIT ANYWHERE" so I chose a booth in the front corner, where I could easily see my car out the window.

The waiter looked about fifteen but was probably a scrawny nineteen. He came sweeping up and tossed napkin-wrapped silverware in front of me, as well as a laminated menu. "Drink?" he asked, almost impatiently, which seemed odd when I was the only patron.

"Ahm...Diet Coke?"

"You want water too?"

"Oh, that's not necessary," I said and smiled.

He lowered his order tablet and looked at me almost quizzically. "You must be a liberal," he said, and I couldn't tell if that was a compliment or an accusation.

"What does that mean?" I asked, honestly curious.

"Well," he explained, "Most people would have just said NO...instead of the whole THAT'S NOT NECESSARY thing."

"Oh. I'm sorry..." but he had already turned to go for my Diet Coke.

I texted Jennifer, told her the assumption that I am liberal based on how I answered whether I wanted water or not. "You've got to be careful, girl," she responded. "You're in Yankee territory now! Watch that high-falutin' vocabulary!"

I answered her that "Necessary" is not exactly a five-dollar word.

"I don't know," she texted back. "Sounds liberal to me."

"I'll try to keep it short and sweet from now on, at least until I know I'm in a mostly blue state."

"Why bother? You ARE a liberal! You've built a whole life helping gay men have babies! To thine own self be true, chickadee."

I responded with an emoji that was laughing itself to tears. It seemed an appropriate response, though it didn't match my mood. I hadn't had enough sleep, I was bothered by the dream, and now I was bothered by the fellow passing political judgements based on my choice of verbiage.

Jennifer was, as usual, correct about my building a life helping gay men have babies. And it was a life I loved.

When I was in my mid-twenties, working my way through my Master's in Counseling at the University of Texas at Arlington, I had bonded easily with a gay couple, Jon Searcy and Bobby Wingo. They had eventually married and now both were Searcy. We were all in the same "Cultural Diversity" class, and I was drawn to them because several other members of the class were outspoken against homosexuality, and I knew this had to make them uncomfortable, though they never spoke up. I spoke out for equal rights and "love is love" and while this didn't make me the most popular person in the class, it made me very popular with Jon and Bobby. We became quite the trio, and they dubbed me their "Trista Bear"

One night, while sitting together in their apartment cramming for an exam and drinking wine, they started talking about wanting to have children. I told them, in my tipsy state, that if we survived graduate school, I would carry a baby for them...but then the conversation got really serious, and I wasn't feeling tipsy anymore. Jon and Bobby had already done a lot of research about the legalities, and how it would work in Texas. They had a friend who was an attorney and had offered to draw up the papers for them. They researched a fertility clinic in Grand Prairie that would create embryos from eggs. Jon's sister was going to donate her eggs, which would be fertilized with Bobby's sperm.

They just needed someone to carry for them.

Bobby explained that to go through a surrogacy agency was going to cost about a hundred fifty thousand dollars, and that's only if it worked right away. If they had to try over and over, it would be much more expensive. Jon and Bobby, of course, didn't actually *have* a hundred-fifty grand.

What they did have was a great deal of charm, and a few helpful connections. Their attorney friend was going to do the contract pro-bono, and the cost of the egg retrieval and embryo transfer would cost them about twenty-five thousand for a single try. *That* they could risk.

Finding a surrogate through an agency would also require a fee of about thirty thousand, but if they could find a *friend* who would do it for free...and this is where I came in, slightly boozy, but wholly willing.

I went into that process, I can see now, completely ignorant. I had a big heart for Jon and Bobby, but no idea what I was doing or where the potential pitfalls were. Looking back, we got really lucky that my insurance never questioned the pregnancy, or why I didn't add a baby after it was born. We got really lucky that I actually could carry a baby—not just one but *two!* —to term (or almost to term) as I'd never been pregnant before. We got lucky that I got pregnant with the first transfer so that it didn't wind up costing a fortune something my friends didn't have— or so that they didn't simply run out of money and have to give up.

I was already married to Jason at the time, and he was supportive of my decision to carry the twins. We weren't ready to have kids of our own yet, and I think he was actually proud of me for volunteering. My mother needed a little more help understanding that this was not actually her grandchild I was going to carry and give away. The first time she met Jon and Bobby, I knew everything would be OK. She set herself up as the honorary grandmother anyway, and a new family was created.

In order to boost the chances of success, the IVF doctor implanted two embryos...and they both decided to set up housekeeping. I was thrilled to get to have the experience of carrying twins. I had a giant red maternity t-shirt custom made which, on the front, had big white letters that said, "NOT MY HUSBAND'S" and a big arrow pointing to my enormous belly. On the back, in equally large letters, it said, "NOT MINE EITHER" ...I had a lot of fun wearing that shirt to Walmart.

I turned twenty-six during the pregnancy, just about three weeks before the twins decided to make their premature debut. I went to my OB for a routine ultrasound and check-up, and they practically set off an alarm because I was in labor, but I hadn't known it. They strapped me down and wheeled me to an ambulance and I was frantically calling Jason, calling Mom, calling Jon and Bobby.

Everyone met me at the hospital, where my doctor put me on a drip of magnesium sulfate to stop the labor, at least for a while, so they could boost the twins' lung development with steroids. That lasted about five days, and by the end of that time the drugs were making me feel like I was fading away. I could almost see through my hand like Marty McFly at the end of *Back to the Future*.

The twins were in no position for an old-fashioned vaginal birth. They were both stretched out sideways, like logs stacked on top of one another, with the girl on the bottom, constantly kicking her brother. The only answer, once we knew we couldn't stop them coming, was the radical "navel to nuts" c-section I mentioned previously. That was the easiest part for me. I relished the magic of epidural, closed my eyes and had some sketchy dream about Danny Bonaduce until the first baby cry woke me up.

The twins were thirty-three weeks along when they were born, which meant some time in the NIC-U, but nothing anyone was deeply concerned about. They needed to develop their sucking reflex. Jon and Bobby named them Elinor Trista and Joshua Baer. My Mom was pleased.

As Elly and Josh grew into goofy adorable toddlers, it was becoming clear that my inner workings were not, in fact, working. I was having almost non-stop bleeding and my OB tried a number of options: birth control, ablation therapy...nothing worked. Finally, he sat in a chair facing me, took my hands, and told me that the only option left was a hysterectomy. Otherwise, this was just going to continue.

I had to let go of the idea of having children of my own. Jason and I talked about it long into the night. I didn't tell my Mom until the decision was already made. I knew how crushed she would feel. More than me, probably. After the actual surgery, my doctor was able to explain to me that, as a result of the radical c-section, endometrial material had begun growing on the outside of my uterus, which was why I was having the unstoppable bleeding. He said that, had we not elected to have the hysterectomy, that would have only continued to get worse.

In the time between the birth of the twins and my hysterectomy, I had finished my Masters, and begun working with a small local group that did home visits for Child Protective Services. I was proud of the work...but I hated it. I hated everything about it. I hated the terrible conditions we had to go into and trying to decide if the kids could stay with the parents or not. I hated the interviews where I asked questions that nobody would answer honestly if the answers were bad. I hated the moments when screaming children had to be whisked away from their parents "for their own good."

I hated it...but I knew it was solid work, and that it would be good on my resume. If I could handle this, I could handle anything...right? And also, in those years, a great many of Jon and Bobby's friends had asked them for their help and advice building a family of their own, and the guys often referred their friends to me, as I had become adept at explaining it forensically: the legal part, the medical part, and the emotional part.

It was almost organic the way I began turning it into a business of my own. I was relying more and more on the kindness of the attorney, Moira, who had done the contract for Elly and Josh. She and I started openly discussing turning this into a real endeavor, where we could focus all of our attention on the would-be parents who came to us.

Moira helped me establish my LLC ("Families in Harmony"), and before long, I had enough business to quit the CPS work and spend all of my time organizing the details and helping couples find appropriate surrogates for the legal requirements in their states. Moira and I were learning as we went, and I wound up hiring two of my earliest surrogates to help guide couples through the process.

That day, sitting in the diner where I, apparently, stood out as a liberal, there were a hundred sixteen babies to the credit of Families in Harmony, and six more on the way. I no longer had to devote all of my waking hours to the business, as my coordinators did most of that. My job was to welcome the new parents, show them the works, and comfort them when things were not going easily. My Master's in Counseling was indeed quite helpful. Moira and I were in regular contact about legal work, and my favorite part was when a baby was born, and I could shower them with gifts and congratulations.

I knew I would never be a multi-million-dollar organization like some agencies were, but I wanted to keep it small, and my services financially accessible. I wanted to know every client by name. That meant keeping my client list limited, but I still made plenty of money to support myself. Moira and I had become official partners, though she still kept her private practice.

On the one hand, the job was deeply satisfying, and made it possible for me to work from anywhere, but on the other hand, it had, for years now, enabled me to just sit in that recliner in my sweats with a dog on my lap. I rolled my eyes in self-deprecation. No wonder Jason started a family with another woman.

My veggie sandwich arrived, along with the bill: a combination that said, "Please eat and leave, you liberal harpy" ...or something like that. Three more tables had been filled since I ordered, so I finished my lunch quietly, and paid the lady at the counter. When she asked me if I needed change, I said, "That's not necess...I mean...no."

I drove into Milton that night, but we didn't try to go all the way out to the island. Instead, we spent the night at the only motel in town: The Red Rooster Inn. It was a quiet little place with a restaurant where no one questioned my political leanings based on my vocabulary. The next day, we would take possession of our island with the afternoon low tide.

It was still remarkably cold in Maine, even though it was mid-April. In Texas, mid-April already meant mosquitoes and sweaty, stinky humidity. Driving down the dirt road of Parson Point, I was glad to see there was no snow on the ground anymore. Perhaps Spring was coming after all.

I parked my car where Lisa had shown me, so that if my "neighbors" were home, I wouldn't immediately be treated to their more litigious nature. As I stepped over the chain and walked up their gravel drive, I could see that there was no other car, and no sign of life in their home. Lisa had told me that she'd only seen the Beardens there once in the two years she'd been coming out to Simple Island, so perhaps I wouldn't even meet them for a long time. Fine with me. I didn't buy an island so that I could deal with difficult neighbors.

I stood for a few moments on the edge of their property, just looking out at Simple. The tide wasn't completely out, but enough that I could splash across in my boots. I figured, however, that by the time I got my stuff unloaded and organized, it would be just a few tide pools remaining. The majority of the crossing would be dry.

I opened the hatchback of my Nissan, and Margaret Mary jumped out, as though she knew this was our destination. There was no need to bother with her leash, and I knew she wouldn't go far, so I let her wander and sniff around while I pulled out the things I wanted to carry over in my first trip.

I had literally put all of my clothes in two white kitchen garbage bags. Vanilla scented. It wasn't that I didn't have a real suitcase, but even empty, a suitcase is heavy, and I knew that if I had to stop mid-crossing to switch hands, a suitcase would get dirty. The garbage bags could be set down in the mud if need be, and then thrown away once I unpacked. This decision had felt smart to me.

I had a zipper-top shopping bag that was lined with some kind of aluminum for keeping food cold, but for now, it was the perfect bag to carry on my shoulder with toiletry items in it, some electronics, and a new set of sheets for the bed (no telling how long since the ones on it had been changed). I called this my "Mary Poppins bag" because of the wide variety of interesting things that it held.

This is all I was taking over on the first day, and I thought I could manage it in two trips.

I carried my bags down the little path, noticing how much more overgrown it seemed just in the two weeks since I was here. Spring was definitely springing. I brushed away branches and wondered if the Beardens ever came down this path. Would they notice if I trimmed it back a little? At the drop off, I tossed my bags of clothes down onto the grass before carefully stepping down the progression of rocks to the lower shore. Margaret Mary whined and wriggled until I lifted her down.

She followed me down the grassy point, but when I turned off the point and into the mud, she just stood there on the last bit of grass and whined. I took a few more steps, encouraging her to come on, but she danced in place and began a real outcry, which carried across the water. People way over on Pinkley Island probably thought I was abusing her.

I turned and took a couple of steps back toward her, and she suddenly stepped off the grass and rushed toward me in the mud. We crossed the ocean together for the first time, and up the grass slope to our island.

I put the first load (one vanilla-scented garbage bag and my Mary Poppins bag of accoutrements) right at the entrance to the path, and then turned to crossed back again for the other bag. This time Margaret Mary danced in front of me, already completely confident of herself in these new surroundings. By the time we got back to the island the second time, she was like a two-tone pickup truck: dark brown on her legs and belly and white the rest of the way up. Lovely.

I made the two trips it took to carry my things from the entrance of the path to the cabin, and then wrestled with the lockbox until I managed to get the front door open.

The sun was already starting to set by that time, and the cabin seemed particularly dark and cold. In my Mary Poppins bag, I had several sizes and types of candles, and a couple of new lighters, and so my first order of business was to light them all and place them strategically about the cabin. Jason might have been surprised, but candle lighters are much easier for me than matches. Straight away, everything looked more inviting. I opened all the blinds to let in as much light as I could, and then turned my attention to the bed.

The sheets on it seemed fresh and soft, but just to be safe, I opened my new package of sheets and changed all the bedding. Now it was *my* bed. Then I opened one of the garbage bags and began pulling my clothes out, one piece at a time, and deciding whether each piece should hang on the rack, sit atop the shelf, or be placed in a basket in the corner of the room.

In the center of that bag, carefully protected by all the clothes, was a bottle of vanilla rum. My favorite. When I got to the bottle, I stopped being productive and went to the kitchen for a glass. Sitting on the dingy white cushion (I meant to change that soon) of the wicker sofa, I called Margaret Mary up beside me and we snuggled in the candlelight and congratulated ourselves on our tiny new home.

Chapter Fourteen

June 28, 1859

My Dearest,

When I turn back the pages of the story of my life, I hope to always come back to the moment you said that accepting your mother's love means accepting her forks. Not even the humor of Thomas Paine, no matter how pointed, could bring me to the rollicking laughter that line of phrase evoked. I was sitting with my father in his study, reading your letter as he worked quietly on his ledgers, and when I found those words in your hand, I was so taken off guard by the hilarity that at first I inhaled sharply and then choked, such that I was subsequently choking and laughing with tears streaming down my face. My father stared at the spectacle I was making, and he just kept repeating, "I say..." and "Well, for heaven's sake..." but I was so caught in my choking and laughing that I could not do more than wave at him with my hand.

You will find that I far prefer the effects of laughter to that of even the finest brandy. I look forward to long years of delighting one another with unexpected moments of pointed humor. If laughter is indeed "the best medicine" then being with you should provide me with a very long life and many happy wrinkles around my eyes.

Please know that on the day when you become my wife, I will be so happy that I would not only procure an entire train for your trousseau, but I would be just as willing should it need to be a train of elephants to carry your belongings from your mother's home to mine. I would perch you in a red velvet carriage, atop the largest beast and I would hire a host of servants adorned in silk and golden bells to feed you grapes and fan you with peacock feathers throughout the journey.

I do understand what you mean about your mother's love. My mother is also quite sentimental about things, and sometimes I sigh at the importance she places on belongings which seem replaceable, or which may be finely made but ultimately do not add to the value of life. I believe, however, that as I grow older, I have a better understanding of her attachment to certain things.

Just as your mother values the importance of good flatware, my mother also has a service of silver that she holds dear. It is, indeed, fine silver, and from a merchant standpoint, I can understand that it has value in that it was originally crafted by the noteworthy Paul Revere, who holds historical significance not only as a silversmith but as one of the founders of our sovereign nation.

But my mother does not hold dear the set of silver because it is of monetary or historical significance, but because it was her grandmother's silver, and every time she brings it out of the cabinet to serve tea, she cannot disguise the mist that comes to her eyes as she tells stories of sitting in her grandmother's parlor in Boston, taking tea like a lady, though she was only a child. My mother has said that her grandmother had a greater influence on the development of her manners and character than any of the other people who were hired to teach her how to be a great lady.

It was a different time. Property passed from father to son, daughters became part of the property of their husbands. A lady had very little to pass to the other women in her descendancy beyond ideals and perhaps a silver tea service.

And so we will happily accept your mother's forks, and someday perhaps you will be sitting at dinner with our daughter, or granddaughter, and you will be unable to disguise the mist in your eyes as you tell them about this flatware and how your mother loved you.

Chapter Fifteen

I dreamed anxiety dreams that first night, but not like the recurring images I'd been having. That night I dreamed that I was walking out behind the cabin, and the island just went on and on until I discovered a huge building—like a factory building—and inside were a number of small shops set up, with a lot of people manning their shops, and I was realizing that these people lived on Simple Island full time. I decided perhaps they had moved there and started their businesses while it was unoccupied, and now I really needed to tell them that they had to go.

In one booth, I met a man who was selling old army uniforms, only they were all filthy and tattered, and all the price tags said the same thing: "Ohio $175." I asked him what that meant, and he said he didn't have time to tell me because he had to take care of these kittens. I looked where he was pointing, and in a little chair, there was a pile of kittens—dozens of them —and most of them were bloody, or missing pieces like ears or legs. Then I noticed that the man was holding a string, like a leash, and it was attached to an alligator who was crouching on the floor. While the man talked to me, the alligator raised up and began eating the kittens that were in the chair. It was very upsetting, so I left his shop and kept walking through the building.

Looking back on it, the dream seemed interminable. It just went on for what felt like hours, as I explored the big building and wondered if I was just going to have to accept that these people lived here. If I owned it, it was still my private island, right? I was repeatedly amazed how much bigger the island was than I had thought.

I met a woman, a pretty middle-aged woman in a long lilac dress and wide-brimmed hat, and she told me that my answer was just down the hall and indicated a sign for "FRESH BLUEBERRIES" that pointed down a long corridor. But when I walked down the hall, I stepped on to a spot where the floor collapsed under me and I fell into a dark hole that was just barely big enough for me. I screamed for help. The lady in the hat came and stood over me, smiled for a minute, and then began shoveling dirt on top of me.

I suddenly woke up, and then laughed at myself. *That* was the kind of crazy dream I normally had.

The day began with sunshine and positivity. I was anxious to start making the cabin my own. I wanted it to reflect my personality, my sense of style, my idea of what a cabin should look like.

I began by crunching on granola bars while finishing the unpacking of my clothes, which had been happily interrupted the night before with the unearthing of the vanilla rum. Now I rapidly finished emptying the two garbage bags, and then went around the cabin filling those same garbage bags with the various wall hangings that even hinted at the word "beach"...anything with a picture of flip-flops or a "toes in the sand" theme went in the bag. Most of the stuff still had price tags on and I could see that it all came from the same discount store. Even so, it all had cost a fortune, $4.99, $9.99, $14.99...it all went in the bag. I knew if Mom were here, she would admonish me to have a yard sale...but how do you have a yard sale on an island? And I was not going to bother with eBay as my first order of business.

Once I cleared the space of the previous personality, I began filling it with my own. In the two weeks since I had been to Simple Island for the closing, I had spent a single Sunday afternoon making cushion covers for the wicker furniture. Currently, the cushions were white, which seemed almost garish against the warm pine walls. I had bought a full bolt of fleece fabric in what, I learned, is called "Buffalo Check": the big squares of red and black check with blended red and black in between. To me, it was exactly what a cozy cabin needed.

These cushion covers had been stuffed in the vanilla-scented garbage bag with my clothes and were now unpacked and ready to work their transformational magic.

I'm no professional seamstress, but I know how to use a machine, and what I made for the cushion covers were basically just big pillowcases. I wrapped each cushion of the sofa, two chairs, and two ottomans (shouldn't that be "ottomen"?) in its cover, pulled it tight, and tucked the extra underneath it. Within ten minutes, the whole cabin felt renewed.

I had also made a new comforter for the bed; I'd made it from an ivy-patterned sheet that I liked, lined with quilt batting and backed with a solid green sheet. Again, really simple sewing that allowed me to have exactly what I wanted. The comforter, however, was still in the car with the rest of my stuff.

I looked at my watch and realized I had about two hours until low tide, so I rolled up my sleeves and prepared to tackle the kitchen. I turned on my little blue-tooth speaker and played Jason Mraz from my phone, loud enough to normalize the clatter I was about to make so that I didn't scare Margaret Mary, who was watching me intently.

Under the bar, which separated the kitchen from the living room, was an absolute treasure trove of *stuff*. A full set of pots and pans that looked unused, a crock pot, a divider box full of silverware, a junk box with odds and ends like a corkscrew, a can opener, a candle lighter, a stack of citronella candles (new) and another box with large utensils like ladles and serving spoons. There were a dozen unopened rolls of paper towels, along with boxes of plastic ware, paper plates, plastic bowls, plastic cups, and several boxes of variously sized garbage bags. Besides all of the useful items, there were also a lot of personal things belonging to the previous owners, and I added a lot of that to the garbage bag while I reorganized the items I would be keeping.

This project completely filled the two hours I had before low tide. As I cinched up the bag of trash, I looked at the clock and realized my "window" was just opening. My t-shirt was grubby from the dusty work and the many times I had used it to wipe the grime off my hands, but I wasn't going out for a fashion show. I ran a comb through my short hair and pulled on my tall red boots.

I needed to use this four-hour window in several productive ways. Yes, I had more stuff in my car that I needed to haul over to the island, but I also needed groceries and supplies. I planned to hit the grocery store to stock the cabin for several days of meals, the hardware store for a gas can and some fire-starters, and then the gas station for gasoline...it was time to get friendly with the generator.

All day, I had been eyeing the wood stove. It was a chilly day, and I knew the rest of Maine was probably lighting a fire, but I found that keeping really busy with all the work had kept my body warm. The truth is, Jason was right when he scoffed at the photo of the wood stove and said I couldn't even light a candle. I was very cautious about fire.

This doesn't seem unreasonable, though. I mean, I knew a girl in school who was afraid—literally *afraid*—of mayonnaise. That's an unreasonable fear. Fire is the sort of thing people *should* be afraid of. Once on Facebook, the system offered me a chance to click on being a "fan of not being on fire." That's totally me. I'm a fan of not being on fire. And I'm a fan of staying away from the various implements that could lead to my ever being on fire: matches, gasoline, wood stoves.

But this was the life I had chosen, and I knew I could do it. Just because Jason always lit the candles in Dallas didn't mean I couldn't light them for myself on Simple Island. I was going to have to learn to do a lot of things on my own.

Milton is the sort of little town where the gas station, the grocery store, and the hardware store are all lined up in a neat little row on the main street. I went first to the grocery store and bought mostly canned goods: soup, beans etc. I added bottled water, some boxed pasta, bread and bagels, and canned dog food to my rather small shopping cart.

Back at the car, Margaret Mary greeted me enthusiastically and began nosing around the bags, because she knew there was something inside for her.

From the outside, "Vincent & Son Lumber and Hardware" looked small, and I was skeptical that it could hold much of a variety of stock, as I was used to a store like Lowes that could qualify for its own zip code. But inside, it looked clean and organized. I realized immediately that what was missing was an entire city of light fixtures to choose from, plus enough bathtubs, toilets, sinks and showers to outfit a New York luxury apartment building.

The little bell on the door jingled to signify my arrival, and just as I was breathing in the clean sawdust smell, I heard a male voice from the back call, "I'll be right out! Don't go anywhere!"

One of the frontmost aisles in the store had the fire-starter products I needed. I'd seen them on Amazon. I didn't want a liquid accelerant—that's the way you set yourself on fire, which I'm a fan of not being—I wanted the little gummy logs that light easily and then catch the kindling. People on You Tube liked them and showed me how to use them, so I felt confident as I put four of them in my little basket.

Next, I found myself standing on the paint aisle, in front of the wall of little color chips, thousands of shades covering the entire spectrum of paint color possibilities. Painting is something I am not afraid of, as it falls in the category of basic crafting.

I'd had the thought earlier that day that a quick coat of cheerful paint on the front door might be just the thing to brighten up the drab front of the cabin. I knew from the inspection report that the cabin would soon need a new roof, and I was partial to the look of a green metal roof on log cabins I'd seen, so perhaps a nice forest green paint for the door...

"I'm not sure that color matches your eyes."

Startled, I turned to face the man who had seemingly materialized behind me. I must have jumped, because he immediately apologized.

"Oh! I'm so sorry! I didn't mean to scare you!"

His apology sounded sincere, but the twinkle never left his eyes. He was about my height, maybe half an inch taller, and muscular in a stocky way. He had wavy strawberry blonde hair and a full beard that was a darker red. His friendly eyes were a clear blue that looked like they would shine in the dark. Inexplicably, I found myself bitterly regretting my disheveled hair and workday clothes.

I couldn't help but smile back. "It's OK," I assured him. "I just didn't hear you come up. Paint chips are so mesmerizing...Do you work here?"

He smiled that smile again. "I practically live here!" he said. "It's my place."

"Oh..." I thought for a second. "You must be the "& *son*" I've heard tell of."

"Nope."

"You're "Vincent" then?" I thought perhaps his son was a young child and he was simply counting on him growing into the family business.

"Nope."

I stared at him, feeling peculiarly aware of my grubby t-shirt, and he just grinned. Finally, he clarified.

"I'm Troy Bowden. I bought this store when Mr. Vincent retired. His son— "& son"—went into dentistry. I kept the name because the town is used to it. If I had changed it, half the people would have stopped shopping here. People don't like change."

"Probably very smart," I said, sticking out my hand. "I'm Trista."

He took my hand in his for a warm handshake and said, "Maybrey, right?"

Surprised again, I asked, "How did you know?"

"It's a small town," he said, and there was that grin again. "People have been talking for weeks about somebody buying Simple Island, planning to live there. You walk in here today in those muddy boots...I just figured."

"Wow...it *is* a small town. People are really talking about Simple Island? Why does anyone even care?"

Troy leaned casually against the wall of colors. "Well, it's been a while since anyone lived there, and there's been a lot of speculation whether the Beardens might reabsorb it into their property. There's been a fellow that came out to look at it several times, and he asked a lot of questions around town. Even brought his own crew of inspectors once, and there was a little trouble when the Beardens reported he was on the island without the real estate agent. Then there was another couple we thought were going to buy it, but I guess they backed out."

"An elderly couple, I think."

"I suppose so."

"Still, it's such a little place. Seems funny to me that anybody is talking about it."

Troy smiled again, comfortable in his domain. "You know how people are. There are all kinds of stories about Simple Island. A few of them have turned into ghost stories."

"Ghost stories!?"

"Oh, nothing to worry about. People love a good ghost story, and they've grown over the years that it's been sitting empty. You don't believe in ghosts, do you?"

I could tell he was teasing me. Everything about him seemed to be teasing me.

"No, of course not," I answered, "But I do believe in my own wild imagination, so let's just not tell Trista the ghost stories, shall we?"

Now I was teasing, and I could tell Troy was enjoying it. Maybe enjoying it too much. I changed the subject back to the variety of green chips in my hand. "My eyes are brown," I said, holding up the chips, "and everything goes with brown, so I just need to pick which green I like best."

Troy took my hint and turned his attention to the chips. "What are you painting?" he asked, suddenly professional.

"I think the front door. I haven't completely decided. The front of the cabin is so plain."

"Oh, that's a great idea!" Troy was beaming at me again. "I've always thought that the outside of the cabin is pretty sad looking compared to the inside. Maybe that's by design. Sometimes clammers park their canoes there, and the plain outside of the cabin may have discouraged anyone from breaking in."

"Clammers?" I asked.

"Sure—but nothing to worry about! You probably won't see anyone now that the island is occupied. It's just been a convenient place for clammers—like fishermen who are specifically gathering clams at low tide—well, they have sometimes used Simple Island as a base to keep their stuff, maybe even camp out. It's probably contributed to the ghost stories, if you know what I mean."

I didn't, really, know what he meant, but I found myself focused on something else. "Wait," I interrupted, "You've been *inside* the cabin?"

"Of course I have," Troy sparkled. "Who do you think turned on the gas and lit the stove pilot before you arrived?"

I must have been gaping, because after a brief pause, he continued.

"I'm kind of Milton's Handyman Laureate," he said. "If anyone needs anything done on their property, they call me. I take care of most of the properties out on Parson Point, especially during the winter when a lot of people have gone somewhere warmer. The people who owned Simple Island were almost never there. I think they bought it as a marital aid that didn't work. They were out there for like a month, fixed it up all cute, then filed for divorce. But of course, they needed it to stay in working order until it sold, so…they called Troy."

I vaguely remembered Lisa's husband saying something about "Troy could do it" in regard to digging up the remains of the old fireplace. This was Troy.

"I've been going out there about twice a month for years, mostly just making sure everything was safe. When the inspectors were scheduled to come out for your purchase, Lisa asked me to meet them and show them around."

"That didn't make it into the report," I said. "I guess I had to find you on my own."

"I guess you did," he agreed. Damn that beaming smile of his. "So, are you looking for an emerald green, or something darker?"

I explained that I knew the roof needed replacing, and that I was considering the green metal roofs I had seen on log cabins in Texas.

"Well, that's easy then!" he exclaimed. "Come on back here and look at the stock; we can match the color as close as you want, and then I'll know what to order when you're ready."

"You do roofing too?"

He stuck out his hand again as though we were meeting for the first time, and, dumbly, I shook it. "Hi," he said, "Troy Bowden, Vincent & Son Lumber and Hardware. We're the only game in town!"

I said goodbye to Troy after checking out with a box of fire starters, a red plastic gas can, a new Maglite, and a quart of paint that exactly matched the green metal roofing.

I'd completely lost track of time while in the hardware store, and Margaret Mary looked concerned. "You knew I would come back," I admonished her as she jumped around in the back seat. "I always come back!" When I turned the key, the clock lit up and told me that my low tide window had only five minutes left. I was shocked and kicked myself for getting so caught up in the shopping. Or in Troy Bowden. Now I had to hurry.

Of course, I knew that the tide didn't come back in all at once. It's not like there would suddenly be ten-foot-deep water separating me from my house. But the longer I took, the more I'd be splashing through in my boots. I looked in my rearview mirror and grimaced at the things I'd be carrying over. This was likely to take more than one trip, and I knew Margaret Mary would be no help; in fact, I'd probably need a whole trip just to carry her across. I didn't dare take the time to stop for gasoline. The generator would have to wait.

As I drove back toward Parson Point, my mood was further squashed by fat raindrops splatting on my windshield. It wasn't heavy rain, by any means, but it would make my repeated crossings more difficult, and certainly less comfortable.

By the time I parked my car in my deeded space behind the Beardens' chain, the rain was falling more rapidly, and I knew I just had to steel myself against it and make the trips. I decided to leave the comforter and some of my other "luxury items" for a sunnier day and focus on my recent purchases. First, I gathered the bag from Vincent & Son, the gas can, and the bag with the canned dog food. Against her protests, I made Margaret Mary stay in the car. I didn't want her following me and getting wet.

Halfway down the wooded path, I realized the folly of carrying the gas can. Because it was empty, I would simply have to carry it back again to fill it up. I cursed my stupidity under my breath and put the can down right there on the path.

I managed to make it across with the other two bags without getting terribly wet. I was pretty well rained on, but the crossing had only been a little bit splashy. About halfway across on my way back, though, it really started pouring down on me. And it was cold.

Back at the car, I scolded Margaret Mary for jumping at me, and then immediately apologized. It wasn't her fault I was wet and cold and stupid and grouchy. I gathered the other three bags of groceries and redistributed the cans into two bags of equal weight.

Telling Margaret Mary to stay, again, I headed back down the path, my head ducked low to keep the rain out of my face. It was really coming down now, like thousands of tiny cold knives, whipping at my skin, making my protective clothing a heavy, unforgiving adversary.

With my head down like that and trying to use my shoulders and elbows to push back the wet limbs that choked the path, I didn't see the gas can...and I tripped, falling headlong into the dirt. My bags went flying and a can of soup rolled up under a fir tree. I landed on my hands and knees and had an instant premonition of the pain I would feel in the morning. Tears sprang to my eyes as I had to resort to using my freshly abraded hands against a rough tree trunk to aid myself in standing.

I gathered everything I could and put it back in the bags. I figured the can of soup would still be there when the sun came out, and if not...it was worth the $1.27 to not have to go looking for it.

When I got to the end of the path and looked through the rain across the 100 yards between myself and Simple Island, I was astonished how much higher the water was already. Even in knee high boots, I would probably get my legs wet, and most of the green grassy point that I followed was already underwater, obscuring my careful path.

There was nothing for it. I had to go—and I'd have to come back again for Margaret Mary. I shook my head, maybe trying to clear the clouds of discouragement, and stepped down onto the shore.

I knew, simultaneously, that under these conditions, I needed to take my time, and also that I had no time to take. I had to hurry. I walked as briskly as the sloshing would allow down what I could see of the grassy point, and then when I came to the end, I turned and set my sights on the shore of the island.

But I turned too soon. Lisa had warned me that if I didn't go all the way out to the last piece of grass on that point, if I turned even twelve inches too soon, I would get "bogged down" ...and suddenly, tragically, I found out what that meant. When I turned toward Simple's shore, I placed my right foot on the mud and then immediately began moving my left foot in front of it, but too late I realized that my right foot had sunk, almost ankle deep, in the muddy mire, and I was already committed with my left foot, which also sank in the mud. I began the slow-motion, arm waving dance that is the inevitable prelude to a spectacular fall.

I could see it all, almost as if I were standing on the opposite shore, watching myself. I could see the various possible outcomes. Trista falls forward, lands on her hands which also sink into the mud, and she drowns, face down in less than ten inches of water. Trista falls to the side, but her feet don't come up out of the mud and so both ankles are badly broken, and she sits there, in the rain, helpless, no one around to hear her cries, until the sea rises and hypothermia lulls her into the sleep of death. Trista doesn't fall, because some hidden neighbor sees her and comes to the rescue with an umbrella, but not before snapping several comical photos which go viral on Instagram.

Thankfully, the winning scenario was that Trista fell backward, landing on my ass, leaving me in a sitting position, waist-deep in the very cold water; I cried like a baby, in big, gasping sobs, as I laboriously pulled my feet out of the mud and scrambled back up what was left of the grassy point toward the rocks that allowed me access to the upper shore and the relative shelter of the trees. Where were my groceries? I figured the canned items were down there somewhere, stuck in the mud where I had fallen. I could see my loaf of bread bobbing on the waves and floating further and further away.

Still sobbing, now completely wet and shivering and feeling magnificently sorry for myself, I dragged what was left of me back to the car. I got in and applied the key without even speaking to Margaret Mary...and drove to the Red Rooster Inn. *Trista Maybrey and the Mysterious Island*: in this chapter...Trista gives up.

A bottle of wine and a hot shower later, I wasn't crying anymore, but I was really nursing the self-pity, like it was a wounded baby bird and I was its mother now. My brain was a long procession of rhetorical questions. Well, not rhetorical, because they had answers, but the answer to all of them was the same: "Because you're stupid" ...or something similar.

Why was this happening to me? Why was my life falling apart? How did this all begin? How did I let this happen? What had I done to bring on this misery? What had I been thinking when I moved here? Why did I think I could handle this? Why didn't I listen to the people who told me to stay in my safe little box? Why did Jason fall in love with someone else? Why was I getting so old and still so incapable of facing reality?

It was really easy to come up with all of these questions, and a hundred more, and the ease of the questions grew in proportion to the diminishing quantity of wine in the bottle. Finally, I was crying again, half-drunk and pitiful, and I crawled under the covers and let the misery sweep me away. Margaret Mary slept under the chair across the room, apparently knowing better than to try to comfort me in my wretched state.

The dream actually started pleasantly. I was on the little sandy beach of the island, and it was sunny and warm, and Troy was with me. We were laughing about something, and then I looked out over the water and I could see my loaf of bread, floating up towards us and I pointed and shouted for Troy to look, but when I turned to him, he was standing holding hands with the woman I had seen in my dream before, the pretty woman with her hair piled up on her head. She was wearing the same dress, with the high lace collar. Troy said, "I want you to meet Em...but I think you already know her..." and he smiled that glorious smile of his.

And then the forest behind us exploded and I was flying through the air and it was suddenly dark except for the flames, and I could hear a man calling to me, reminding me to "Find me at the temple!" and I was falling and falling, falling toward the water and thinking that, if I could just land on that loaf of bread, then maybe I would be able to float and wouldn't drown. But as I aimed for the bread, I suddenly saw that there was an alligator circling in the water, waiting for me to land. And then the face of the man, the man with red hair and freckles, loomed toward me again, and came so close that I thought his face was melting into mine, and I felt like he was trying to tell me something, but then I hit the water and woke up.

The morning period of low tide was before my check out time, and I wasn't interested in even pretending that I was leaving the Red Rooster before I absolutely had to. I went outside at about eight, only long enough to let Margaret Mary have her morning walk, and then I came back in and crashed again. When I woke up the second time, it was ten A.M. and I called Mom.

At first, I groveled in the self-pity again, telling her about falling, twice, and losing my groceries and giving up and coming back to the motel. But even as I was doing it, I was glossing over it, because I didn't want Mom to start telling me to come home. In glossing over it for Mom, I was glossing over it for myself as well, and I was realizing I felt better.

"Well, honey," she said, "It sounds like you just have to learn the ropes. I know you will."

"Sure I will," I said, actually starting to believe it. "And there's always more bread. But, Mom...there's something else."

I started telling her about the recurring images in my dreams. The explosion, the fire, falling into the water. Mom was used to me telling her my dreams, but she also understood that recurring nightmares were a new thing for me. I thought she would comfort me by saying that my quest for a new life was just wreaking havoc with my subconscious, which had always been like a dog on a leash that would turn and bite me in my sleep.

But her response surprised me. "That's...interesting," she said, and the way she dragged out the words, I could tell she was thinking, trying to remember something.

"What is it?" I queried.

"Well..." she began, "It reminds me of something. It reminds me of a poem you wrote when you were just a little girl, something about fire and falling into the sea. Do you remember? It was the one you got a ribbon for. I think you won third place in a state contest your teacher sent it to."

I did have some vague remembrance of winning in a poetry contest, and my fourth-grade teacher being really proud of me, but I categorized that win along with my blue ribbon for the sixth-grade field day Frisbee Toss which had been entirely due to the wind. I kept both awards, and happily accepted all accolades, but recognized that I was no more a poet than I was a Frisbee Athlete. Is there such thing as a Frisbee Athlete?

"I think I still have it somewhere," Mom continued her musing. "I'll have to find it and show you what I mean."

I said goodbye to Mom feeling much better than when I'd said hello. Moms can be good like that. I was thirty-three, but she could still kiss my boo-boos, even long distance.

Next, I called my two coordinators to let them know I was only available by phone for the day. My laptop was on the island, no doubt with a dead battery since I hadn't ever gotten the generator going. Then I checked us out of the Red Rooster and drove to Elmore for the day, hanging out in a variety of antique stores while I waited for the tide to go out.

When finally, on dry land, Margaret Mary and I crossed back over to our island, I walked up the long damp path to the cabin. On the front porch, lined up neatly, were all of my canned items, including the soup that had rolled away on the path, and on the bottom step was my new red gas can, filled to the top with gasoline.

Chapter Sixteen

July 11, 1859

My Darling,

If you laughed to the point of choking over my comment about my mother's forks, then I surely mirrored your level of mirth when attempting to picture myself in a red velvet carriage atop an elephant, leading an elephant train carrying my trousseau from my childhood home to yours. While the image of an elephant train is fantastic enough in the typical setting of an African desert, it is only made more comical by imagining such a caravan trudging down the thoroughfare in, for instance, downtown Philadelphia.

And so, it occurs to me that my ability to envision your home—which will soon become my home—is as difficult as picturing those elephants in Philadelphia. While this city where I was born and have lived my life to this point carries its unique traits, they are no more unique than the traits of any other city, and you have visited so very many cities.

Though I have not yet traveled the world, I imagine that you could lift me bodily out of Cincinnati and transplant me in Boston or Charleston or Atlanta or Albany and within a couple of hours I would have gathered my bearings and begun to find my way around the shops and restaurants and millinery establishments. Even so, when I try to imagine myself in the new setting that is the home of your birth, the home where our children will also be born, it is as though I am staring at a blank artist's canvas, trying to imagine what picture might be purposed there.

Within the moments we have thus far spent in one another's company, I came to recognize the love you have for your part of the world, and I desire nothing more than to share that love with you, but still you will, I hope, forgive me for the present moments when gazing upon the blank canvas is at least a little bit frightening for me.

I will learn to love it as you do, and until then I will rely upon your lifetime of knowledge to welcome me into your world and comfort me as I grow accustomed to the differences, the magical differences, that my new life and environment will offer.

Chapter Seventeen

Whether it was the wine or the talk with Mom or the unintentional baptism in Black Bay which affected the change for me, my return to Simple Island was accompanied by pure determination. I just knew that my tearful retreat to the Red Rooster would be the last one.

There was a small part of me which knew absolutely that Troy Bowden had brought up my groceries and filled my gas can, and that same small part also knew absolutely that this gesture meant that he knew, or at least had guessed, about my floundering failure. But because this was a small part of me, it was only bothered in a small way. It had been a long time since anyone had successfully lived here, and I was going to show them all...it had to be excusable that I had an early misstep, and equally commendable that I had returned the very next day. I congratulated myself on my show of heartiness.

The gifted gasoline meant that I could figure out the generator. It was a modern model, with a pushbutton starter; thank god, again, for the YouTube uploaders, because I had seen several helpful videos that taught me to turn the knob for the gas line, flip the top switch on, pull out the choke as far as I could, then push and hold the bottom button until the engine kicked in. I'd love to say it all came together like poetry the first time, but in truth it took several tries and several masterful streaks of profanity before it finally caught and held...but when it did, I was the superhero of my own story!

As soon as the generator engine fired up, every light in the cabin came on, and suddenly my world was warm and bright, and all things were possible. I went inside and immediately plugged in my laptop to charge, and also began charging several external batteries that were supposed to allow me power even at times when I was not running the generator.

The generator, of course, was loud, and this quite spoiled the lovely quiet atmosphere of the island, but I saw it not merely as a "necessary evil," but more like that friend in high school who was garishly loud and tacky, but who knew all the cheat tricks for Algebra, so you valued the friendship even though you looked forward to her going home at the end of the day.

Now that the lights were on in the cabin, I abruptly realized how much I disliked them. Not the light emitting from them, of course, but the fixtures themselves. There were six ceiling lights in the cabin: one in the bedroom, one in the bathroom, two in the great room (which is an ironic thing to call such a very small room), one in the kitchen, and the chandelier over the bar. The five fixtures that were not the chandelier were all extremely plain, just little white upside-down cups stuck to the ceiling, each with a single lightbulb inside. The chandelier, however, looked like something from a nineties rave club, ludicrously out of place in this island-forest cabin. It was a long silver rectangle attached to the ceiling and hanging down were four elongated glass pendants with bubbles in the glass such that when the light was on, they looked like they were boiling. I had not cared for it with the lights off, but with them *on*, I knew it had to go.

Taking advantage of the period of electricity, I used the microwave to heat up a can of soup, and while I sipped it, I scrolled through several websites looking at light fixtures that seemed more appropriate for a cabin. Of course, there were some amazing chandeliers made with antique wagon wheels and wrought iron, if one was interested in spending a thousand dollars. I soon found myself enamored of some little brass hanging lanterns which could replace the ceiling fixtures, and a wooden-accented chandelier which culminated in three lanterns to hang over the bar. I put all of these things in my online "cart" and then realized I had nowhere to send them.

My informal address was "#1 Simple Island" ...but it wasn't like I had a mailbox that the FedEx guy could put my packages in. I'd need to get a post office box, for regular mail, but I didn't even think they'd let me receive massive and multiple packages for all the things I wanted to order for my new home.

When my computer was fully charged, and the external batteries were showing all their little dots of power, I went outside into the near-dark, and turned off the generator. I was almost shocked by the silence. With Margaret Mary at my heels I wandered over to the west side of the island where there was an overgrown patch of blueberry shrubs, and I picked my way through the greenery to the edge of the rocks where I had a clear view of the ocean and the sky. The tide was very much in, and the sinking sun was a ball of muted gold wrapped in pink clouds. The water was pink in its reflection of them, and I felt as though I could just melt into the sky, merge with those pink clouds. The sun was a friendly eye, winking at me. "You did well today, Trista. You're gonna be OK,"

And I knew that I was.

✳ ✳ ✳

The photographs of the cabin roof had been pretty disturbing. The inspector had climbed up there with a ladder and taken pictures from several angles, writing in his report: "Original roof has reached life expectancy."

The cabin was built in 1996, so this roof was now more than twenty years old. The individual shingles were curling and holding them all together (and in place) were enormous, amorphous blobs of living, growing, thriving moss. This combination of decay and plant life meant that a tragedy was brewing and would ultimately manifest in water leaking through onto my beautiful pine walls and ceiling. I knew that no matter how cute I made the inside of the cabin; the condition of the roof would ultimately ruin it all.

Early the next morning, I got up with the tide and headed for Vincent & Son. This time, however, I was more conscious of what I was wearing, and even put on a little mascara. I told myself it was good to look professional when I was going to do the sort of business that would cost several thousand dollars...and that it had nothing to do with seeing Troy Bowden again.

When I pushed through the front door and heard the little bell jingle, I could instantly hear Troy's voice back at the checkout counter, explaining something to another customer. I walked back toward the counter, and could see an older gentleman standing there, with his back to me, evidently trying to decide between different brands of deck sealer. Standing behind the counter, Troy was facing me, but deeply engrossed in the conversation, expounding on the pros and cons of the two cans of sealant the gentleman had carried to him.

I stopped several yards away from the counter, not wanting to interrupt, and just listened to Troy's voice, so easy and confident, and then he turned to reach for something on the shelf behind him, and as he turned, his gaze slid into mine for just a quarter of a second...and he winked at me. It was a wink that was so slight, anyone else watching might not have caught it, but I definitely caught it. At the end of that quarter second, he was already back in full conversation with the other man, but in that tiny gesture, he said so many things to me...some of them things I wasn't ready to think about.

The main message that I took from the wink was that Troy was saying, "I know you. You're important to me. I have to do what I'm doing, but I'm especially aware that you're here; give me a minute, and I'll be all yours."

I could feel myself blushing, so I took quick refuge in the lightbulb aisle. Why are there so many different kinds of lightbulbs, and how many lightbulb purchases happen in a town this size? Did Milton really *need* this many lightbulbs in so much variety?

Finally, I heard the older man's voice, very close to me now, thanking Troy for his help, and then I saw him pass by the end of the lightbulb aisle, on his way out of the store. Inexplicably, my heart started beating faster, and as I turned to step back out into the main part of the store, Troy was already turning the corner of the aisle to meet me.

"Hi there!" he said cheerily, and I felt myself blushing again. Dammit.

"Hey...hey, did you...pick up my groceries?" I honestly hadn't meant to ask that at all. What was wrong with me?

"Grocery delivery is not usually in my job description, but...well, they were just lying there, at the bottom of the ocean..."

"Well...thank you..." I winced, "I guess..."

Troy's smile melted into something even softer. Compassion. Understanding. "You'll get the hang of the tides, Trista. It's not easy. Not for anyone. It took me at least a year to get the hang of it...took me more than a month just to get used to consulting the tide charts. You've got a lot to learn but look at you...you're still here!"

"Wait," I said, confused. "You're not...you're not *from* here?"

"Oh, no," he brightened. "I'm a Southern boy, born and raised. I moved to Maine to finish my degree in electrical engineering. I just fell in love with it, tides and all."

Something about the way he finished that sentence left us just quietly standing there, looking at each other. For a moment, it wasn't awkward, just...familiar.

And then the awkward kicked in.

"Roof," I said at last. "I wanted to talk to you about the roof."

"That's right!" he said, the spell broken. He turned to walk back to his counter, and I followed him. He was chatting back at me, over his shoulder as he walked.

"I'm glad you're making this a priority," he said. "That roof is definitely on its last legs, so to speak. Now that it's

Springtime, the heavy rains will come, and all that moss will really thrive up there. Have you been up to see it?"

"No," I answered. "But I've seen the pictures. The inspector's report was pretty graphic."

"I'll bet!"

Troy reached the counter and crossed behind it. I stood on the customer side as he leaned on one elbow and gave me that lazy grin again.

"How soon do you want to start?" he asked.

"As soon as you can get the materials. I guess you'll need to come out and measure so you can work up an estimate."

"Nope," he grinned, and there was silence while I waited for him to explain.

Finally, he broke the tension and stood up straight. "I know that cabin pretty well. The other day when you were talking about replacing the roof, I went ahead and took the initiative to work up an estimate."

Troy reached under the counter and pulled out a yellow legal pad. I could see a scrawl of numbers and figures on the top page. He studied it for a second, then turned it around to face me, and with a ball-point pen, he circled a number in the middle in the page, indicating that this would be the total cost for the roof.

"That's it?" I said at last. "That's the whole cost? I was thinking it would be a lot more..."

"No reason for it," he said. "It's a really straightforward roof, nothing fancy. There is a little something extra here because you need ice breaks."

He circled another number and tapped on it with the pen.

"Ice breaks?" I asked, wishing I didn't sound completely ignorant.

"Yes—you need ice breaks on the roof so that, in the winter, the snow doesn't just slide off in one big heavy sheet."

I guess I just blinked at him dumbly, so he continued.

"You know, on both sides of your roof you've got gutters. Now, usually, if I'm installing a metal roof up here, I just tell people the gutters need to come down, because the sheets of snow, when they slide off, well they'll just rip the gutters right off the house. But your gutters can't come down, because..."

"Because they're the water collection system!" I interrupted him, proud to finally have a clue.

"That's right!" (Did he look impressed?) "The rain and melted snow run into those gutters and then funnel into the cistern, and that's your water for...whatever. Washing dishes, showering. Probably not cooking. So, we can't take the gutters down, and we sure don't want them ripped down by giant heavy sheets of snow so...ice breaks."

With that, he tapped on the circled number again.

"Well, let's do it!" I said, trying to match his smile. "I'm ready when you are!"

"Ok, then..." Troy pulled a desk calendar from under the counter and appeared to be reading the multicolored hieroglyphs that covered every date of the month of April. "If I place the order tomorrow morning, I should have the materials by next Wednesday. I could come out next Saturday to do the job. Shouldn't take more than half a day."

"Really?" I said, incredulous. "Half a day?"

"Like I said...it's not fancy."

When I left Vincent & Son, I stopped by the grocery store for bread and a couple of impulse purchases, mostly of the chocolate variety, and then to the gas station to refill my gas can. I didn't actually know how long a single gallon would last, and I wanted to have more on hand. As I was driving back down Parson Point, I got a text message from Mom: "Check your email. I found the poem."

Margaret Mary was so happy to see me when I got back to the cabin that she was literally dancing in little circles on her hind legs. I put away my groceries and then turned on the gas stove to heat up a can of baked beans and some rice for lunch. I sat at the little dining table and opened my computer, looking for Mom's email among all the emails that were work-related. I finally found it, titled: YOUR AWARD-WINNING POETRY.

In the body of the email, Mom had simply typed up the words of my fourth-grade poem:

The water's cold
The fire is hot.
The night is bold
But I am not.
The Sultan's wife,
That crocodile,
She spits me out,
I fall a mile.
I look around
This endless ride,
And see tin soldiers
Side by side.
I think they'll save
Me from the sea.
But I am wrong.
They fall with me.

I read it through three times. Maybe four. I was trying to recapture the little girl who wrote this. What was she thinking? What did this mean to her? The Sultan's wife...who was that? I had been really into Aladdin in the fourth grade. Like every other little girl, I wanted to be Princess Jasmine. That probably explained the bit about the Sultan's wife.

But what about the rest of it? The fire, the sea, the fall...Mom was right. It sounded like my dreams.

I spent the rest of the afternoon catching up on work emails. I had a surrogate who was due to deliver within a week, and I wanted both her and the baby's parents to think I was totally paying attention to them. I was grateful for my little staff, who had so expertly kept things rolling comfortably while I had been distracted over the past weeks...months, really.

It was nice to have something else to focus on for a while, and when I finally closed my laptop at about seven o'clock, I took a moment to realize that, during those hours, I hadn't even considered that I was in a whole new environment. Surely that must be a sign that I was settling into my new world.

I didn't feel much like cooking dinner, so I made myself a peanut butter and banana sandwich and carried a lawn chair down to the overgrown blueberry patch by the water. It was the perfect place to watch the waves and the sunset, and Margaret Mary lazed at my feet. I sat there, focused on being mindful of the moment, the sea, the sky, the breeze, the incredible silence.

In Texas, there was always noise at night. Locusts and frogs, countless life forms scurrying and croaking, clicking and chirping, barking and crowing. Even in the city, the evening noises were incessant. But here...it was breathless silence. Occasionally I might hear a lone crow, or a

Laughing Gull, or something less natural, like the drone of a generator, carried across the water from a neighboring island. The water carried even the smallest noise. I had heard, a couple of times, neighbors' conversations as clearly as if they were taking place in my own yard, but in truth, they were so far off, I didn't even know where these phantom conversants were. The only house that could be considered "near" to me was the Beardens' place, and I had not seen any movement there at all.

As I sat there, focused on the still beauty of that moment, I realized I heard quiet footsteps behind me, and the hairs on the back of my neck stood up. It was high tide, so no one could have wandered over to say hello, and yet, I was physically aware that someone was approaching to stand right behind me.

I whirled around and came face to face with a woman I recognized from...where? She was a middle-aged woman, maybe in her fifties, wearing an old-fashioned lilac dress and a wide-brimmed hat. She was smiling at me warmly, but before I could choke out a single word of query or protest, the ground beneath me gave way, and I found myself crashing through weak wooden boards. I felt my hands and arms cut and scraped by the broken boards as I fell through, suddenly screaming and desperately trying to grab at the boards, at the overgrown blueberry weeds, at the dirt of the ground itself, anything to stop my fall. I caught a glimpse of Margaret Mary, but she had not changed position. She just looked at me quizzically as I cried out and strained to hold on...and then I fell. I landed hard on the ground at the bottom of a perfectly symmetrical hole, which was just big enough for me to sit in.

Breathing hard from the terror and the impact, I was no longer screaming, but I looked up through the broken boards and saw the woman as she stepped over to look down at me. Still smiling, she nodded, then reached over to the side where I couldn't see...and produced a shovel. The first load of dirt hit me directly in the face as I looked up at her in horror. It went all in my nose and mouth, down the front of my shirt. I choked and gagged and tried to cry out before she threw the second load of dirt on top of me, burying me alive.

And then, abruptly, I was back in my chair, sitting on top of the overgrown blueberry patch, looking out over the water with Margaret Mary lounging on the ground beside me. I leapt up and spun around, but there was no woman in a wide-brimmed hat. There was only me, alone on my private island.

My heart was pounding, slamming against my ribs, and my breath came hard and fast. Determined not to let myself hyperventilate, I sat back down and attempted to control my breathing. Margaret Mary was on alert now, aware that something was happening to me, and I focused on offering her comfort, cuddling her on my lap and letting her concern and kisses help regulate my palpitations.

What the hell was that? I hadn't been asleep—I was certain of it. I wasn't one to just "fall asleep" in my chair like that. And yet I was positive that I'd seen this woman before in a dream. Yes! It was the dream I'd had about the island being much bigger and having all the people who sold things in a big warehouse...she was the woman who had told me all my answers were—somewhere—and then, in that dream, I'd fallen in a hole and she had started burying me with dirt. This was that same imagery except...this hadn't been a dream.

Of course, it hadn't been real either. Reality was sitting here in my foldable chair, facing the water with a half-eaten peanut-butter and banana sandwich on the rock in front of me. Reality was Margaret Mary whimpering and licking my face. If this was reality and that was *not* a dream, then it could only have been one thing.

Hallucination was a scary word. I'd never known myself to have a hallucination, and I didn't want to add that to my psychiatric repertoire now that I was living alone on an island.

Needing to ground myself, I walked back to the cabin and settled down in front of my laptop again. I needed to start doing what Trista always did: using logic. I opened a new Word document, and began writing down dates and details of my recurring dreams...everything that I could remember, starting with the dream on the airplane, just before the first of my seat companions had spilled my own melted ice on my lap.

That first dream had been followed by a longer version of the same thing in the hotel room on that first trip. The next dream in the sequence had been that night in the awful motel in Hagerstown Maryland, and this time, the images of fire and water and falling had been accompanied by the pretty young woman, whose name was Emily or Emma, something like that—Em for short—and that was also the first time I'd seen the man with red hair and freckles, the one calling desperately for Em, and telling her to find him at "the temple."

On my first night in the cabin, I'd had the anxiety dream that had, at the time, seemed completely disconnected from the recurring images. This was the dream where all the people were manning little shops in the big warehouse, where the man was selling old army uniforms that were all marked "Ohio $175," but he was tending a mass of bloodied kittens, which were being eaten by an alligator, and the pretty woman in the hat was burying me in the small, symmetrical hole. I had discounted this dream at first, but after this...I still didn't want to call it a "hallucination" ...I now had to consider that it was connected, somehow, to the others.

The final dream in the sequence, if I was ready to admit there was a sequence here, had been the night I retreated to the Red Rooster Inn. This most recent dream had included Troy, introducing me to Em, but commenting that he thought I already knew her.

I could find the common elements in the dreams about the fire and the water and some kind of explosion, the falling. I began using the Word highlighter to color code the elements that matched on my list, and I went back to Mom's email to copy and paste my fourth-grade poem onto this new document, and added my color-coding system to the matching elements in the poem as well. Assuming that, in the fourth grade, I simply didn't yet know the difference in a crocodile and an alligator, I coded those images and references together as well.

With the dreams of fire and falling, and the coordinating poetry, all colored up, I turned my attention to the details in the longer dream that had seemed disconnected, and that evening's vision of the older woman in the wide brimmed hat. The most obvious connection was that this woman had appeared both in the dream and the waking vision. In both cases, I had fallen through boards into a hole in the ground, and she had begun shoveling dirt on top of me. Besides the concern over discovering my island had not been all to myself after all, the only other memorable part of the long dream was the man with the bloody kittens and the alligator, and all the tattered army uniforms for sale.

It seemed a weak connection, but I color coded the bit about the army uniforms to the mention of "tin soldiers" in the poem I'd written a quarter century ago. By this time, I knew I was probably just grasping at straws, as my mother would have said, but the soldier/uniform connection was the only possibility I could see.

Sitting back, looking at my pretty colors, I knew there had to be more here than I was seeing, and I decided it was time to call in my one resource.

Jennifer answered her phone before I even heard it ring on my end. "Hey! Hey! What's going on?"

I decided to start slowly. "Everything's great!" I assured her, confidently. "I'm getting settled in. It's a lot to learn all at once, but I'm getting the hang of all the details of living off the grid. I'm still alive, anyway, and Margaret Mary seems to think we're doing ok....so, yeah."

I realized that my confident note kind of went sour by the end of my little speech, and I knew Jennifer heard it as well.

"I'm glad you're figuring it all out," she said. "You're a lot more flexible than I am, that's for sure! I'd have already drowned myself in the ocean by now!"

"Well, I guess I almost did," I admitted, "But I decided to think of it as a baptism into my new life."

"Baptism..." she considered my choice of verbiage. "In all cultures, baptism carries a significant spiritual element. So...tell me what's happening."

"Jen," I began, tentatively, "I need you to not think I'm crazy..."

"That's an easy deal to make," she laughed. "I've been relying on you to not think I'm crazy for thirty years!"

Jennifer made it so easy for me to tell her about what I was experiencing. I told her my story, step by step, chronologically, and then described my Word document with all the color coding, linking the elements of the dreams, the poem, and the waking vision. I heard myself clearly trying to apply logic to what I knew she was thinking of as a purely spiritual experience.

She listened attentively, asking a question here or there to gain clarification for herself, and when I was finished with my description of events and how I supposed they connected, she said, "I have two things to say about this."

"OK...shoot."

"First of all, and I know this is already obvious to you, all of this is connected to that island. You didn't have your first vision until you were on your way to the island, and then the second one once you were already there. Then they stopped when you came back to Texas and started when you headed back toward Maine. Do you remember I said I thought something there was calling you home?"

"Yes, but..."

"No but! This is as clear as day! Trista...I think you're having a past life experience."

"Jennifer, that's too much! All of this—my finding the island and moving here—all of this is just circumstantial!" She was silent, and I continued, not so confidently. "Isn't it?"

"Is it?" she asked quietly. "Or is it the Universe, reality itself, bending to bring you exactly there at exactly this time." She paused again to let me consider.

"What if the entire goal of your life was to be right there. What if elements you know nothing of, and your own subconscious, have been conspiring since the day of your birth to help you become the woman who might marry a man like Jason and build the business you've built so that when Jason turned out to be what he had, clearly, always been, you might be free to seemingly stumble upon just the right episode of just the right TV show so that you'd go home and seemingly stumble upon just the right website to find just the right listing for this exact island, such that you would be irresistibly drawn all the way across the country, away from everyone you know and count on, to start all over on an island. An island that brings you these dreams and visions you can't ignore, things that circle back and connect to your own childhood! Seriously, you think you got Pillar Loans to change their policies all by your little old self?"

At that last bit, I laughed out loud. "Yeah," I agreed, "that part seems pretty fishy."

"Let me tell you something I've never told you," she said, and she sounded very serious again.

"I'm ready..."

"I think I killed someone."

I was silent, waiting for her to continue, but she didn't.

"Jennifer..."

"I mean, I have what I'm really sure is a solid memory from a past life; it's just a fragment of a memory, but it's very clear. I'm in the living room of a house that I've never known this version of myself to be in. The décor looks like, maybe mid-1970s. There's a big braid rug on the floor, and on the rug, face down, is a young woman with long brown hair. I know she's dead, and I know I killed her, and I'm filled with heavy remorse. I didn't mean to kill her. It was an accident somehow. I don't know what happened, but in that fragment of memory, I know my own life is over because I've somehow brought about the end of hers, whoever she is. I've worked with three different psychics, and a past life hypnotherapist, and I can't get any more of the memory than that...but what I have is vivid."

"Jen...why didn't you ever tell me this before?"

"I couldn't risk it. Not until now. I know you've always prided yourself on having your head squarely on your shoulders, and no time for nonsense like the fluff in my head. If I'd told you this a year ago, do you think you would have heard anything more than just bla bla bla, Jennifer is crazier than we all thought...?"

"Probably not," I admitted with a sigh.

"And now?"

"Now I don't know what to think!" I almost shouted into the phone. "You talk about past lives, and I'm seeing visions of strangers in explosions and bloody kittens...I don't have anything like the solid memory you've just described. If any of it is a memory then it is only a memory of my death: a death by burning, or by drowning, or by premature burial. Tin soldiers and alligators and old dresses and screaming and falling and...Troy."

"Troy? Who is Troy?"

"Nobody."

"Not nobody! I know that voice when you say 'Troy' and try to make it sound like nobody!" Now she was my Jennifer from high school, picking on me for having a crush on the guy who starred in the school play. I felt myself blush and tried to hide the betraying smile that she couldn't see through the telephone, but I knew she knew was there anyway. My only salvation would be to change the subject.

"Wait," I stopped her, "What's the second thing?"

"Second thing?"

"Yeah...you said you had two things to say about all of this, and then you said, 'first of all...' So, what's the second thing?"

"Oh!" Jennifer laughed, suddenly remembering. "The second thing is that, while you were talking, I zipped over to Expedia and bought a plane ticket. I'll be there on Friday morning!"

Chapter Eighteen

July 20, 1859

My Dearest,

It simply will not do to have you experiencing any emotional discomfort as you prepare for our union. I apologize for not having considered that the geographical and cultural differences between "your world" and "my world" may have given you even a moment's pause. That shows my own ego, still immature enough to imagine that the elements of my daily environment which are commonplace to me would also be commonplace to you.

I choose instead, now, to think of this entirely differently. I could, I suppose, attempt to allay your fears by insisting that you will not find it so different living here than living anywhere else, and in many ways that is true...people in "my world" follow the same basic pursuits of which you are already aware. Everyone wants to maximize their pleasure, to minimize their discomfort and, in general throughout the whole wide world, people simply want to find someone to love, and to sleep in on the occasional morning.

But rather than emphasizing these commonalities of which I know you are already aware, I will endeavor to emphasize the differences, not so that you will feel more afraid or less familiar, but so that you can anxiously anticipate adding these unfamiliar elements to the list of things you consider commonplace.

Here, we are ruled by the sea, governed by the tides. I cannot remember a time in my life when I was not perpetually cognizant of the ebbing and flowing of the tides, but I can step back from that simple acceptance and recognize that it will be all new to you, and you will simply have to learn that which I was born to. I believe there will be a period of adjustment, but your body, which is almost entirely constructed of water and therefore equally subject to the pull of the heavens as is the enormity of the deep dark Atlantic ocean, will at last remember itself and the rhythm of the tides will become a natural part of who you are.

There are several thousands of islands that line the coast of this region, and in order to reach any of them, one must become as comfortable on the deck of a boat as you might be on a rocking rail car. Boats will become an integral part of your life, and I hope you are excited about that. There is simply nothing in life to compare with travel on the water.

The shores of your new home, My Dearest, are rocky and pine covered. The deep green of the trees and the deep brown of the rocks and the deep blue of the sea will become the patchwork colors of your life, the calico quilt that wraps you warmly until you forget that it is a quilt and not your own natural skin. That's what Maine does: it becomes a part of who you are. While you may take your time acclimating to this *world, our children will be born ready to skip across the rocks and chase crabs in the tide pools.*

Still in all, this description is of the coastal area where we will make our home, gazing out every morning at the sun rising over the sparkling sea, but at any moment that you wish, I will arrange for the short carriage ride that will take you into town where you will, with no difficulty, find the shops and restaurants and millinery establishments that every other city offers, and in that you will find comfort and familiarity.

Oh, that I could hurry up the day when I get to bring you, forever, into my world!

Chapter Nineteen

The call with Jennifer was on Saturday night, so I had basically a whole week to prepare for her visit. It was annoyingly important to me that everything be perfect, so that she could see that I was doing as well as I'd tried to convey. I knew, of course, that she would be giving a full report to my mother as well.

On Sunday, the first reasonable low tide was in the mid-afternoon, so I timed my day and my chores so that I could leave the island as early as possible and make the drive for Elmore...and Walmart. The grocery store in Milton was adequate, but when my best friend was coming to town, I needed the big boy.

I was quite proud of myself for remembering to finally remove the lock box from the front door and carry it with me back to my car so that I could return it to Lisa's office while I was in town. I texted her quickly and she told me to just leave it in the black mailbox by the back door of the office, as no one was likely to be there on a Sunday. When I pulled into Elmore, that's the first address I asked Siri to take me to, and once that chore was complete, I set my sights for the big blue sign.

Elmore was a much larger city than Milton, but nothing so busy or crowded as any part of Dallas. Although my stress level was elevated due to the traffic, I could clearly see every turn that I needed to make, and by the time I pulled into my parking space on the grocery side of Walmart, I felt I had conquered Elmore. There would be no crying on the side of the road here.

It was almost eerie how familiar the sameness of Walmart was. With the exception of the rack of Maine-related bumper stickers near the checkout, the monstrous store was so very familiar, so very like the one I had shopped in weekly in Dallas. Welcome to Generica.

With very little stopping to think, I was able to maneuver the store as though I'd always shopped there. I found my favorite scented candles—the ones that smell like Crème Brule in the oven—and my favorite cleaning products. I bought what I'd need to make pasta shells with button mushrooms and kalamata olives. I bought cookies.

I came out of the store with enough bags of groceries to require at least four trips back and forth across Black Bay...but I wasn't even worried about that. My best friend was coming to visit me on my private island, and I had been shopping at Walmart. What more could a girl want on a sunny Sunday in the Spring?

The answer to that question was fluttering in the wind, tucked neatly under the windshield wiper of my car. I lifted the wiper to free the paper and discovered it to be a full-color extravaganza of stars and exclamation points and promises. "CLEANING, CLEARING, HAULING! NO JOB TOO BIG OR TOO SMALL! SERVING ALL OF DOWNEAST MAINE! CALL TODAY FOR A FREE QUOTE!"

Could this day get any better? This was *exactly* what I needed! Before Jennifer came, I needed someone to clean away all the *junk* around the outside of the cabin, and maybe to clear some of the brush that obscured the view of the ocean from the back deck. I didn't even care what it cost, I just wanted it done. Besides, the roof estimate was much less than I'd expected, so I had extra money that could be used for this...

The roof. Ugh.

I'd forgotten Troy was going to be there on Saturday to do the roofing. Jennifer was coming Friday, and Troy would be there Saturday. I don't know why I didn't want Jennifer to meet Troy, but I just didn't. I knew that if she saw him, if she saw me *with* him, she would see the very thing I'd been trying to hide from myself...and once she saw it, I wouldn't be able to pretend it wasn't there. Damn.

I got in the car and started the air conditioner, but before I buckled my seatbelt, I called the big red phone number on the flyer in my hand.

The phone rang once, twice, and then a man's voice said, "The only thing we have to fear is fear itself."

Startled into confusion, wondering if I'd gotten a machine, I fumbled, and then said, "Excuse me?"

The man on the other end of the line laughed softly. "That's your free quote. If you called this number, you were promised a free quote, so there you go. Franklin Delano Roosevelt. If you want another quote, I'll have to charge you."

"Oh..." I wasn't sure how to proceed.

"Sorry if I caught you off guard. It's just a little joke to break the ice. The flyer used to offer a *free estimate* and then when someone called, I'd say something dumb like, 'I estimate that you're 46 years old and have a long history of alcoholism.' That didn't always go over so well."

"Is that true?"

"Not at all."

I was both charmed and confused. Thankfully, the man was prepared to guide me back to solid ground.

"Well," he said breezily, "Now that we know each other, what can I do for you?"

"Oh. I just bought a little island off the coast of Milton...do you know where Milton is?"

"Sure! Cute little town. Hasn't changed in twenty years."

"That sounds about right. Anyway—I bought a little island, and on it is a little cabin, and around the cabin is a lot of junk."

"Junk? Can you clarify? How do you define 'junk'?"

"Oh, overturned barrels, shredded tarps in many colors, dozens of those bobbers that people attach to lobster traps, broken buckets, broken tools, random bits of lumber..."

"Ah," he said, as though suddenly wise. "Junk."

"Junk," I repeated. "Plus, there are places where it's just overgrown with brush and a little clearing would give me a prettier view of the water."

"So, how does one get to your little paradise?" he asked. "Do you have a boat?"

"Oh! I should have mentioned that part! No—you don't need a boat. At low tide you can just walk out. If you want to meet me in Milton, I'll show you the best way to walk out to the island. Just let me know what day you might come, and I'll consult the tide charts."

"How interesting," he said, and I could hear paper shuffling. I imagined he was looking at a calendar. "When did you want this job done?"

"Well," I said, suddenly feeling apologetic, because I knew I was asking a lot, "I was hoping you could do it one day this week. I have company coming next weekend, and I'd really like the place to look nice."

"This week...this week..." he considered, consulting...what? Notes? Dates? Finally, he said, "That should be doable. I could send someone out on...probably Wednesday. Would that work?"

"Wednesday would be great!" I enthused. I could already see how pretty Simple Island would look with the junk gone.

"Two things we need to discuss," he said.

"Sure!"

"I'll need a deposit up front, and I'll need to see the area to work up the total price."

"OK...just tell me what to do!"

"Well, I've already locked the office for today, but I could meet you somewhere with my little credit card swiper. If you just got my flyer, I assume you're at the Elmore Walmart."

"Yes!"

"There's a little Asian place right across the highway from the Walmart...it's called *Thai-Tanic*...I know; that's terrible...but I could meet you there in about twenty minutes, if you like."

I looked at my watch. I still had a solid two hours on my low tide window. "That's fine!" I said, happily. "I'm driving a cranberry-red Nissan."

"Great. I'm in a silver Beemer. I'll see you in twenty!"

"Wait!" I stopped him before he could hang up on me. "What's your name?"

"Oh, sorry! You probably thought it was Franklin Delano Roosevelt! I'm Ian Andrews."

"Nice to meet you, Ian. I'm Trista Maybrey. See you in twenty!"

* * *

The man who climbed out of the silver Beemer parked in front of the *Thai-Tanic* did not look like the sort of person who made a living doing hard labor. I remembered what he'd said about "sending someone out" and realized that he was the businessman *behind* the hard labor. He probably had a crew of several workers.

Ian Andrews was tall and lanky, almost stunningly handsome, with thick shiny black hair and sparkling green eyes. When he came into the restaurant, I was already seated in a booth facing the front door, and he looked right at me and struck a perfect smile. He moved fluidly, almost lazily, across the restaurant and slid into the booth across from me, offering his hand for a firm shake. His hands were perfectly manicured, unlike my own, which had fallen into disreputable disrepair since taking possession of my island. I found myself purposely hiding my hands under the cover of the table so that he couldn't see.

Getting the business out of the way first, Ian told me that every job, no matter the size, required a $100 deposit, and he offered me a little contract to sign with all manner of fine print about his liability and insurance. That out of the way, he smiled at me and asked if I had time for lunch. "The owner made a terrible decision when he named the place," Ian laughed softly, "But that's no reflection on the quality of the food."

I told him I had a few minutes before I needed to leave, and the next thing I knew, he had ordered several appetizers and two martinis. As the food was brought to the table, I calculated that he had already spent the bulk of the hundred bucks I'd just given him.

While I picked at the various meatless options he had ordered, I listened to Ian tell me this and that about other places he thought I might like in Elmore. Restaurants, night clubs, a bed and breakfast with an Eastern European flair. I asked how long he'd lived there, and he laughed and told me he didn't live there at all. He lived in Bar Harbor, but had a second office in Elmore, and just happened to be there on that day.

"Lucky for me!" I said, dipping a triangle of fried tofu in the spicy ginger sauce, and popping it into my mouth.

"Lucky for us both," he said, and flashed those green eyes at me.

We were saying goodbye in the parking lot, but I could tell Ian was trying to stretch it out. He didn't want to say goodbye. He was scheduled to come out to the island on Tuesday to take a look at the work that needed to be done, but I could tell he was flirting with me, and as I turned to open my car door, he put his hand on my arm.

"Trista...please know that this isn't usually part of the routine when I book a job but...could I take you out for dinner later this week?"

It had been so long since a man had stumbled a little over getting up his courage to ask me out that I almost melted on the spot. I hadn't dated, obviously, in all the years since Jason and I had met and married. It felt unspeakably nice to suddenly find myself the object of a man—a really good-looking man! —whom I'd just met.

"Out for dinner might be a little difficult..."

"Oh," he said, disappointed.

"No! I mean because of the tides! And also, I have company coming..."

"That's right. You said that."

"But..." I didn't want to let this possibility pass by me. "What if you come over to Simple Island on Wednesday evening at the beginning of the second low tide period. That's the time your workers will be leaving, so I know the island will look absolutely fabulous, and I can cook dinner for us. That way, we can spend the whole low tide time getting to know each other, rather than spending half of it driving."

Ian brightened visibly with my suggestion. "That sounds perfect!" he said. "And that way, if you don't like the work that's been done, you'll have something like three hours to tell me everything that was done wrong!"

"Exactly!" I laughed and opened my car door. "I'll see you on Tuesday morning, and then Wednesday evening!"

Ian took my hand quickly in his own and gave it a squeeze. "I'm looking forward to it, Trista," he said, and there was an undercurrent of intimacy in his voice that was impossible to miss.

★ ★ ★

I spent Monday deep cleaning the cabin. This included my very first time to empty the composting toilet, which was an adventure unto itself.

Sitting in the bathroom, the composting toilet looked modern and innocuous, but I had already decided that it was more like a litter box than a toilet. Every day, I was to add just a handful from the bag of special sawdust, but every once in a while, I was going to have to empty it, which I assumed meant digging a hole in the yard and burying whatever had been collected in the little bucket receptacle.

The design of the toilet was ingenious, such that it never actually *smelled* like a litter box. At least, not until I took the top half off of the toilet and began hauling the half-full bucket outside. *Trista Maybrey and the Mysterious Island*: in this chapter, Trista does the least glamourous thing she will ever do.

I had already located a shovel among the other implements under the house, but as I forced it into the ground to lift out the first scoop of dirt, I was flooded with the imagery of the lady in the hat, and the look on her face as she shoveled the earth down on top of me in my little hole. I shook my head rapidly to try to expel the image and continued with my chore.

The litter successfully buried, I rinsed the bucket in the outside faucet and then sprayed it thoroughly with Lysol before putting it back in its hidey hole inside the toilet. I felt quite accomplished. It made me think of the old saying: something about if you start every day by eating a live toad, everything else after that seems easy.

Trying to remember what that exact quote was made me think of Ian Andrews and the way he'd thrown me off by answering the phone with the FDR quote. Ian was, as my mother would say, "a caution." I couldn't quite figure him out. He was definitely "tall, dark, and handsome" in the most cliché way, but there was something in his easy manner, something about the way his facial expressions and quiet voice worked together that made him, on the whole, mysterious.

A mysterious, tall-dark-and-handsome stranger...that was definitely straight out of a dime-store novel. Could I be so stereotypical that I'd fall for that kind of man? Well, maybe not fall...at least not yet...but I could certainly let him flirt with me.

I felt entirely out of practice with flirting. My relationship with Jason had jumped that particular shark years ago, and in the life I had built, there had been little opportunity to meet new men who might even consider me desirable. I guess I'd thought that part of my life was just over. I was a divorcee, destined to be single.

But, now that I thought about it, just in this past couple of weeks, I'd encountered two men who looked at me like a woman, not a divorcee. I allowed my mind to drift back to that moment when Troy winked at me from behind the counter of his store...and enjoyed, for a second, my own quickening pulse, before shoving that away.

Why did Troy both attract and annoy me? Trying to answer that question for myself, I realized that it was almost like he was a pesky brother I was trying to be mad at, who charmed me back into sibling love and rivalry over and over. On the one hand, that's how it felt...but on the other hand, there was an undeniable current of decidedly *non*-sibling attraction, and I had no doubt that the current flowed both ways.

And yet, *how* did I know this? Troy had never said or done anything to indicate more than a friendly, small-town familiarity, as well as his generally professional enthusiasm for the job ahead. The wink may quicken my pulse, but in truth, he may wink at lots of people in his store, as a way of saying, "I see you. You're next in line."

As I cleaned, I indulged myself in going back carefully over my two encounters with Troy Bowden, and the text of the conversations. There was nothing more there than congenial professionalism. But still...

What I sensed from him wasn't in the text. It wasn't even in the body language. It was something else that I couldn't put my finger on. Something that I just inherently knew...and that's what I found so *annoying*.

It wasn't like that with Ian. He wasn't familiar to me at all...he was entirely the sort of man I was wholly *un*familiar with, which was exciting.

What would Jennifer think of all this? Of me, sitting on the floor of my cabin, scrubbing the baseboards with a rag on my head, daydreaming about two men like a melodramatic high school cheerleader.

I laughed out loud at myself and decided this job needed music. I called up the *Yentl* soundtrack on Spotify and spent the rest of the afternoon belting with Barbra while Margaret Mary attempted to harmonize.

On Tuesday morning, at almost exactly the stroke of low tide, Ian called me to say he was in Milton and ready to meet me. I told him how to get down to the end of Parson Point and park behind my Nissan, and that I would meet him there and guide him over.

I'm embarrassed to admit how much thought and effort I had put into my appearance that morning. I had studied deeply into how to look unstudied. The goal was to look casual and comfortable, as though I hadn't a care in the world and I always looked this good in jeans and a casual shirt...a casual shirt that I had changed four times before settling on the right one. I'd trimmed and painted my toenails to look their best in sandals, and I'd scrubbed and manicured my fingernails as well. I even turned on the generator long enough to blow-dry my pixie hair to perfection. I'd never put so much labor into accepting a price estimate for yardwork.

Of course, at first, I had to cover up my pretty painted toes with my now-muddy red boots in order to cross the ocean to meet him, but I liked that effect too. *Trista Maybrey and the Mysterious Island*: in this chapter, we see our heroine in her natural habitat, cool and collected in her mud-streaked boots which speak volumes to her competence in this setting.

I ducked under the fir tree to step out onto the Beardens' gravel drive just as Ian was getting out of his car. I smiled and waved...and saw him click the button on his key to lock the doors of the BMW. That gesture struck me as funny out here. Who was there to try to break into his car?

"Nice place you've got here!" he called out in greeting, and I looked up at the Beardens' country waterfront mansion.

"You know this isn't it," I said, smiling, as I approached him, and he reached out to shake my hand professionally. I figured that was a habit too, like locking his car. He followed me the few steps to where we could see Simple Island across the way, through the trees that lined the Beardens' property. "That's it!" I said, pointing majestically toward my little kingdom.

"Wow," he breathed, impressed, I could tell. I was pleased. It was my first time to get to show it off to anyone. My island.

"Just wait till you see it without all the buckets and bobbers!"

He followed me down the trail to the crossing point, offering ideas about how his crew might trim back some of the foliage and branches to make the trail more comfortably navigable. I knew he was already assessing for his estimate, but I kind of wanted him to not be thinking about that. I was already thinking of this kind of like a date, and I wanted him to look at it that way as well. I mean...I'd done my toenails and everything.

We chatted lightly as I led him down the long grassy point. I tried to explain about not turning too soon, but Ian stepped off just about a foot before he should have, and he wobbled as his boot (which was far too dressy for this crossing) sank into the mud. I instinctively reached to grab at his hand to stabilize him, but once he was back on solid ground, he didn't let go of my hand. He just kept holding it as we crossed the rest of the way to the grassy base of Simple Island. I decided to pretend I didn't notice...that I was still just helping him across the unfamiliar terrain...but he was definitely, and purposely, holding my hand.

"Yes," he mused, "this could be really pretty with just a little bit of clean up."

Once we'd climbed up onto the level ground of the island, Ian released my hand and began turning around to survey what he could see of the property.

"Oh, you haven't seen the worst of it yet," I assured him, leading him further in toward the cabin where the array of leftover trash and junk had collected around the house.

"Ah," he said, fully understanding now that he could see it. "I can see why this would bother you, for sure, but it's not a big deal. Just a matter of hauling it off. I'll have my crew come in a pickup so they can just gather all this up and cart it away."

"You make it sound simple," I smiled at him.

I walked him around to the back of the cabin so that he could see the area that could be cleared to offer a prettier view of the ocean from the deck. He asked me if I had any ribbon, and I offered him a roll of pink duct tape, with which he marked a number of small trees to be cut down.

When the trees had been properly tagged, I asked him, "So what's the final estimate?"

Ian looked thoughtful for a moment, doing the math in his head, I supposed, and then said, "I estimate that you're 46 years old and have a long history with alcoholism."

I threw back my head and laughed. "You're right," I said agreeably. "That doesn't go over well!"

He joined me on the deck and suggested a sum for the job, a sum which I thought to be very fair, and we shook on it. He pulled his little credit card swiper out of his pocket, and we sealed the deal. He Googled the tide chart on his phone and assured me that his crew would arrive the next day for a morning crossing and would be done by the beginning of the evening low tide...at which time he would arrive for our dinner date.

I was tempted to walk him back across to his car, but he didn't seem concerned about making the crossing by himself, so I stood on the grassy slope and waved goodbye to him, then turned back into my island. As I approached the cabin, I could already see it with all the junk gone, and I was so excited. Excited about my new home, excited about Jennifer coming, excited that I had a date—a real date! —the next evening.

Things have a way of working themselves out.

★ ★ ★

Early the next morning, as I was sitting answering the emails that had come in overnight, Margaret Mary burst into barking, desperately clawing at the front door as though she might open it with sheer will. I opened it *for* her, which was the same thing, really.

As she went tearing down the front steps and out into the yard, I heard voices. I think I had expected Ian's crew to call and wait to be led across to the island, but apparently, Ian had simply given them directions...and here they were.

As they came into view, with Margaret Mary sniffing at their heels, I could see "the crew" was a pair of Mexican men, one older and one younger. They might have been father and son. I called my hello, and the younger man replied with his own.

When they reached the cabin, the older man immediately busied himself with creating a pile of what was obviously trash, while the younger man stood with me and chatted about what I wanted done. He was offering things that Ian and I had not discussed, like rebuilding the tumbled fire pit, but I declined the offer, as I didn't want to complicate things on a price that had already been agreed and paid.

They had carried over a big Rubbermaid tub of tools, and I asked if they needed me to turn the generator on, but no. None of the tools required power. They emptied the tools on to the back deck and began filling the tub with junk to be hauled away.

In her intense curiosity, Margaret Mary was making a real nuisance of herself, so I beckoned her back inside and returned my focus to work. I had scheduled several phone calls that day with expectant parents, and in between calls I had a lot of catching up to do on my caseload spreadsheets. Only occasionally did I hear any noise from the workers outside, and a couple of times I heard them speaking to each other in Spanish.

I had to take a moment to wonder if Mexican immigrants were very common in Maine. Of course, in Dallas, I expected to see them everywhere, and had learned some basic working Spanish, as had everyone that I knew back home. A bit of curious Googling taught me that Maine had nearly 50,000 immigrants, and another 120,000 were American born, but had at least one immigrant parent. It wasn't exactly on par with the Texas statistics, but it was more than I'd thought it would be.

At about noon, I opened the front door and offered the guys some lunch. The younger man walked over to the porch and thanked me for the offer but said that they had brought their own. I took a moment to look around and was quite pleased with the work they had already done. The junk was gone. Just gone. I supposed they had taken it to the edge of the island, ready to load it up when the tide was out again and would spend the afternoon on the clearing work.

As I stood there, the older fellow walked up to the porch and leaned the rake against the rails. I recognized it as the rake that had "conveyed" with the property. He smiled at me and nodded, and just by way of making idle conversation, I asked him, "How long have you worked for Mr. Andrews?"

He looked at me confused for a second and cocked his head slightly to one side the way Margaret Mary did when she was trying to understand me. When he finally spoke, I realized his English was much less fluent than the younger man.

"Only one day, Ma'am," he said, and waved his right arm to indicate the island. "We work one day."

I nodded and smiled, and realized he hadn't understood what I was asking. It wasn't a question that required an answer anyway...just small talk. I hypothesized to myself that perhaps they were, indeed, father and son. The father was the immigrant, and the son was American born. The son's fluent English made it possible for the father to earn a satisfying living, despite his own handicap with the language. I felt so proud of myself for moving "all the way" from Texas to Maine...what this man had done to make a better life for his family made my move seem pretty insignificant.

My phone rang, and I stepped back inside to answer it. It was one of my clinic contacts letting me know that one of my surrogates, Ronda, had just suffered an early miscarriage. She had only been about 5 weeks pregnant, but this was still a tragedy for everyone involved.

Working in the fertility industry, I knew that I saw a lot more joy than sorrow, but the sorrow, when it hit, could be devastating. At five weeks pregnant, the "baby" was little more than a tiny peanut with a barely detectable heartbeat, but to the parents, it was already their long-awaited child, and now it was lost. I hated these days; even when the parents took it well, it was so hard for everyone.

Most of my clients were gay couples, and most of them came to me from referrals from other gay couples who had babies through Families in Harmony. But about a quarter of my clients were hetero couples, and their stories were always the hard ones.

The gay couples, or "same-sex" couples as we called them, always came to us like shiny new pennies; they'd been happy in their relationship, confident in its longevity, and were now ready to enrich their lives with children. They reached out to us with enthusiasm, excited to start down this road toward parenthood.

But, with the rare exception of a situation where a woman was born without a functioning uterus, such that she had known all her life that she would not ever carry a child of her own, the hetero couples came to Families in Harmony already broken. Most of them had spent years of their lives and a fortune of their money—or even the money of other family members and friends—unsuccessfully trying to have a baby that was made of her egg and his sperm and carried in her womb. Some of the women had suffered ovarian or uterine cancer, which was the reason they couldn't carry a child, and so they had to factor in concern that the cancer might return, and the father would be raising their child alone. Some women had been trying for so long that their eggs were no longer recommendably viable, and they would need the assistance of an egg donor. The prospect of raising and loving a child that was created with the biology of her husband and another woman was, to some women, an element they could accept and ignore...but to other women, coming to this acceptance was like grieving a death.

An early miscarriage like the one I'd been alerted to on that day was unfortunately common, and many couples took it in stride, understanding that it was no reflection on whether they would have success next time. But with this particular couple, because I knew their long, tearful quest for parenthood, I was prepared for a protracted period of counseling.

I spent the afternoon on the phone, between the clinic, the surrogate, and the parents. The parents sounded more exhausted than sad, which pulled even harder on my heartstrings. Ronda, the surrogate, cried. She couldn't help blaming herself, though intellectually she knew there was nothing she could have done to prevent the loss. The IVF doctor repeatedly assured everyone that this was a fluke, and that there was no reason to believe the next try wouldn't be successful. He told Ronda to stop all of her medications and let him know as soon as she started her menses.

By the time I said goodbye on the last phone call and finished updating all my files with their new information, I realized that the workers had finished...and left. I went out onto the back deck and looked through the now-cleared area out to the ocean. It was beautiful. If I hadn't known where to look for the stumps of the trees they had cut, I wouldn't have seen them; they were cut off flush to the ground, and easily hidden by the ground mulch.

I walked through the cabin to look out the front and was smitten by how nice it looked with the colorful collection of plastic debris gone. As I turned to go back inside, something caught my eye, and I stood and admired my rebuilt fire pit, which the guys had completed even though I'd told them not to bother with it, and I was pretty sure I hadn't paid for it. Now if only I wasn't quite such a fan of not being on fire.

I glanced at my watch and realized that Ian would be there within half an hour, expecting dinner. I'd decided to go ahead and cook the pasta with mushrooms and olives that I had planned for Friday night with Jennifer. I had some English muffins which would be lovely cooked with garlic, and I thought we might carry our meal down to the overgrown blueberry patch to watch the sunset while we ate and chatted. That sounded romantic. Was I going for romantic?

I changed into a more feminine top but elected to keep the blue jeans. If I *was* going for romantic, I wanted Ian to see me for myself. *Trista Maybrey and the Mysterious Island*: in this chapter, we see Trista trying hard to not try too hard for her first date.

I refreshed my makeup while waiting for the water to boil, then poured in the whole box of pasta shells, and started another pot with the sauce and vegetables. About the time I was turning down the heat to "simmer" on the sauce, there was a knock at my door.

Ian entered, leaning in to kiss me on the cheek, and presented me with a bouquet of flowers and a bottle of wine, both of which, I could tell, were expensive. There went the rest of the deposit I'd given him, and probably a good chunk of the other payment as well.

I offered him a seat and a room temperature beer, which he accepted with grace. We chatted pleasantly while I tended the pots on the stove, and he talked about how his business had just sort of grown organically, but that his first love was antiques. I gushed to tell him that I spent a great deal of my free time pawing through antique stores, and that any time I was in a new town, I always tried to make time to find the local Goodwill. I laughed and apologized if that sounded a little gauche.

"Not at all!" he reassured me. "There's nothing so much fun as finding a treasure that didn't know it was a treasure, and the best place to do that is in a junk shop or a charity store. When you buy something from a proper antique store, you can bet they have already researched what it's worth, and then priced it even higher. Whenever I find a prize that I can get for a buck or two in a junk shop, I'm as happy as I know how to be!"

He very carefully looked around the cabin and commented on various elements. I felt so proud, seeing it through his eyes. I talked freely about how I had tried to rectify its "personality disorder" and he complimented me on my choices of cushion covers and wall hangings.

"It's got a long way to go," I admitted as I was serving the plates, "But I'm definitely seeing the end game."

Before his arrival, I had already dragged a second lawn chair out to the blueberry patch, and so once the plates were served, I gathered the muffins and some napkins and utensils into a picnic basket, and Ian helped me carry it all down to the chairs at the shore. "Wow..." he said, with awe in his voice, as he settled into his chair and looked at the sky which was, thank you very much, already putting on a lovely array of colors for our dinner date.

Even with pasta to occupy us, conversation flowed easily. When the plates were empty, he told me to "stay put" while he walked back to the cabin for the wine and a couple of plastic cups. He pulled the cork expertly, and we enjoyed the wine along with the last bit of the sunlight for that Wednesday. As the last sliver of sun slipped into the ocean, Ian took my hand and held it, softly caressing my skin with his thumb.

We walked back to the cabin quietly, and I picked up my phone from the kitchen counter. I had missed four phone calls, all from a Milton number which I instinctively knew was Troy. I scowled at my phone.

"Everything OK?" Ian asked, catching my expression.

"Well...probably. I had a crisis at work today, and there's still fallout." I decided that talking about work was better than musing to Ian why I'd had so many phone calls from another man. As I loaded the dishes to soak in the sink, I talked a little bit about my work, about the day's unhappiness, and he listened intently, offering all the right clucks of compassion. When everything that had marinara sauce on it was thoroughly covered with hot, soapy water, I dried my hands on the nearest towel, and then turned to find Ian standing *very* close to me. Too close.

Before I could step away or query him, he put his hands on my waist and pulled me in for a hard, overly passionate kiss. It wasn't romantic. It wasn't even nice. It was almost angry in its fervor. I didn't want to hurt his feelings by pulling away too quickly...though I can't tell you why; I sometimes think Southern women are raised with too much consciousness about preserving a man's ego no matter what...but I discontinued my portion of the kiss as quickly as I could.

Pulling away, I kind of gasped his name, "Ian..."

And just in that moment, there was a loud knock on my door and an almost simultaneous burst of barking alarm from Margaret Mary. Almost grateful for an excuse to disentangle myself and push past my would-be suitor, I answered the door in surprise, and found Troy Bowden on the other side.

"Trista, I'm sorry to just show up like this...I tried calling, and then I tried calling again, and you didn't answer, so I just wanted to make sure everything was ok. I didn't want to think you'd floated away."

He was trying to sound friendly and funny, but I could tell he had actually been worried about me. I was going to begin reassuring him, but then Ian took a step or two into Troy's line of sight, and his expression changed.

"Oh...I'm sorry..." he began, but then he looked more intently at Ian, and his eyes widened. "Hey..." he started.

Ian grabbed his keys off of my counter and began pushing past me. "I've overstayed my welcome," he said, almost gruffly; that Southern woman thing kicked in again and I chastised myself internally for bruising him by not fully returning his kiss. He brushed past me, then past Troy, and was out into the night without even looking me in the eye. He called a goodbye over his shoulder and was gone in the darkness.

I turned my frustration onto Troy. "What the hell was that? You just show up at my door? Don't you think maybe that's why I moved to a private island...so that people didn't just show up at my door?"

Troy looked completely shocked by my tirade. "Trista...I...I really was worried about you. I mean, it's only been a few days since you tried to float away in a rainstorm." His voice was filled with his genuine concern, but I don't know. I couldn't stop.

"You're not my Dad! You're not my husband, you're not my big brother. You're...what? The handyman? You don't get to just show up here. If you didn't notice, I was *trying* to have a date. Like a grown up!"

His expression changed as he remembered something. "Your date...do you know who that is?"

"Of course I know who that is! His name is Ian Andrews, and he runs a yardwork company in Elmore. I hired him to have his crew clean up the ton of junk in my yard, and he asked me to have dinner with him...a dinner which you just interrupted!"

Troy just blinked at me oddly for a second, then said, "A yardwork company? That's what he told you?"

At this point, I felt myself boiling over. "What do you mean is that what he told me? I just told *you*, I hired him...and we just kind of hit it off, I guess. I literally haven't been on a date in twelve years...an even dozen...and you want to play Daddy-Daughter sleuth on my first one."

Now I could see his ire rising to the occasion I had created. "Wait a minute. I didn't come here to play sleuth or to ruin your romantic evening," his voice was hollow with sarcasm. "I came out here while it was still low tide so that I could make sure that you were OK, and to tell you that all the materials have arrived except for the ice breaks, and they won't be here until next week's truck, and maybe I thought it might be nice to have a casual conversation here on your island which I have taken care of for the past several years, and to see what you've done with the place...or whatever...but then when I get here, I see you have company and I'm shocked to see him because...well, whatever he told you, *that* is the guy who made several offers to buy Simple Island, and almost got arrested for showing up out here without the real estate agent. That seemed sketchy...*really* sketchy...at the time, and now he shows up here again, suddenly owning a yardwork company in Elmore, and having a dinner date with *you*."

He was almost panting by the time he finished that diatribe. When he had said the part about having taken care of the island for the last several years, I had prepared myself to retort something loud and lame about his services no longer being needed...but that argument died in my throat after he finished talking about Ian.

Now it was my turn to blink oddly, blindsided by this news that I couldn't seem to make any sense of. "Are you sure?" I asked, dumbly.

"Yeah, I'm sure!" he said, still loud and breathing heavily from the exertion of his argument. "You don't forget a fella like that. He looks like he stepped out of a 1930s vampire movie, oozing charm and money, and looking like he doesn't quite have all his wheels on the track."

I couldn't help laughing at that. For some crazy reason, I wanted—seriously wanted—to stay mad at Troy in that moment, but I couldn't do it. He had absolutely nailed it. That's why I was able to admit that I found Ian attractive, but I wasn't quite able to actually be *attracted to* him. 1930s vampire movie. All mesmerizing handsome, but with a kiss of death.

And so, I laughed. I just let myself laugh, a full indulgence in the moment until ultimately, I was laughing at myself for laughing, and Troy was laughing with me, a rolling guffaw, his eyes sparkling like the first day I had met him, and in that moment, we were the dearest of friends, completely understanding one another and no walls between us.

When the laughter ultimately died, and we were both left catching our breath and wiping tears from our eyes, Troy said, "They really did forget your ice breaks. I wanted you to know that."

"Do you think my cabin will survive if we put off the roofing until *next* Saturday?"

He put the index finger of his right hand in his mouth and licked it, then held it up as though testing the direction of the wind. "Yes," he said at last, with serious gravity. "I believe it will."

This, of course, made me laugh all over again, as even the slightest bit of humor can when you've just come off of a good laugh. Laughter is an addiction that takes an immediate hold and quickly seeks its next fix, even if it is a milder version of the original drug. The expensive bottle of wine I'd shared with Ian was no doubt a contributor to my odd sense of humor.

When I finally sighed the last of the hilarity, Troy and I stood just staring at each other for a moment. I was suddenly very aware of how small the cabin was, and how close he was standing to me in the little kitchen. The front door was still open behind him, and he took a step back, toward the waiting night.

"It's ah...It's getting close to the end of low tide. The water will be coming back in, and it's dark." He waited, as though I had the next line in this dialogue...but if I'd ever known what I was supposed to say in this moment, I'd suddenly forgotten it.

"I should go, then."

But as he turned his back to me, I impulsively reached out and put my hand on his arm.

"Troy..." I said.

And then, for the second time that night, a man I hardly knew took me in his arms and sought my mouth with his.

But this time was very different from the other. This time, I wanted it. It made no sense, and I didn't need for it to make sense. He pulled my body against his own and wrapped his arms so tightly around my waist that I felt I might melt into him. My arms went around his neck, and my hands tangled themselves, almost of their own volition, in his thick, curly hair.

Our feet were never still. He turned me all the way around as if we were dancing, and even as my tongue found his, I realized he was maneuvering me toward the couch, where we fell together in a tangle of limbs and lips. Troy laid me back, bumping my head unceremoniously on the arm of the sofa, and then he was on top of me, kissing my face, kissing my neck, his hands all over me. I was groaning as if in relief that we were finally together like this.

He was the first one to speak. "This probably isn't a good idea," he said huskily as he unbuttoned my blouse and began a trail of kisses down my cleavage to the plunge of my bra.

"No. Definitely not," I whispered back, gathering the bottom of his shirt in my hands so that I could pull it over his head and then tangle my fingers in the dark mahogany hair on his chest. "It will probably ruin our professional relationship."

"And I'm the only roofer in town," he replied, his mouth so close to my ear that I could almost hear his rapid heartbeat in his voice. "I mean, you could hire someone else, but you clearly have terrible judgement when it comes to contracting labor."

I giggled, "Of course you're right. I hadn't thought of that. We should get up off this couch immediately!" I dug my nails into his back and arched my body in an attempt to be even closer to his.

"Definitely. Any minute now, I'm getting up."

"Good," I breathed. And then, "Meet you in the bedroom?"

"Only if I don't get lost in this massive house!"

I made it to the bedroom first, leaving a little trail of my clothes as I hurried. I flung myself across the bed, and Troy was only a second behind me, and then he was beside me, above me, inside me.

The heat created by the friction of our bodies, the sweet comingling of our breath and our sweat and our souls in that moment, this was more than sex had ever been to me. We moved almost in silence, just the heavy sound of our breathing, I inhaled his every exhale, and he then inhaled mine. The candle by the bed guttered and extinguished itself, and then the darkness was almost a third party to our passion. In the heavy shadows, I heard

Troy whisper, "*Astra inclinant.*" Without thinking, without even the ability to think, I responded, "*Sed non obligant*" and then he was kissing me again, rolling me over so that I was atop him for the resplendent finish.

Popular music loves to have men sing their promises to "make love to you all night long, baby" as though this is something most, or even all women seek. I've never known a woman who wanted to actually have sex all night long. Women want, ultimately, to sleep in the arms of their lover. Or just to sleep, period. Sex that is accompanied by the kind of energy and desperation that Troy and I were experiencing cannot keep up with that level of vigor. There must, ultimately, be the rush of climax, and then the quiet glow that slows the pulse, relaxes the breathing, and returns the sense of reason that was temporarily suspended.

It was about half an hour from the moment our lips connected to the return of reason, and when reason returned, it did so with a crushing sensation of regret.

Oh, God, what the fuck had I just done?

Troy tried to hold some levity in the moment, but I imagined he was asking himself the same questions that I was. He spoke softly, but he got dressed really fast as I continued to lay there on the bed.

"I'm not going to say I'm sorry, Trista," he said as he sat beside me to pull on his shoes. "I'm definitely not sorry that this happened, and I want you to know that. No regrets...but I really did just come over to talk about roofing materials. I just didn't know you'd get so turned on by that."

The last was obviously an attempt at humor, but I hadn't found my sense of humor about any of this yet. His shoes on, Troy leaned over and kissed my forehead. A brotherly kiss, now that the deed was done. "I've got to go before the water gets any higher. I probably need waders already. Can I borrow a flashlight?"

"There's a Maglite on the counter behind the sink," I said flatly, hating the sound of my own voice.

"Ah...probably the one I sold you."

I didn't answer. He didn't need an answer. He just needed to go.

Without another word, he left the bedroom. I heard a bit of clatter as the Maglite bumped against the faucet of the kitchen sink, still filled with dishes from my date with another man, and then I heard the front door close as he left.

★ ★ ★

There was so much to think about what had just happened as I lay there, alone, and yet I wanted more than anything to just not think. Unfortunately, that was not an option my brain offered me...and so I thought.

I had known Troy Bowden for less than two weeks. We had not yet spent a total of an hour together before tonight, not counting his solo rescue of my canned goods.

I had found myself annoyed, aggravated, by the attraction I felt to him, and so I had done my best to push those sensations away.

I had never been the sort of woman to have wanton physical desires, much less to give in to them. I'd had one sexual relationship in college before meeting Jason, and those were, until tonight, the only two men I'd ever been with. The sexual part of my marriage had been...dependable. We each knew what the other expected, and after the first year together, rarely deviated from a regular pattern. In my relative inexperience, it hadn't really occurred to me that there might be more.

What I felt that night with Troy was definitely more. We had been, at once, the fire and passion of a brand-new relationship, and the comfort and ease of lifelong lovers. In this new light, it was as though we knew each other as well as any two people can. And yet, when the light changed, we were strangers again, seeking to retreat as quickly as possible from the flame we had mishandled.

In an effort to distract myself from thinking about Troy, I turned my thoughts to what he had told me just before the fire had started. The part about Ian.

If Troy was right, and Ian Andrews really was the man who had made "three lowball offers" (as Lisa had said) on Simple Island, and then, when his offers were refused, had come uninvited to the island to...what?...look around some more?...then was there any possibility that my meeting him was a freaky coincidence?

Maybe...maybe he really did own a yardwork company in Elmore, and when I called the number on his flyer, he dealt with me like any other customer, and he decided he wanted to ask me out before he realized the uncanny situation that I had bought the little island he was interested in. Sure...that was all possible.

But, at what point did he figure out that this was the same island? When I directed him down Parson Point? When he parked behind me at the Bearden's place? As we walked the little trail? Did it not hit him until he saw the cabin? At what point did he figure it out, and why did he not tell me? There would have been no reason for me to be angry if he'd revealed this incredible coincidence; indeed, it would have been a great base for conversation.

His silence on the topic made it pointedly probable that it wasn't a coincidence at all. Instead, it was likely that this had all been a ruse. How could he have known that I would be the one to call the number on his flyer? Well, on the one hand, he certainly knew that the island needed tidying up. On the other hand, had there actually been flyers on the windshields of any of the other cars in the Walmart parking lot? I hadn't noticed, hadn't looked...but now that seemed unlikely. I was the target.

Which meant he'd been watching me. Following me. That's how he knew I was at Walmart, where I would think less of a flyer under my wiper.

And yet, his work crew had done a lovely job of cleaning up. Wasn't that proof that Ian was who he said he was?

But I smacked my palm to my forehead remembering the older man saying, "Only one day, Ma'am. We work one day." His English had been broken, but he understood my question, and had answered it correctly. Ian Andrews had hired them for just the one day, to clean up my island.

I reached up to wipe my mouth with the back of my hand, as though trying to wipe away the kiss I had allowed him for too many seconds. What had this all been about? Had he planned to seduce me into *giving* him the island? Had he hoped for a quickie marriage so that Simple Island would become community property? None of this made any sense, but the more I thought about it, the more grateful I was that Troy had shown up when he did. What might Ian have done if I'd had the opportunity to rebuff him, as I surely would have? He'd put a lot of effort into his cover story, and the kiss had seemed so...so angry and determined. Troy's perfect timing may have saved me in many ways...even if it had also ruined me, or at least ruined my reasonable image of my own self-control.

There was no sense in continuing to lie there, pretending I might fall asleep, so I got up, put on pajamas, and went to the kitchen to wash the dishes. It was about midnight, and I wasn't going outside to turn on the generator, so I cleaned up by the glow of the LED lantern, and wondered if I might get my Maglite back.

How was I going to face Troy again? How could we have a casual business relationship after this? I'd already paid him half the cost of the roof job, so there was no way to get around that, unless he offered me a refund...and then who would do the roof? This was ridiculous. Why had I let this happen?

And Jennifer was coming, day after tomorrow. No...tomorrow, technically. Would I be able to smile through a whole long weekend without telling her about this enormous debacle with two men I hardly knew? Even if I didn't tell her, she would probably sense that something was up, and I didn't want to play the game of "What's wrong with Trista?" "Nothing." "What's wrong with Trista?" "Nothing."

I'd have to cross that bridge when I came to it.

Sitting on the counter was the bottle Ian had brought, still containing about five ounces of wine. I poured it into one of the glasses I had just washed and carried it to the sofa. Margaret Mary was glad to see me sit down so that she could take up temporary residence on my lap. This had probably been a stressful day for her as well...four different strangers to assess, pasta that she wasn't allowed to share, and the business on the sofa with Troy had to have worried her. I almost laughed at that image from her perspective. What must she have thought of her mother's behavior?

The wine helped remind my body that it was way past bedtime. I carried my little LED lantern into the bedroom, clicked it off, and climbed under the covers. Something had changed over the past hour, with the distraction of the dishes and the comfort of the wine, and now, drifting off to sleep, my memories of the half hour with Troy had lost the hard edges of regret and self-chastisement, and were lulling me into my dreams with a sensual sweetness. I may never be able to look him in the eye again, but I also knew I'd never forget the enthralling power of those few moments together.

At first, I didn't even know I was dreaming. It seemed like I was awake, lying in my bed in the cabin, but the room was filled with candles and in the soft glow, I realized that Troy was sleeping beside me. I rolled onto my side to look at him, to watch him sleep, but just as I was reaching over to touch his hair, I realized that, beyond him, in the bedroom (which was suddenly much larger than in reality), was another bed, with another couple, only they weren't asleep. They were tangled together in the tender intensity of lovemaking, and I could hear the soft sounds they cooed at each other, unaware that I was watching.

I felt embarrassed. I knew that I needed to lie perfectly still so that they wouldn't realize I was awake and observing this intimate moment. I thought I might cover my head with the comforter, but then I began to realize that I recognized them. It was the woman, Em, and the man with the red hair and freckles. I said, aloud, "These are the people from my dreams!" and in that moment, I knew I was dreaming. I knew it, but I couldn't wake myself up or affect any change.

In the dream, I decided to wake Troy up, to bring his attention to the other couple in the room, and when I shook him, he opened his eyes and smiled up at me. Without even turning to see the other couple, he raised up on one elbow and spoke to me. "That's Em," he said, smiling lazily, "But I think you already know her. She belongs to me."

And then I heard the sound of an explosion and I leapt out of bed, my heart pounding. The other bed, the other people, were gone now, and I ran to the window to look outside and realized that the cabin was floating on the dark water. The water was full of people, people who were screaming and crying and clawing at each other; drowning one another as they tried to keep from drowning themselves. There was fire everywhere, fire on the water.

And then Troy was beside me at the window. He took my hand and nuzzled his face close to my ear, and he murmured, "Find me, Trista. Find me at the temple." I turned to look at him, but now it wasn't him. It was the man with red hair and freckles, and again he spoke and said softly, "Find me. It's time."

I was flying through the air again, as in the previous dreams, and, looking down, amid all the people who were screaming and thrashing in the water, I saw my bed floating there, looking completely peaceful amid the turmoil and terror of the drowning masses. An alligator was in the water, circling my bed, but because it was a dream, I was able to maneuver myself and angle the fall so that I landed, gently, on the bed. I pulled the covers up over my head and lay there, hiding from the frightening scene around me and feeling the gentle rocking of my bed on the water.

★ ★ ★

I woke up softly, without the startled alarm this recurring dream usually brought. Possibly because, on some level, I had known it was a dream. Daylight was just beginning to whisper behind the curtains, and it was tempting to just go back to sleep, but I knew it was important to remember as much of the dream as I could.

I tumbled out of bed and pulled a sweatshirt over my pajamas. The cabin was very cold out from under the protection of my blankets, but I didn't plan to be awake long enough to start a fire in the woodstove. I hadn't yet tackled that chore, and I didn't want my first try to be just then, when I had other things to think about.

I booted up my laptop and then opened the document I had begun two days before. Scrolling to the bottom of the page, I began a new paragraph, and wrote out this most recent dream in as much detail as I could remember. As I was trying to describe the desperate scene in the water, I closed my eyes to try to recapture what I'd seen, and I realized something I hadn't made note of before. The people in the water were all in various states of dress or undress, but most of them were, at least partially, dressed alike. They were all in uniforms, uniforms like the ones in my dream with the salesman who had the chair full of bloody kittens. The men in the water were soldiers.

Once I'd written out the details of the dream, I began the color coding. Yellow for the appearance of Em and the freckled man, green for the explosion. Lavender for falling through the air to the water, and pink for the soldiers, connecting them to the uniforms for sale, and the mention of "tin soldiers" in my childhood poem. Olive for the alligator/crocodile.

This time I needed to add a new color, grey, for the appearance of Troy. In this dream he had, again, been introducing me to Em and commenting that I already knew her. Also, this time, it had been Troy who first said, "Find me at the temple," though it had quickly become the other man speaking to me.

This was the longest, most detailed dream I'd had that actually included the explosion and the water and the fire.

Like a movie for which I'd only previously seen the commercial trailer. Sitting there, looking at my color-coded list, I realized that these were merely the dreams I could *remember*. What if the details that would tie all of this together were coming in a constant wave of nightly dreams that I simply wasn't able to retain in my conscious awareness? That was a frustrating thought. Maybe I was getting the full message, the entire movie, but I just wasn't able to carry it into my waking life.

Finally outdone by the chilly morning, I saved the document, closed the laptop, and retreated to my warm bed. As I relaxed back into slumber, I could almost feel the rocking of the bed as it floated on the water.

Chapter Twenty

July 31, 1859

My Darling,

Last night I dreamed that I was there with you on that rocky shore you described to me. The sea and the sky and the whole landscape looked like an oil painting and only we two were real in that idyllic setting. You held my hand and led me to a small house hidden within the trees. Even inside the house, everything appeared to be a painting, but it was a picture that I could walk through and touch the things, the chairs, the shelves, even the fireplace had a painted fire that stood suspended, frozen flames. It was all very beautiful, and I was trying to tell you so, but then all I could do was cry. I cannot tell you if my tears were of joy or sorrow, only that I could not stop or lessen them, and I just sobbed and sobbed, standing there in that painted house with you.

Then you placed your hand on my shoulder and you said, "My Dearest, we can always come back to this place. This place belongs to us, and if either of us is ever lost, we can find each other here."

I think there was more to the dream, but it is unclear. There was a ship on the sea, but it was not the right kind of ship. It was the sort of ship that travels on rivers, and yet there it was, afloat upon the painted sea outside of our painted house. I do not remember the significance or story of the dream beyond that. I woke up feeling strange, and yet happy, peaceful.

I am always fascinated by dreams, by the cluttering images that my mind sorts through in my sleep and then offers up odd combinations to weave together stories from the unrelated fragments. I sometimes imagine a little man in the cavern that is my mind, and all day, when I am wakeful, he crouches on the floor, protecting himself from the non-stop influx of information that I am taking in through my eyes, my ears, my nose, my mouth, my fingers. I imagine countless reems of individual pages flying in through the windows of this room, bombarding the little man on the floor, and all he can do is cover his head and wait for the barrage to stop.

When I close my eyes to sleep at night, I am also closing the windows to that room, and in the quiet, when no new information is coming in, the little man rouses himself and begins sweeping up the mess, collecting all of the papers and organizing them into stacks, deciding which bit belongs to which pile, and in doing so, he occasionally holds two or three overlapping pages up to the light, and the odd combination of those illuminated pages becomes the dream.

And so this dream was built of a number of elements: I suppose my inability to fully picture the coastal landscape you described led to the oil painting world of the dream, and my own excitement which is equally yoked with insecurity at the thought of such an enormous life change led to the *uncontrollable tears. But then, there you were, comforting me, reassuring me, and that was the overarching element of the dream, larger and more powerful than the sea itself.*

Perhaps you are raising an eyebrow over my penchant for dream analysis. You will learn over the course of our years together that I have a uniquely rich dream life, and one that I cherish. If you are indeed raising an eyebrow in this moment, then you should be prepared to have that eyebrow almost permanently raised as I will likely tell you of my dreams every morning for as long as you will allow it, and should you disallow it, I am likely to defy you occasionally and tell you my dream anyway.

Chapter Twenty-One

I cannot fully express how grateful I have always been for the stabilizing force that Jennifer is in my life. When I saw her step out of her rental car just outside the Bearden's chain, I suffered an unexpected mist of tears across my vision. These last couple of weeks had been a unique recipe of exciting, frustrating, triumphant, failing, frightening, angry, confusing, embarrassing, thrilling...but when Jennifer rushed to hug me, I felt something I'd not even realized I'd been missing: *safe*.

Because of the tide and the timing of her flight, I had not been able to pick her up at the airport, but by the time she drove herself down Parson Point, the tide was out, and I was able to cross to meet her there at the blue gravel drive. As we walked the little wooded trail to the crossing point, dragging her luggage, I relayed the details of the most recent dream, and I discussed the various connections to the other dreams. Jennifer's enthusiasm for this story was helpful. I'd been viewing it all from a perspective of fear and upset, and it was nice to be reminded that this could all be really exciting, that I was experiencing something uncommonly peculiar, something to be studied and cherished rather than escaped.

Jennifer's enthusiasm for my past life experience (which she insisted upon calling it, as though this were an absolute given, and now it was just a simple matter of connecting the dots) was rivaled only by her enthusiasm for Simple Island. As we stood at the edge of the rocks, before climbing down to cross over the floor of Black Bay, she looked across at the island and just gasped.

"Oh, Trista...look at her!"

"I know!" I said, almost crowing in my pride and excitement. "Wait till you see it up close!"

"Then let's go!" and Jennifer led the way down the rocky "stairs." I carefully guided her to the very tip end of the grassy point, entertaining her with the woeful tale of my earlier misfortune which had landed me, sloppy-drunken and sobbing, at the Red Rooster Inn.

We climbed up to the main floor of Simple Island, and Jennifer turned to look back at our light footprints in the mud behind us. "This is...this is all going to fill up with water?" she asked, almost incredulous as she surveyed the vast expanse of seemingly dry land around us.

"Completely," I assured her. "See those enormous boulders out there? If we walked out to them, which we won't because of the mud, you'd see they're several feet taller than you, but at high tide, they're completely covered by the ocean."

As we approached the cabin, I chattered about the junk that had been removed, my plans to paint the door, the new roof that was coming. I could talk safely about the roof now that I knew Jennifer and Troy weren't going to cross paths that weekend.

Once inside the cabin, Jennifer just gasped and gushed over my tiny house. It was unspeakably gratifying. I had left everything in place so that she could see my arrangement of the furniture, but I knew that, in a few hours, I'd have to move all the furniture to make room for the air mattress.

A queen-sized air mattress, still sealed in its original packaging, and several big blankets, had been among the treasures under my bed in the bedroom. I hadn't quite gotten over feeling guilty about how very much I was benefitting from the previous owners' marital misfortune. They had, no doubt, bought that air mattress with plans of having guests of their own on their island, just as they had bought the brand-new set of pots and pans with plans of cooking many of their own meals. I was sorry things hadn't worked out for them...but I couldn't actually carry that sorrow very far, because if things had worked out for them, I wouldn't be here listening to Jennifer gasp and gush over my tiny home.

Hurling her suitcase on my sofa, Jennifer unzipped the cover and dug around in the middle until she pulled out a little paper bag. "I brought you a present!" she announced and produced from the bag a silver chain with a pendant, which I could see was in the shape of a classically pointed crystal but was solid black.

I reached to cup the crystal in my hand. "It's beautiful," I said, and Jennifer raised it up out of my hand as though my assessment were not worthy of the gift.

"Yes," she said, "It's beautiful, but it's also powerful. This is obsidian, and obsidian has many healing properties, but I chose this for you because obsidian is often linked to past life connections."

My natural instinct in a moment like this with Jennifer was to go into "patting her on the head" mode...but I couldn't do that this time. I was definitely experiencing something that I couldn't explain, and her explanation was as good as any. Indeed, her explanation was better than an assessment that I was simply losing my grip on reality.

Spinning me around bodily, Jennifer put the chain around my neck and clasped it behind me. "You can make the best connection if you place the crystal over your third eye. I like your hair, by the way," she said as she worked the tiny lobster-claw into its ring. "You've never had it so short. How will people *not* be able to tell us apart?"

I had to laugh at this. Jennifer was not, by any means, my doppelganger. She was at least six inches shorter than me and looked very much like her own family. Her own family, however, were all blonde and blue-eyed, and

Jennifer's almost-black hair and rich brown eyes did have quite the similarity to mine. When we were children, playing together in the dirt, people often mistook us for sisters—twins even, as we were only three months apart in age.

In our teens, Jennifer's family had moved from Texas to Vidalia, Louisiana, and we had stayed in touch through email as well as old-style snail mail letters and packages. Jennifer stayed in Louisiana for college, and then moved back to Dallas for a job opportunity in 2010.

In the Spring of 2004, my undergraduate history class took a select group of students, including myself, on a pilgrimage to visit the antebellum homes in Natchez, Mississippi, which is just across the river from Vidalia, Louisiana. Jennifer and I tried very hard to match her schedule to mine so that we could see each other, if only for a few minutes, while I was in Natchez with my history group...but with no success. Her own college schedule and various obligations simply could not be synched up with any "free" time I might have on the trip. This was sad, because the only reason I had enthusiastically applied to be included in the pilgrimage was in the hopes of seeing Jennifer.

After the long bus ride to Natchez on the first day of the weekend trip, we arrived at the pre-Civil War home (which definitely counts as antebellum, though it was thoroughly lived-in and in rather tumbledown condition) of the family who would be hosting us for this pilgrimage. As we filed into the house, the elderly gentleman whose home this was, stopped our procession as I passed him, He called to his wife who came quickly to the door, pointed to me, and said, "Look here, Amy...doesn't she look like someone we know?"

I just smiled because, though I didn't know how they knew her, I wasn't even slightly surprised to hear Amy say, "Why, she looks like our little Jennifer."

And so, fourteen years later, in my tiny cabin, "our little Jennifer" was clasping around my neck an obsidian charm for connecting to my past life, and chattering about how she probably ought to get a pixie cut so that we could go on being twinsies.

As Jennifer unpacked some things from her suitcase and put her toiletries in the bathroom, I opened my laptop to check email. It was Friday, and I had told my coordinators that I would be available all day, though not really "working," but I still wanted to check email now and then to make sure everyone was doing OK.

Jennifer came back in and stretched out on the couch. "So, what adventures are you going to treat me to today?" she asked.

I closed the laptop and said, "I don't know...what's your pleasure?"

"So, I was thinking about all the stuff you told me, and the history of this island and the people who lived here, and I figured there must be somewhere around here where you can learn some solid facts. So, I just googled and came up with lots of little museums in the area, and some of them are in cool places like old lighthouses, and some of them have boat tours to go see whales and sea lions and puffins...and I thought we might check some of that stuff out."

Leave it to Jennifer to come up with exactly what I needed to help ground me. I hadn't even thought once about seeking historical information on Simple Island, but surely the information was out there. I opened my laptop again.

"This is a really small island," I said, as I began typing into the search engine. "Any information would have to be very local, definitely Washburn County, if not Milton itself."

"OK!" she said, enthusiastically, as she came to stand behind me, reading the search hits over my shoulder. "Oh! What's that one?" she said, just as I was clicking on a link for "Washburn County Maritime Museum and Island Registry."

We scrolled through the home page, skimming the text about the history of Washburn County and the wealthy families who had brought it to life. Lots of information about the importance of the forestry and lumber industries.

"Bla bla bla," Jennifer said at last, "When are they open?"

I clicked the link that said, "Hours and Tickets" and learned that they were open every day from March 15 through October 15, and tickets were $8 for adults.

"Let's go!" Jennifer crowed in my ear, and I laughed out loud at the way she made me jump in my seat. She was already slinging her purse onto her shoulder, but I had to be the bearer of bad news.

"We can't go," I said, soberly. "The tide is coming in, and by the time it goes out again, the museum will be closed."

Her face fell under the weight of this new reality, but then almost immediately brightened as she dropped her purse on the sofa and said, in an equivalent crow, "Then let's paint the front door!"

✳ ✳ ✳

To the ageless grinding rhythms of George Michael's *Faith* album, Jennifer and I made a glorious mess of masking tape and green paint, and the drab front door of my cabin came to life. While we let the final coat dry in the sunshine, I led Jennifer out to the overgrown blueberry patch where the two lawn chairs were still there, waiting to be occupied. By now, the water was at its full depth around the island, and Jennifer was astonished how very different everything looked with the tide in.

I pointed out the area where the large boulders could now *not* be seen under the water. The grassy point and the rocks we had climbed to reach the island were also now entirely underwater. I told her again of the night I had waited too long to come back and showed her where I had ultimately gotten stuck and fallen. The story seemed much more funny than tragic when telling it to my friend.

We sat there in the golden light that preceded the sunset, sipping room temperature beer and enjoying the kind of silence that is only comfortable between true friends. At last, I thought I might actually tell her about Troy, and about Ian, in the hopes that that story might also be reframed by the telling.

"So, Jennifer..." I turned to her.

Only, Jennifer wasn't there. Instead, sitting improbably in the multicolored folding lawn chair, was the lady in the wide-brimmed hat, smiling sweetly at me as she always did.

In shock, I leapt out of my chair, and immediately the ground collapsed under me and I was falling through the hole, grasping at the earth with my newly manicured fingernails as the broken boards drew blood from my bare arms. Unable to gain any purchase to pull myself out, I finally fell, landing hard on the ground at the bottom of the little hole. I felt the incredible pain of the fall as my ankle twisted with the landing.

I was screaming uncontrollably for help, there must surely be someone to help me, but only the lady came to stand over the hole, just smiling at me, and holding her shovel. Just before she threw the first load of dirt onto me, Troy Bowden came to stand behind her. Looking down at me over the lady's shoulder, Troy said, "*Astra inclinant*," and the lady nodded and answered, "*Sed non obligant*."

Then the first load of dirt fell, filling my open mouth and choking the scream. I slammed my eyes shut against the falling earth, but then I opened them again, and I was sitting in my lawn chair next to Jennifer...who was staring at me, obviously concerned.

I let go a long exhale now that it was over, and Jennifer said, "What was *that*?"

Still catching my breath, I returned her question with a question of my own. "What did it *look* like?" I asked.

"It looked like...nothing. Like you turned to stone. I was starting to say something about going to the museum tomorrow, and when I turned to look at you, you were...catatonic or something. I'm not sure you were even breathing."

I was definitely breathing now, too hard and too fast. I leaned over deeply, angling my head between my knees to try to control it. And then, in that awkward pose, my breathing turned to sobbing, and I asked Jennifer the question I'd been afraid to ask myself: "What is happening to me?"

Jennifer didn't answer, just caressed big circles on my back as I leaned over like that, until I finally sat up straight, the hyperventilating and the sobbing both subsided.

The sunset was in full bloom now, and we walked back to the cabin. I gathered the ingredients I'd bought for a simple chili, to be served over Fritos in true Texas style, and as I opened cans of beans, Jennifer stepped back out the newly painted front door, calling, "Meet me outside when dinner's ready!"

As the chili simmered on the stove, I peeked out the front window and saw that Jennifer had built a small fire in the fire pit and was coaxing it to life. She had carried the lawn chairs from the blueberry patch and placed them just outside the fire ring, such that we might eat our chili by the fire in the growing darkness. Lovely.

I filled my little picnic basket with napkins and spoons, two beers, and the bag of Fritos. I served two bowls of steaming chili and, with the handle of the basket over my arm, managed to carry it all out to the waiting fire.

Jennifer had been remarkably patient, not asking me for the details of my catatonic experience. She knew I would tell her about it when I was ready. About halfway through the bowl of chili, I was ready.

"It was almost the same as before," I began, and Jennifer put down her spoon. "It was the same scenario where I was falling through a hole in the ground and the lady in the hat was burying me alive."

"Like the other hallucination...not like your dreams."

"Well, I did have the dream that ended with me falling through a hole and the lady in the hat was burying me, and at first I didn't see the connection between that and the other dreams, until I had that same vision the other day, just before I called you."

"So...this vision today was the same as the other day?"

"No...not entirely. Almost, but there was one thing that was different. This time...Troy was there."

"Troy?" Jennifer's face brightened from the intensity with which she had been regarding my experience. "Troy is a name that keeps coming up...tell me about Troy!"

I rolled my eyes, knowing that I was going to have to tell her. If she was going to be able to help me sort this out, I'd have to tell her about Troy. I began vaguely.

"Troy Bowden is like the local handyman. He owns the hardware store and he knows everybody, and he's been the one looking after Simple Island for the last few years while it was for sale. I met him when I bought the paint we just used today, and he's also the one who's going to put a new roof on the cabin."

"So...the local handyman figures into all of this...how?"

"I don't know," I cried in exasperation, throwing my head back and rolling my eyes. "But he's shown up in a couple of the dreams, and then today...and today, he was standing over the woman in the hat just before she threw the shovel of dirt on me, and he said something in Latin, and she answered in Latin, and then threw the dirt."

"Latin?" Jennifer queried. "What did they say?"

"How am I supposed to know?" I exploded at her. "It was Latin! The only thing I recognized was the word *astral* which I know means something about stars. The rest of it was...Greek."

"Latin," she corrected me.

"The thing is," I continued, rushing now because I knew I had to tell her this part, "It's the same Latin phrases, at least I'm pretty sure it is, that we said to each other the other night when we were...when we were having sex."

Jennifer jumped to her feet. "What?? You were having sex with the handyman?? I've been here like twelve hours and you're just now telling me this?"

"I know, I know..." I groaned, my hands over my face in embarrassment. "I knew I needed to tell you, but it's so...*unlike* me."

"Unlike the old you, you mean!" Jennifer was back in her chair, but smiling, her eyes bright in the firelight. "The old Trista also never bought an island and moved to Maine all by herself." Then she called over her shoulder toward the front steps of the cabin, "Sorry, Margaret Mary...not quite all by herself!"

"I guess I haven't really had time to get used to the new me, and the old me is still telling me that all of this is wrong, somehow. Well—not all of it, but definitely the Troy parts."

"Ok, so I'm going to need you to tell me that story, and I mean the *whole* story, later on...but for now, tell me what you were saying about the Latin? You said that you were saying those things to each other during sex? I don't understand that part."

"Oh my god, I don't understand it either! I didn't even think about it until after the vision today. I think I was so thrown off by the whole event, the whole 'new me' sleeping with the local roofer, that I didn't even remember the exchange of Latin until after I heard those same phrases today."

Jennifer just waited until I gathered the scraps of memory.

"When we were together that night, just when things were really hot..."

"You will not get away without telling me every detail of the hotness..."

"Right. Sure. Later. Anyway, that night, in the hotness, Troy said that thing to me about the stars. Astral something. And the weird thing is, though I didn't think anything of it at the time, I responded to him the same phrase that the lady said to him in my vision this evening."

"That's so weird," Jennifer mused. "And you can't remember it at all?"

"Something that sounded like something about obligation...but I'm not sure. I don't speak Latin."

"Apparently, you do. At least in the right circumstances."

Again, I threw my head back and groaned. "But how can any of this be right? No part of me feels like throwing myself at Troy was right."

"*No* part of you?" Jennifer teased.

"Ok, in the moment, it felt completely right—righter than I've ever felt, and I know how melodramatic that sounds—but the second it was over, I was just drowning in regret. It all felt wrong."

"That was just the old Trista talking," she said softly.

"Then how do I make her shut up?"

Jennifer shifted her chair slightly to be facing me more fully. "Listen," she began, "One of the psychics I worked with a few years ago told me that the way you can spot an *old soul* is by their level of acceptance. See, we go through lifetime after lifetime, mostly not remembering the details of previous lives, but still, we've learned something from them that carries into the subsequent lives, and that learning is manifested in acceptance."

"I...I don't understand."

"Well, look at you! How long has it been since Jason Barnes told you he had a whole other secret life and then left you. Not even three months, I think! And in that time, you've built an entirely new life. You divorced, took back your name, bought an island; you ensconced yourself in a new minimalistic, off the grid life, you've learned about tide patterns and how to live without a refrigerator..."

I laughed. "I didn't have a choice. Jason made the choice for me. I had to move on."

"No, you didn't," she corrected me. "Not like this. Think about it. How many people do you know who, when their marriage fell apart, would have just crumbled, moved in with their parents, cried for weeks, stopped washing their hair? How many people do you know who would still be blaming Jason for the ruin of their lives ten years later? Twenty years later? It's been barely three months, and you haven't mentioned him once since I got here. He's history. You've accepted it."

"Two months," I said quietly into the darkness. "It's been just over two months."

"See?"

And then we sat quietly while I thought about what she'd said. I really had been through a major life change, and I had rolled with the transition much better than I might have predicted at the beginning. She was right: why hadn't I just moved in with my Mom and cried for a year? That hadn't even presented itself as an option. I had seen my life like a baseball game that was called for rain, and I'd started the new game as soon as I saw the sun peek through the clouds. But in this analogy, the new game also included a new diamond, all new team uniforms, and quite a few new players.

"And so sometimes," Jennifer continued, "when you're an old soul, you meet another old soul, and you just know it. I'm positive that's why you and I were drawn to each other almost in infancy. The relationship between old souls needs very little nurturing. It's just there, because they recognize each other out of all the people on earth. The old soul relationship has no drama...because of the mutual levels of acceptance. Maybe that's what's happening with you and the handyman."

"Troy," I reminded her. "And there has definitely been drama in our relationship."

"Tell me," she coaxed with a smile, and so I did.

I told her, in as much detail as I could remember, about Troy, beginning with the first time I heard his name when Lisa's husband had suggested Troy might be able to help me remove the remnants of the ancient fireplace, through the first meeting over paint chips and roof colors. I told her how, after my defeated night at the Red Rooster, I had come home to find my groceries lined up on my porch, and my gas can filled, and how I'd known, immediately, that it had been Troy.

I told her about the second time I'd been to Vincent & Son, and the way I'd been affected by his almost undetectable wink. I detailed the conversation we'd had, and how he encouraged me, congratulating me for getting out of the mud and going back to try it all again.

I tried to weave in, as best I could, where and how the various dreams and the vision had timed themselves through all of this, leading to my calling her, which had led to the trip to Walmart where I'd found Ian's flyer.

"Ian??" she said, laughing out loud. "There's also an Ian??"

"Just listen!" I admonished her, and I explained about meeting up with him at the *Thai-Tanic* ("Oh, that's awful!" she interjected) and how he'd asked me out to dinner. I described his first visit to the island, how he'd held my hand. Telling this part seemed really creepy now that I knew the rest of the story.

I told about the Mexican fellows who had cleaned up the island, and then Ian's return for our date, which ended abruptly when Troy had shown up. I described the argument, which turned to hysterical laughter, which turned into Latin-laced lovemaking, and then his friendly, if not hurried, retreat.

Then I described, for the first time, the lengthy dream I'd had that night after Troy left, where I'd seen the other couple making love and Troy had said "Find me at the temple" and then the water was filled with hundreds of drowning soldiers and I was floating on my bed.

The fire was dying, and the night was cold. We cleaned up the remnants of our dinner and went back into the warmth of the cabin. I lit half a dozen candles as well as the LED lantern, and then I showed Jennifer the color-coded document where I'd written out all the elements I was collecting of the dreams and visions. As we sat there, I wrote out the vision of that afternoon, and colored it to match the other elements of the lady, the burial, and Troy. I didn't know how to indicate the Latin phrases or how they connected, since the other time I'd heard them spoken, it hadn't been a dream or a vision, but a strange, overwhelming reality.

"So, what do you think this is?" She asked me finally, when we were settled on the couch.

"I was kind of hoping you'd tell me."

Jennifer laughed. "I can't tell you. You have to tell me. You're the one experiencing it."

"Then I'm at a loss. None of it makes any sense to me. And this didn't all start when I moved up here...not really...it started as far back as when I wrote that poem in the fourth grade."

"Mmm..." Jennifer mused to herself. "Your whole life, you've been aiming at this, long before you knew it."

"I just hope I don't have to wait the rest of my life to understand what it all means."

"I think you're going to find some answers at the museum tomorrow...but whatever it is, Trista, Troy is involved."

"Ugh," I said, rising from the couch and stepping to the bedroom to get the air mattress. "Troy Bowden is the goad of my old age," I called back at her.

But I knew what she meant. Troy was involved. And I wasn't ready to say how, but I was pretty sure I knew the role he played.

I just wondered if *he* knew.

Washburn County Maritime Museum and Island Registry was a name that was almost bigger than the facility it represented. The "island registry" part was probably just a book under the counter, and the "maritime museum" part was two little whitewashed rooms with pictures on the walls, and a single glass case with an ad-hoc assortment of relics from the bygone days of the Maine shipping industry. By the time we got to the counter to pay for our $8 tickets, we'd already almost seen everything the museum had to offer.

The weather-beaten gentleman behind the counter took our money good-naturedly. We were the only customers at that moment, and maybe we would be the only customers for the whole day.

"You ladies here on holiday?" he asked as the register dinged and he handed us the receipt.

"I am," said Jennifer, chipperly, "but my friend here is a local. She just bought an island."

"Oh?" he said, looking at me with interest, "Which one?"

I smiled and almost brushed off the question. "Just a little one-acre place off the coast of Milton. At the end of Parson Point."

"Parson Point?" he repeated, and his voice creaked like the wood floors of the museum. "Then you must mean Temple Island."

I know my eyes must have betrayed my dismay, and I tried to sound calm as I corrected him. "No...Simple Island."

"Oh, sure," he agreed. "That's what they call it now, but in the island registry it's still listed as Temple Island. It was named that for being at the end of Parson Point, and for being shaped like a steeple. But then when it was sold as a separate property back in the mid-century, the new owners thought the name was silly for such a little place, and they started calling it Simple Island, almost as a joke, but it stuck. I mean it stuck colloquially. The real name is still Temple Island. It's actually very difficult to get the government to allow an official change to an island's name. Otherwise, every time an island sold, we'd have to update all the maps and registries; people would want to name all the islands after themselves or their dogs, or their favorite TV character. Can't be having that."

Jennifer was clutching my hand, and I knew she was thinking what I was thinking. Temple Island. Meet me at the temple. Find me at the temple...that's what the temple was! It had to be.

The old man was bringing a big dusty book out from under the counter; he flipped it open to the middle and I could see that it was an atlas. Page after page of maps, all angles of Washburn county.

"This atlas is from 1862," he said, as he searched the pages for what he was looking for. "Back then, every year they did a census, they would make these atlases, and if you participated in the census, you could buy one of these for two dollars. In this condition, this one would sell for about eight hundred now...not that I'd sell it. Ah!"

Having found what he'd sought, he turned the big book around to face me, and poked a gnarled finger almost in the seam between the two facing pages. "There it is!" he said, and I looked closely.

Right away, I could see the check-engine-light shape of Pinkley Island, which then drew my eye up to where Simple Island...Temple Island...should be, but I didn't see it. If it was there, it was caught exactly in the seam.

The museum curator saw the problem. "Oh, it's there all right, but back then, it all still belonged to the Sutter family."

"The Sutter family?"

"Sure! The Sutters owned all of Parson Point, from the main road all the way down to Temple Island. They owned that whole area even before Maine was granted statehood in 1820. My history don't go back no further than that, I'm afraid. You know, it's funny...I didn't know much about the Sutters, other than the name, until about five or six months ago when another fella came in here asking about Temple Island. He offered me a thousand dollars to do the research and get him some information, but that's not how I do business. I do the research for the sheer pleasure of it, and I told him if he wanted to pay me, he could buy an eight-dollar ticket like everyone else. I think he thought I was putting him off, but I did the research and I called him up about a month later and told him everything I had learned. I don't actually think he ever bought a ticket but...no matter."

"This man," I interrupted, "Was he tall, with black hair?"

"Yes...yes he was. Someone you know?"

I just looked at Jennifer and said, "Ian."

Turning back to the curator, who was looking at me blankly, I encouraged him to continue. "I'm sorry for interrupting you. I'd love to hear more about what you learned, now that the island is mine. I love history, and I don't know a single thing about my little island except what you've just told me. I obviously didn't even know its name!"

Happy to have an audience, the gentleman continued, and Jennifer and I stood, entranced, as we listened.

"So, all that land belonged to the Sutter family. Old man Sutter and his wife had only one son, Lawrence, and when he married his wife, Helena in about 1830, they inherited everything, including the family's lumber business. Not sure what happened to the old man and his wife, nor how long they lived. Couldn't find much about them.

"But Lawrence and Helena, they had two sons. Maybe daughters too, but history is pretty ragged about mentioning daughters unless the daughters later married someone of note. Sorry about that. But they had two sons, Samuel and Jonathan. Interestingly enough, Samuel and Jonathan met a pair of sisters from Ohio and married them. Two brothers married to two sisters. Jonathan, the younger boy, well, he moved back to Ohio to live with his new wife's family, but Samuel stayed. Story is, Daddy Lawrence had a little house built on Temple Island and gave it to Samuel and his bride for a wedding gift. Guess they were pretty happy Samuel stuck around after Jonathan had moved so far away."

"On the island," I interjected, "I can still see the remains of the brick fireplace from that original house."

"Can you now? I'd like to see that sometime. Might pay you a call for the history of it."

"I'd like that," I beamed at him. "Anytime!"

"So, what happened to Samuel and his wife?" Jennifer asked, pushing the storyteller back on track.

"Well, now, let's see," the curator said, finding his mental bookmark. "Seems like Samuel never did go into the lumber business. He studied medicine, which probably made his parents both proud and disappointed. When the war started, the *great* war, you know, Samuel didn't join up with all the other men; he stayed in the area and was the local doctor. Someone had to be the doctor, you know. Lots of young men went off to fight for the Union, and Samuel, he stayed and took care of their families, and then took care of them when they came home...if they came home.

"But the war kept dragging on, and it looks like Samuel finally joined up, almost at the very end, though I'm sure folks back then thought it would never end. I'm not sure he fought in more than one battle, before he was captured."

"So, what happened after he came home?" I asked, anxious for any other tidbit that would tie all of this together.

"Oh, no...he didn't come home," the gentleman corrected me. "No, no...he died in the *Sultana* disaster. Sad, sad business. Almost made it home, all of 'em."

"The...Sultana disaster?" I asked, with a sudden tremor in my voice.

Jennifer chimed in, "A Sultana...that's like...a Sultan's wife, isn't it?"

"A Sultan's wife, sure, or daughter, or sister. Pretty much any woman connected to a Sultan is called a Sultana. But this *Sultana* was a steamship on the Mississippi, carrying over two thousand of our boys in blue home from confederate prison camps. Lots of speculation why, but she exploded in the middle of the night on the trip home. The ones who didn't die in the explosion, or the fire, died in the water. Terrible, terrible stuff."

I know I was staring at him; I absolutely couldn't find my voice. Here it all was, the Sultan's Wife from my fourth-grade poem, the explosion in the dark water, the soldiers fighting for their lives, the uniforms, the fire.

While I choked on all of this new information, Jennifer kept a cool head. "Do you have any photographs of the Sutters?" she was asking.

"Oh, sure! I'm glad you thought of that, because I did come up with one photo in the archives when the tall fella was asking me about them. Just a minute," and he ducked through a door behind the counter, and was back a second later, carrying a photo album with a broken binding.

"Just this one," he was saying, "But it's a good one. It's the wedding photo taken on the day Samuel and Jonathan married their brides."

He presented the book with a proud flourish and turned it sideways so that we could see the landscape 8x10 photograph, moldering on its edges, but the faces still clear. It was a large wedding party, almost all strangers to me, but there they were, right in the center: Samuel who, even in this sepia toned photograph, I knew to have red hair and freckles, and his new wife standing beside him, in a lovely long ivory dress with a high lace collar, and her hair piled on her head. Standing directly behind Samuel was his mother, Helena Sutter, in her wide-brimmed hat.

My heart skipped a beat, and I felt weakness creeping into my limbs. I placed a finger on the bride, and said, "What was her name? Was it Emily? Or Emma?"

"No, no..." the gentleman thought for a second, and then gingerly lifted the back of the photo off the page to consult the handwriting there. "Her name was Marilla. Marilla. That's right. I remember now."

So...not Em, short for Emily...it was just the letter "M" that her husband called her, as a nickname, a pet name. M for Marilla.

"What happened to her?" asked Jennifer.

Closing the book, the old man shrugged his shoulders. "Don't rightly know. She just disappeared. Some folks say she threw herself in the ocean when she found out Samuel weren't coming home. Some folks say she's still on that island, haunting around, seeking Samuel. Folks love a good ghost story, you know.

"The story stops being so interesting after that. The property passed to Jonathan after Lawrence died, but

Jonathan never did come back from Ohio. He sold it to someone else, and they started breaking it into parcels, selling Parson Point off in bits and pieces. Temple Island sold off by itself. I'm sure I could find the whole list of previous owners if that's helpful. You've paid for your ticket after all."

I found my voice, and my smile. "Thank you so much," I said genuinely. "You've been so much more helpful than I could have even asked for. If I have any more questions, can I call you?"

"Oh, sure!" he said, and handed me a card from a little holder on the counter. It said, "Washburn County Maritime Museum and Island Registry- Calvin Barstow, Curator."

"Thank you, Mr. Barstow," I said, pocketing the card.

"It's no trouble," he said. "Lovely talking with you!"

As Jennifer and I turned to go back out through the front door of the little museum, Mr. Barstow called out to us. "Also, there's a fellow in Milton who's been taking care of Temple Island for the last few years. He might have some information for you too. He runs the little hardware store...Troy Bowden's the name."

"We've met," I called over my shoulder as we stepped out into the very beginnings of rain.

We hurried across the parking lot to the car, and once seated and out of the drizzle, Jennifer fairly sparkled at me. "Isn't this exciting! I just knew you'd find the answers here!"

"I don't know what all you heard," I said gravely, buckling my seatbelt, "but I'm going to need some time to process all of this. I...I can't even believe it."

"I would think what you just heard would help you believe it even *more!*" Jennifer chastised my determination to be obtuse. "I saw your face when you looked at the picture. That's her! That's the one you've been dreaming about...the one Troy keeps telling you that you already know. You know her because you *were* her! You were Marilla Sutter...and now you're back to finish whatever she started. Whatever she put on hold when she threw herself into the ocean at the end of the Civil War."

"She didn't throw herself in the ocean," I said flatly. "She didn't die on Simple Island...Temple Island...because she was *on that boat*, the *Sultana*. She was on that boat...I remember it."

Chapter Twenty-Two

August 8, 1859

My Dearest,

Far from disallowing your dream discussions, I will actively seek to hear your stories each morning. Like you, I also cherish a "rich dream life" as you called it.

In fact, it was because of my dreaming life that I began to open myself up to the possibility of having lived multiple lives, as Eastern Mysticism suggests. I have had dreams, on occasion, within which I seem to be an entirely different person, experiencing things that I have never experienced, fully knowing things that I have no cause to know. I have dreamed of families that I love deeply, but with whom I have no connection in the waking world. I have dreamed skills and endeavors that have no connection to this version of myself.

I believe I have dreamt you, My Dearest, and please do not allow your opinion of me to be altered by this revelation. I had thought I might never tell you this, or that at least I would wait until long into our marriage, but your description of your own relationship to dreaming has moved me to tell you now, and somehow I do not feel that you will "raise an eyebrow" at all. I believe that you will understand me in this, as you seem to understand me in all things.

I have told you before that, upon meeting you on that evening in New York, I felt that I was not meeting a stranger, but rather that I was finding you after a long separation and my heart sang to have finally recovered you, having been missing you for so long. I did not immediately recall having seen you in a dream; that would have been a little bit too precious, don't you think? But it was about a week later that I had a dream that was very familiar, a dream I was sure I had dreamt before, and it was in this recurring dream that I saw you. You were standing across from me in a terribly crowded train station. I could tell you were beckoning me to join you in boarding a train, and I was struggling to reach you through the crowd, knowing that if I could but board that train with you, all would be well. I woke feeling like I had been drowning in the pressing crowd that had kept me from reaching you, and yet immediately upon waking, I knew that I had dreamed this before, had dreamed you before, though previously I had no ability to connect the you in the dream to any part of my reality.

Even so, when I saw you across the room in New York, though I didn't recall the dream in that moment, my heart knew. I knew that if I could breach the crowd and stand by your side, we could board the train, we could take this journey of life together.

And so, we shall.

Chapter Twenty-Three

We drove through the rain in silence, just contemplating all that we had learned and how it might connect to my dreams—my memories—of Marilla and Samuel Sutter. I still had no connection for Helena and her shovel; that didn't fit anywhere. Not yet, at least.

I thought about the repeated admonitions to "meet me" or "find me at the temple." This was Samuel calling to Marilla, even as they were drowning in the burning, churning river. Had he meant...like this? Living a whole new life in a whole new century, but each finding their way to Temple Island to meet again, to be together again? And if Marilla had come back as me, then that had to mean that Samuel had come back as...

I thought about the dream after the night with Troy, when I could see Samuel and Marilla making love in the bed next to mine, and Troy was saying, "That's Em, but I think you already know her. She belongs to me."

How much of this was Troy aware of? Did he know the story of Samuel and Marilla? Did he have memories of being thrown in an explosion, falling through the night sky, calling out for Marilla from the freezing water? Did he know *any* of this? I thought that he must not. He seemed so cool, so unflustered. If he was having these same memories, he would definitely be flustered. Like me.

Maybe it wasn't Troy at all. Maybe it was Ian...he'd been the one obsessed with the island, asking for answers, finding sneaky ways to study it.

But it didn't feel like Ian. It didn't make any sense to me that it was Ian. If I was Marilla, and I was seeking Samuel, wouldn't I have felt something more solid with Ian...like what I felt with Troy?

I pulled past Jennifer's rental into my own little designated spot at the end of Parson Point. Stepping out and opening my umbrella against the thickening sprinkle, I looked back and noticed something under Jennifer's wiper blade. It was a blue piece of paper, tucked into a page protector. Written on the paper in bold Sharpie, it said, "THIS IS PRIVATE PROPERTY. REMOVE THIS CAR OR IT WILL BE TOWED."

"What is it?" called Jennifer through the rain as she struggled with her umbrella.

I looked over at the chain that blocked vehicular entrance to the Beardens' property, and noted that, for the first time since I'd been on the island, it was unlocked, and lying on the ground. Craning my neck to see around the trees, I could also see that there was a black SUV parked by the house. I could see something else, too: a portly man, pointing at me with a long bony finger, his head down in the rain, but his eyes glaring at me, was hurrying across the gravel drive to intercept me.

"Trista," Jennifer called again, finally getting her umbrella open, "What is it?"

"I think I'm about to meet the neighbors," I said, as softly as I could so that Jennifer might hear me, but Mr. Bearden might not.

In that moment, I decided that I would pull out all the Southern Woman Charm my mother had so carefully taught me. She'd always said that when I "bat my big brown eyes" I could accomplish anything I wanted. Never minding the blatant sexism inherent in that phrase, I sensed this was a moment to use every weapon in my arsenal.

"Good morning!" I called cheerily through the rain, "You must be Mr. Bearden! I wondered when I might get to meet you!"

Mr. Bearden was not to be discouraged from his mission.

"I know what you're thinking, young lady," He spat at me as he stepped over the chain, never lowering the accusing finger.

"Oh?" I said, batting the aforementioned big brown eyes.

"You're thinking you've got a quitclaim deed that says you can park here, and that's right. There's nothing I can do about it. But that deed says you can park a car. CAR!

Not *cars*! You can have your wild party on your own property," (here he glowered at Jennifer, who was not choosing Southern Woman Charm, and scowled back at him), "but you can't park more than one car on my property!"

"Mr. Bearden," I said, placing a feminine hand on his arm. "I completely understand my mistake, and I promise I won't make it again, but as it's raining right now, can't we just..."

"NO!" he bellowed, jerking his arm away from my touch. "If that car is still here in five minutes, I'm calling the police to have it towed!"

With that, he spun around in the gravel and marched back to the house in almost the same attitude he'd marched out, but without the pointing finger.

I watched him for a few seconds, then turned back to Jennifer. "Get in," I said, indicating her rental car, and as she unlocked her car, I climbed back into the driver's seat of mine.

Before I'd started my motor, Jennifer texted me the obvious question. "Where are we going?"

"I really only know one person in town," I texted back with a sigh of resignation. "I'll have to ask him if we can park the car at his store."

Once back at the main road, I led the way into the parking lot of Vincent & Son. There were two other cars in the lot, and it occurred to me I had no idea which one was Troy's. I'd slept with him, but I didn't even know what kind of car he drove. I could add that to the long list of simple things I didn't know about Troy Bowden: his middle name, how he took his coffee, whether or not he liked Star Trek...the important things at the foundation of a relationship.

I pulled into a parking spot and was out of my car before Jennifer was parked beside me. I knocked on her window and when she rolled it down, I said, "I'll be right back!" But Jennifer wasn't having it.

"Are you kidding?" she said, unbuckling her seatbelt, "I'm not missing this for anything!"

The little bell on the door jingled as Jennifer and I stepped in out of the rain, and I could hear voices toward the back of the store. I walked back toward the counter, but as I approached, I could see that it wasn't Troy behind the counter, but a young man, maybe not even twenty. As I approached, the lady at the counter had finished her business. She turned, smiled at me and said hello, then passed us on her way out.

"Hello," the young man said expectantly.

"Hi," I responded. "Is...Is Troy here?"

"Oh, no," he answered. "Troy went home for a few days. He always does about this time of year, to visit his family." He grinned broadly. "He usually leaves my Dad in charge when he takes a trip, but this year he said he trusted me to handle it."

I could tell the young man was proud to have been given this responsibility, and it sounded just like the sort of thing Troy would do, valuing the pride he could instill in someone over any concerns for his store.

"Well, I was hoping to talk with him. I needed to ask him a favor."

"I'm sorry," the young man said, then his face became quizzical. "Hey...are you Miss Maybrey?"

I must have looked equally quizzical. "Yes...that's me..."

"Oh, wow! Cool! Troy told me you might stop by, and he left a package for you."

Before I could ask another question, he dropped behind the counter, and I could hear him rummaging. When he popped up again, he offered me a small box whose flaps were folded in upon themselves rather than taped shut. Assuming this wasn't the sort of package that needed to be opened in private, I pulled the flaps apart. Inside was my Maglite, and a note that simply said, "I've been assured that your ice breaks will be on Wednesday's truck, so we're still on for next Saturday. -Troy."

Reading over my shoulder, Jennifer teased, "Still on for next Saturday..." and I elbowed her in the ribs.

Turning back to the boy, I asked, "Listen, do you know the Beardens who live at the end of Parson Point?"

His smiling face went sour. "Yeah...everybody knows about them. Are they home?"

"Yes, they're home, and this is the first time I've met them. My friend here is visiting and they're just *not* going to let her park her rental car there, so I came here to ask Troy if it was OK for her to park the car here. She's going home tomorrow, so it would just be for one night."

The boy looked sympathetic. "I guess it's OK," he agreed. "I'm sure Troy would say yes, and he left me in charge..."

I took that as an affirmative. "Thank you so much!" I gushed, "and thank you for this!" I held up the box with the Maglite to indicate my gratitude, and we left the store.

Once back in my car, Jennifer said, "I don't care what you say, I know you well, and you looked positively disappointed when he told you Troy is out of town."

"Shut up," I growled, and drove us back down Parson Point in silence.

We spent the rest of Jennifer's visit researching the *Sultana* disaster. We were both absolutely shocked we had never heard of it. The websites we found with information all touted it as "the worst maritime disaster in the history of the United States," having more casualties than the *Titanic*, which Jennifer pointed out was actually a British maritime disaster, though it had been headed for the United States.

We learned, in our reading, that the *Sultana* had been a Mississippi River steamship with a legal passenger limit of 376, but because of greed, corruption, and carelessness, she was carrying more than 2000 passengers in the wee hours of April 27, 1865. The numbers of passengers and casualties varied widely from one set of statistics to another, because apparently, at some point in loading the paroled Union soldiers, they just stopped counting. One website said there was a whole trainload of soldiers brought at the end of the loading, and no one even bothered to register them.

These were all soldiers who had been held captive in the prison camps at Andersonville, in Georgia, and Cahaba, in Alabama. One website offered gruesome details of what life had been like for these men in the prisons: the disease, the starvation, the desperate measures for survival. There were photographs of some of the men, taken after their release, and they were little more than skeletons…just absolutely emaciated.

Because the United States government was offering $4 per soldier and $10 per officer for any ships that would bring them up North, the captain of the *Sultana* had conspired with the quartermaster in Vicksburg to grossly overload the *Sultana* for maximum profit. There was a photograph taken from the Arkansas side of the river as the *Sultana* passed, and the deck of the boat is just absolutely black with uniformed soldiers. How did they even sit down, much less lie down to rest, in that horrific crowd?

All the articles and web pages agreed that the captain had been aware of a leak in one of the *Sultana's* four boilers, but his desire for the money involved made him choose to cover the leak with an inadequate patch rather than take the time to replace or truly repair the boiler. Had he taken that time, other steamships would have taken the soldiers home, and he would have missed out on the money.

The *Sultana* left Vicksburg Mississippi on April 24, 1865, just ten days after the assassination of Abraham Lincoln. Amongst the extreme overcrowding, there were also about 70 paid passengers from New Orleans, and a crew of 85. Apparently, there was also quite a bit of livestock, including several Army mules, and an alligator that the *Sultana* crew kept as a pet.

"An alligator after all," I said to myself. "Not a crocodile."

The Mississippi was experiencing a record-breaking flood at that time, with melted ice from the north coming down, and the already-crippled *Sultana* was working hard against the current to move upstream with her heavy load. In fact, the load was so heavy, that the lower decks had to be braced with boards because the weight of the soldiers on the top was causing everything below to creak and sag. I'm sure that was lovely for the seventy passengers who had paid to travel "in style."

On the night of April 26, the *Sultana* stopped in Memphis to offload several tons of sugar, and to take on more coal. There were stories of some of the soldiers getting off the boat in Memphis to drink or gamble or otherwise pass the time. One fellow missed getting back on the boat and had to pay someone with a private boat to catch him up to the *Sultana*, and he counted himself lucky. He was not among the survivors.

At about 2 am, when the *Sultana* was seven miles north of Memphis, the patched boiler exploded, and two more boilers exploded in a chain reaction. Most of the soldiers were asleep at the time, and some survivors later reported waking up to find themselves flying through the air.

The number of casualties was as variable as the number of men who had loaded on the *Sultana* in Vicksburg. There was no way to know how many bodies were simply never found, or found, but never identified. It was estimated that, of the men who initially survived the disaster, more than 200 died in the following days due to their horrible burns and other injuries. There had been women and children on board, among the paid passengers, and very few of them had survived.

The name Marilla Sutter was nowhere in what I'd read, not that there was a comprehensive passenger list. Why was she on the *Sultana*? Where had she boarded? How had she known that's where Samuel would be?

Jennifer was piled up on the sofa, reading articles on her phone. "Hey," she called to me, "It says here that all the soldiers loaded onto the *Sultana* were from Ohio, Michigan, Indiana, Kentucky, Tennessee and West Virginia. Not Maine. In fact, there was a *New York Times* article that week that said, "No troops belonging to states east of Ohio were lost.""

"I know," I answered heavily. "I'm seeing the same thing. But...well, they didn't count everyone, so..."

I didn't need to finish the sentence. I knew Marilla had been on the *Sultana*, and Calvin Barstow, the museum curator, had said without question that Samuel had died in the disaster.

Even if, somehow, Marilla had been one of the paid passengers, Samuel was among the troops which didn't include Maine...but also, there was that trainload of men that were never registered or accounted for.

I think I had been hoping that, somewhere in all of the historical research, more of my "memory" would kick in and the answers would be among them, but all I was getting was a headache from reading page after page of small print on my computer screen. I began closing out the pages, one by one, and I came to the page with the photograph of the emaciated parolees. Stopping to study the photograph again, to be nauseated all over again by the idea of what humans can do to each other, I began having a feeling of something gnawing at the back corners of my memory. Not a memory from a previous life, just something from so far back in *this* life that I couldn't quite...

I texted my mother. "Can you send me a picture of my award-winning poem? I need to see my original handwriting."

Mom didn't answer, but within three minutes, my phone dinged and there was the photograph.

I immediately emailed the picture to myself so that I could open in on my laptop and study it, enlarged. Once I opened it, I looked at the careful handwriting on the specially lined paper. For the contest submission, I had written the poem out in pencil, and then gone over each letter with a black magic marker and signed it at the bottom in tenuous cursive. In the top corner was my fourth-grade teacher's handwriting, documenting my full name, my age (9), grade (4), and the date of the submission, October 17, 1994.

Jennifer came to stand behind me. "Is that the original?" she asked.

"As close as we can get, I guess. I mean, I must have written it somewhere else first, because this was the final draft for the contest. No idea where the *original* original would be now."

I zoomed in as far as I could before the image lost cohesion. Scrolling around, reading through each line carefully, I finally came to the reason I'd asked for the picture.

"Look," I said, pointing.

"I see it..." Jennifer answered.

Between the first two letters of the word TIN, between the T and the I, which were both carefully traced in black marker, was another letter that my nine-year-old hand had tried to squeeze in when I had realized my mistake; a tiny letter that had not been traced in magic marker, but was, instead, still scrawled in pencil, but dwarfed by the surrounding letters. This hastily included afterthought was the letter H; a lower-case H almost completely lost between its towering, magic marker neighbors.

"Not TIN soldiers," I said. "I never meant TIN soldiers. It was supposed to be *THIN* soldiers. Thin soldiers...emaciated and starving from their time in the Confederate prison camps."

I turned to Jennifer who was just staring at me in amazement. I began quoting the poem. "I look around this endless ride, I see *THIN* soldiers, side by side. I think they'll save me from the sea, but I am wrong. They fall with me."

"Oh my god, Trista," Jennifer said, finally finding her voice. "You were having a full memory back then, at nine years old, and you probably didn't understand it, so you tried to capture it in poetry."

"I can't say what I did or didn't understand back then," I said. "I don't *remember* remembering, which is so frustrating. It seems like if I remembered it back then, I would remember even more now...but it's just all a tangle."

"So, what will you do next?"

I hadn't really thought about that, at least not deliberately, and yet when she asked the question, I knew the answer.

"I think I have to go there."

"There?"

"To the various sites. There's a monument in Memphis and another in Knoxville. A lot of the unknown bodies are buried in Memphis."

"You think Samuel is there?"

"I don't know...maybe. If he'd been identified and brought home, there would have to be some mention of at least one soldier from Maine, right? Also...Marilla *must* be there. She was also never brought home, which is why they tell stories about her throwing herself into the sea and still haunting Temple Island."

"Well, in a way," Jennifer said with a grin, "She *is* still haunting Temple Island. But now she has a cute haircut and blue jeans. And she haunts the island by, like, painting the front door. Wooo-ooooo!"

I wanted to smile back at my best friend, but I felt too overwhelmed to even raise the corners of my mouth.

"So, when will you make this epic pilgrimage?" she asked.

"Honestly, I feel like it can't wait. I'm thinking I might leave tomorrow when you head back to the airport."

"You're going to *drive*?"

"Yes, well, last minute airfare would cost more than this island, plus I'll need a car to go from site to site...besides, I'll need to take Margaret Mary."

We played around on Google Maps, finding that the drive from Milton to Knoxville was 18 hours...too far for one day. But if I left the island at the earliest low tide and made the goal for Sunday night to be in Baltimore, I could make it there in about ten hours, twelve hours allowing for stops to eat and walk the dog. That would put me at my first hotel before midnight.

The rest of the drive, from Baltimore to Knoxville, would be, including stops, only about ten hours, so I'd still reach Knoxville at a reasonable hour on Monday night, and could visit the Mount Olive Cemetery Tuesday morning, then drive on to Memphis, another six hours, to visit the two sites there on Wednesday morning.

While Jennifer arranged the covers on her air mattress for the night, I logged in to my Hotels.com account and booked myself into "pet friendly" hotels in Baltimore and Knoxville. I figured the trip home could be sorted out once I had seen what I went to see. Oh, how easy navigating the world had become just in my lifetime.

That night, lying in our separate beds, Jennifer and I were still able to communicate softly across the little cabin.

"Why do you think we were never told?" she asked.

"About the *Sultana*?" I queried, knowing that's what she meant.

"I mean, I took U.S. History in 7th grade, like everyone, and I took American History in High School, and both of those included entire units on the Civil War. Of course, I took those classes in the South, where history is still a little skewed."

"Well, I took a college course that was a full semester of the Civil War, and it was an online course, using the Ken Burns documentary like a textbook. It wasn't skewed, and yet, I don't remember anything about this. If it was mentioned, it was like a footnote." I rolled over and propped up on my elbow so that I could see Jennifer on her air mattress.

"I think a lot of the historians agree that there was just so much going on right then. The war had ended, Lincoln was assassinated...John Wilkes Booth was found and killed just the day before the *Sultana* exploded. All the soldiers were coming home, trying to rebuild their lives. It was too much."

"News overload. I get that," Jennifer said into the darkness. "I mean, I get that back then, but why is it *still* a footnote? Where is the blockbuster film with a John Williams score?"

I flopped onto my back and stared up at the ceiling. "It's in my head," I said. "I mean, minus the music, the movie is in my head, and I can't bring on the closing credits."

"Maybe the closing credits are somewhere in Tennessee."

"I hope so."

Chapter Twenty-Four

August 19, 1859

My Darling,

This morning my tears have not been part of a dream, but real salty drops running down my face. I awoke to my father and brother arguing loudly, and my sister came into my room, drowning in her own tears.

It was the same argument I have tried to avoid, tried to ignore, as I tried to pretend that nothing will change, that life will go on the same as it always has. But more and more each day I do not believe this is the truth.

And so, my father and brother were arguing about the coming war. At least, they insist that a war is coming, is unavoidable, and the argument is about what our role will be in it. My father insists that the family has a responsibility to the nation to keep the railroads moving, and that in this effort, we will support and contribute to the swift resolution of the conflict. My brother, however, believes that his duty will be to don the uniform and fight.

My mother, of course, denies that there will ever be any fighting. She insists that the government will resolve the difficulties without bloodshed, and then my brother argues that there has already been more bloodshed than we will ever know, centuries of bloodshed on the part of the Africans who have been enslaved since the foundation of this country. My mother has no answer to that, and I know it is because she cannot reconcile the comfort of her own life with the suffering of those in bondage, and she is too delicate to try to do so, and so she simply attempts to forget that this is the central issue to the coming conflict. If she can believe that the central issue doesn't exist, then she can believe there will be no war, and that her son will not go and fight.

My sister, of course, is almost as delicate as our mother, but her tears are also for her own soon-to-be husband who may also choose to fight. I believe this is a large part of the reason she feels unable to leave Cincinnati even when she has become a wife. I understand this in her. She has not the constitution for change, she does not desire adventure. She is happy in a very small world, surrounded by people that she loves and an environment that she knows.

As you can imagine, it is to the great joy of my mother that my sister will not be leaving our home after all. Perhaps you think I will be sad coming to Maine without her, but please do not be concerned. I love my sister dearly, and all I desire is her happiness, but she and I are quite different people; I would have enjoyed having her along on this new life, but all that I require for my happiness and security is you.

My heart swells just to be able to write those words.

Chapter Twenty-Five

I wondered if Margaret Mary thought we were going back home, to Dallas. It had only been two weeks since our journey to Temple Island, as I had decided to forever call it. She settled into her favorite spot on the back seat and appeared to be resigned to another long trip.

But this time, she wasn't sharing her seat with a crowd of bags and boxes of my belongings. This time, there was just one big suitcase in the trunk, along with my smaller bag of toiletries, and Margaret Mary had the back seat to herself.

To keep me company on the long first day of the drive, I had downloaded an audiobook version of Alan Huffman's *Sultana: Surviving the Civil War, Prison, and the Worst Maritime Disaster in American History*. It was a harsh book, and I was grateful for my driving to keep me partially distracted from the horrors the author was laying out for me. The narrator followed a small series of young men from when they mustered into the Union Army, through the battles they fought, to being wounded and captured, then the horrible life in Andersonville and Cahaba prison. Then through the journey out of prison to the parole camp, the excitement of finally going home, loading on the *Sultana*, and then the nightmare of the explosion, and the hundreds upon hundreds of men trying to survive in the water.

There were so many stories from the survivors, the almost unimaginable terror they went through, as well as the survivors' stories of the victims, of how and where they saw one another give up and go under the water, many of them simply too weak to manage the long swim to shore. Thin soldiers.

The water that night was probably about 60 degrees, which is cold enough to pull the body heat out of a human pretty quickly, bringing on irrationality as well as numerous physical points of decline.

Alan Huffman, the author, spared me none of the graphic details he had gathered in his research: the horrible deaths, the men drowning each other in an effort to survive, the bodies on fire, desperate soldiers attempting to float to safety on the bodies of dead mules, the men so scalded by the exploding boilers that their skin slipped off of them in the water like boiled potatoes. I winced as I listened, but I had to listen. Samuel and Marilla were in there.

I stopped for gasoline, and realized I was in Hagerstown, where I'd stayed before at the awful little motel and where I'd had the third of my dreams about being on the *Sultana*. When I got out of the car, Margaret Mary didn't even stir in the back seat. She'd been very quiet the whole trip, always excited to get out and stretch her legs, but never complaining about getting back in.

As I was pumping the gas, suddenly Margaret Mary jumped up and began barking ferociously, as ferociously as a little white Wookiee can come across. She was looking out the window facing me, but she wasn't barking at me...it was something behind me.

I guess because of my focus on the tragedy, and my own dark memories and fears of losing my grip on reality, the hair on the back of my neck stood up, and I was afraid to turn around. Would I find Helena Sutter and her shovel? Was the asphalt of the gas station about to give way and I'd be falling through the broken boards?

But no. In the bay next to me, a man had begun pumping gasoline into the tank of a big brown UPS truck, and I laughed out loud. The man looked at me with a friendly, if slightly concerned, smile, and I explained.

"She hasn't made a peep all the way down from Maine, but you pull up in a UPS truck, and she sounds the grand alarm!"

"Well, it's good to know you've got a brave protector," he said.

"Yes...only from mail carriers, though!"

We pulled into the circular drive of our hotel in Baltimore just before eleven o'clock. The lady at the front desk told me that all guests with dogs get rooms on the first floor, which I thought was a lovely plan. It's a challenge in the early morning when your dog is practically crossing her legs in her desperate need to go out, but you have to take her first on an elevator ride. All hotels should have this policy.

I'd hit a convenience store for granola bars and fig newtons, and this was my late-night supper while Margaret Mary picked daintily at a bowl of kibble. I slept dreamlessly, and we hit the road again by nine the next morning.

We made excellent time on Monday and checked in to our hotel in Knoxville at about six that night, which meant we still had a couple of good hours of daylight. After unloading my suitcase, and turning on the AC in the room—and of course realizing that I hadn't even considered needing AC in Maine, but here in Tennessee, April 30 was already summertime—I left the hotel, without Margaret Mary, to go find the Mount Olive Cemetery.

I only knew to look for the Mount Olive Cemetery because of something I'd read on the internet, but what I actually found was the Mount Olive Baptist Church, and in the churchyard were a number of small gravestones as well as a few large monuments. I parked my car in the parking lot and walked across to begin reading the stones in the yard.

Most of them were small, classic gravestones with rounded tops, and the majority of those were so weathered that most or even all of the engraved information was long gone. I focused on the larger monuments, as this seemed more likely than that the *Sultana* memorial was on a tiny headstone.

The largest monument in the yard was a grave marked McCARRELL, and smaller letters said this was the resting place of Reverend P.B. McCarrell and his wife Sallie, who had died in 1897 and 1902, respectively. A nearby, more towering monument turned out to be the grave of "our mother" Elizabeth Hall, who died in 1879, at the age of 43. I began realizing that these were all just individual gravestones, the most recent being that of Nancy French, who was born during the Civil War, and died in 1939. The *Sultana* memorial was not here in the churchyard.

There was no reason to think that anyone would be at the church on a Monday evening; in fact, if I worked at a church, Monday would definitely be the day I would want *off*. Still, I followed a sign that said "Welcome Center" which led me down a long, shaded sidewalk to a heavy door with a keypad lock.

Cupping my hands around my face to block the glare of the setting sun, I peered through the window of the heavy door, and down a hallway to the right, I could see there was a light on. I knocked firmly on the window, and I could definitely detect movement in the sliver of light. Within about 45 seconds, a gentleman with thick white hair and a royal blue polo shirt answered the door with...not quite a smile, but at least with a friendly curiosity.

While I'd been standing there, hoping someone would come to the door, I had realized that, when I had checked in to the hotel, I should have availed myself of the facilities. It had been about five hours and three Dr. Peppers since I'd emptied my bladder, and this was becoming abruptly and urgently apparent.

"Hello!" I said to the man, just glowing my Southern Woman Charm. "I actually came all the way here from Maine just to see the *Sultana* Memorial. I thought it would be here, maybe, but I can't find it."

"Oh, no," he said, smiling now. "We haven't put anything new in the churchyard in a very long time. The memorial you're looking for is in the Mount Olive Cemetery, which is up the hill, behind the church."

"Thank you," I said, sincerely, and then, "Could I just use your restroom?"

The man opened the door wider and pointed me down the hall and around the corner. I hurried, because I wanted him to know that my request was sincere and not that I was just using the restroom as a ruse to get into his empty church on a Monday night. You never know with people.

He was still holding the door for me as I exited, thanking him sincerely for his help and hospitality. He responded with the standard "you're welcome" but I was pretty sure that was an empty platitude. He had not, actually, wanted to be disturbed at his work on a Monday night by a crazy woman with a full bladder.

I was halfway back to my car in the parking lot when I stopped still and groaned. Both my hands were empty. My pockets were empty. My cell phone, in its wallet case which contained my driver's license and credit cards, was still sitting on the counter of the Ladies Room in the Mount Olive Baptist Church.

For about 0.72 seconds, I actually thought that it might be easier to cancel my credit cards and report my phone stolen than to have to go back and knock on the door. But reason took over quickly, and I turned around.

This time, the man with the lovely white hair didn't even pretend to be smiling at me. "I am so sorry," I began stumbling over myself as soon as the door cracked open. "I left my cell phone in the bathroom." Wordlessly, he widened the door to let me pass, and I moved even faster than the first time, opening the door to the bathroom, sweeping up my phone from off the counter, and back to the door within thirty seconds.

"I'm so sorry," I reiterated as I breezed out the door, "I promise I won't bother you again." He closed the door behind me without comment, and I couldn't blame him. I hoped that, whatever work was keeping him there at dusk on a Monday, that he would finish soon and go home to his family.

My embarrassment of that moment was almost forgotten as I drove around to the back side of the church looking for the coordinating cemetery. Knoxville, at least this part of Knoxville, was absolutely beautiful. Both sides of the road were lined with aged oak trees and looming Magnolias. The cemetery, once I spotted it, was indeed on a hill, and a stone retaining wall lined the side of the road. Even in the waning light, the play of sunlight and shadow through the reaching arms of the old trees was too beautiful to describe.

I had to drive quite a distance around the cemetery hill before I found an entrance. I had been concerned that I might be too late, but the gate was still open, and I could see a crew of landscapers working busily on the grounds. I pulled in through the gate and then drove the length of the cemetery on the lower level, and I parked my car as I came to a sort of point at the far end from where I had entered. This is where the landscapers were working, though their big truck was parked more centrally, and I had passed it as I drove from one end of the cemetery to the other.

As I got out of my car and made the difficult climb through the grass up the steep hill, one of the men spotted me, guessed correctly that I was headed for him, and turned off his noisy edger. I made quick business of asking him if he knew where the *Sultana* memorial was, and he pointed me back toward the center of the cemetery, but the upper level. Where he pointed, I could only see his landscaping truck.

I opened the compass on my phone and noted that I had parked on the Southwest end of the cemetery, and needed to head Northeast, toward my original entrance, to find the monument. I decided to walk rather than drive, as I had already climbed the hill and didn't want to have to climb it again.

On the internet, I'd seen a photo of this monument, but the photo was taken without any context. It was a picture of the monument, and nothing else, so I had no idea how big it might be, or what other monuments were around it. It did appear, in the photo, to be sitting on concrete tiles, not grass, and I thought this might be helpful in my search. I could easily discount all the large expanses of green lawn that were dotted with other stones and markers of various size.

When I reached the landscaping truck without having found the monument, I almost turned around to go back and ask the men for more detailed help, but, as I was just coming off the humiliation of repeatedly disturbing the man in the church, I decided to trudge on a bit more. I made a semi-circle to walk around the big truck and then there it was, right in front of me, just on the other side of where the truck was parked.

It was a very large monument, the main part of the stone as high as my shoulder, so probably five feet tall, and wide. The long lists of victims' names were engraved down both sides of the pink marble, as well as on the front and back. On the front was a carving of the *Sultana*, brandishing an overly large, almost comically large, American flag, and the words: "IN MEMORY OF THE MEN WHO WERE ON THE SULTANA THAT WAS DESTROYED APRIL 27, 1865, BY EXPLOSION ON THE MISSISSIPPI RIVER NEAR MEMPHIS TENN. FROM IND. KY. MICH. OHIO. TENN. VA. MO" and under each of the listed states there was a number of casualties, at least the best they had figured by the time the monument was erected in 1916. The numbers ranged from just 2 from Missouri to the largest number, 460, from Ohio. Near the bottom, it said, in smaller letters, "THIS STONE WAS DONATED BY GRAY EAGLE MARBLE CO."

Looking at the numbers of casualties listed, I had a thought about Ohio. Calvin Barstow at the little Washburn County Maritime Museum had told us that Samuel and Jonathan Sutter had met and married a pair of sisters, and that Jonathan had moved back to Ohio to live near his wife's family. This would mean that Marilla, Jonathan's sister-in-law twice over, was originally from Ohio, but, unlike her sister, had settled in Maine with her new husband, Samuel.

I remembered back to the dream on my first night in the cabin. The man who was tending the kittens who were being eaten by the alligator, he'd been selling Army uniforms which all had the same price tag: "Ohio $175."

This all connected somehow. Somehow. But I couldn't see it. I stood skimming through the hundreds of names, almost hoping to see one that would be familiar, but no. On the Northern-most side of the monument, the stone was greatly weathered, and many of the names were almost illegible. A hundred years of wind and rain had lost those names to history almost as the disaster itself had become lost. But on the Southern side, the names were more legible, and I could even see places where other names had been added, much more recently. The effort had been made to carve them in the same lettering, but they were carved more deeply, and just slightly out of line with the others. I wondered who they were, and if their family members had petitioned to have their names officially added, maybe even decades later.

On top of the monument, there was an odd addition that I believed had to have been an afterthought. It was like a stone pole rising another two feet into the air, and a different color marble from the original structure. Was it supposed to represent a smokestack? There was no explanation, of course, and so I was just guessing.

The sun was thoroughly set; I was beginning to feel cold, and suddenly thinking of how long I'd left Margaret Mary alone in the hotel room. In the dwindling light, I walked back across the hilltop and climbed down to my car.

I don't know what I had expected to experience at the monument. I hadn't known that it had names carved on it, so I hadn't been looking for a familiar name. Maybe I had hoped that connecting with the history like that would help more of my memories to coalesce and make sense. That hadn't happened, but still, I had appreciated the ability to be there, to imagine the handful of old men, in their seventies, no doubt, who sought to erect this monument to their comrades who had perished in the disaster they, themselves, had survived.

Back at the hotel, I heated a can of soup in the microwave and settled in to catch up on emails. Finally snuggled under the covers, waiting for sleep to find me, I recounted for myself the details of the trip so far, and thought about the drive to Memphis the next day.

I had to admit that, for me, this trip was a major undertaking. The "old Trista," as Jennifer would say, would have been too fearful to drive from Dallas to Fort Worth, and here I was, driving from Maine to Tennessee, with multiple destination points, and not once had I experienced the nerve-wracking fear that I might have predicted a few months ago. Something important was changing inside me, and I knew that the changes had their roots in Marilla and Samuel Sutter.

Marilla must have made this trip as well. Unknown to anyone else, she must have traveled alone from Temple Island down to Vicksburg to board the *Sultana*. Was she afraid on that journey? Whatever she had been feeling, she exhibited a great deal of courage to undertake her private mission to find Samuel and bring him home. Perhaps it was her courage that was bolstering me now.

The original plan had been to drive all day Monday, then visit the Knoxville monument on Tuesday, but timing had been such that I managed to visit the monument Monday night. This meant I was ahead of schedule and could indulge myself by sleeping in on Tuesday. The hotel had a continental breakfast, so I brought a bagel and peanut butter back to the room to enjoy with coffee while I answered some emails and made a couple of work-related phone calls.

I showered, repacked, and Margaret Mary and I hit the road by noon. It was roughly a six-hour drive to Memphis, through very pretty country. I finished the Alan Huffman book and, when we stopped for lunch, I downloaded something much lighter, a historical romance novel, to keep us company for the rest of the trip.

When we finally made it to our hotel in Memphis, there was still enough daylight to go to at least one of the cemeteries on my list, but I decided to wait until the morning. I found *Groundhog Day* on TV, and quoted along with the film while I did what amounted to a full day's work on my laptop before turning in.

I dreamed that I was back in the Knoxville cemetery, standing by the monument, and when I looked across the lawn, I could see Troy sitting cross-legged on the grass. He was turned away from me, so I walked over to him, and touched his shoulder from behind. He was startled, and jumped to his feet, but then he was glad to see me. He pointed off in the direction he had been facing, and I could see that, in the distance, Marilla Sutter was standing in the grass in her long ivory gown, holding a bouquet of colorful flowers.

"Look," he said, smiling at me, "That's Em...but I think you already know her. She belongs to me."

And then he leaned in to kiss me and it was so nice, so sweet and simple, that it made me cry. Troy just smiled at me as I cried, and then I was sobbing uncontrollably, and Samuel came to put his arms around me, and he whispered, "This is good, Trista. You're almost ready. Find me at the temple."

When my alarm went off, I lay there for a few minutes processing the dream. It had been peaceful, the serenity of the cemetery, Troy's smile and kiss. Even my own fit of sobbing had been more cathartic than upsetting. It was a purge that I had needed. The presence of Marilla as well as Samuel's comforting words at the end...all of this was peaceful, in contrast to the frightening imagery of explosions and fire and falling. I thought, maybe, coming to understand about the *Sultana* meant that I didn't have to keep being reminded of those memories. Perhaps this peaceful dream was significant of my growing more comfortable with Marilla's life experience and my role in it.

We were, again, enjoying an unhurried morning. I had breakfast, and then bathed Margaret Mary before I showered myself. The long days in the car had made my little Wookiee start to smell overly doggie, and I was going to have her with me today in both cemeteries, as I wouldn't have a hotel room to leave her in.

There may be parts of Memphis that are pretty, but I didn't see them that morning. The part of the city I was treated to was, at first, a long row of "buy-here-pay-here-slow-credit-no-credit" used car lots, and when that ended, I found myself in what felt like an industrial ghost-town. Surrounded by empty warehouses with broken windows, barricaded by rusting razor wire, I couldn't imagine how the historic Elmwood Cemetery could be in this neighborhood...but Siri assured me that it was.

And then, I rounded a corner and saw the iron gate, welcoming me out of the wasteland and into the green, shady lawn of Elmwood. Once inside, I wouldn't have even known the wasteland was out there...once inside, it felt just like Knoxville, except that the Elmwood cemetery is much bigger, and there were no landscapers to ask.

Again, I had no frame of reference for the monument. I knew from the internet that the monument was there, in the cemetery, and the photo I had seen showed that, beside the *Sultana* memorial was a little green sign that simply said, "*Sultana* Memorial." I thought the little green sign would help me find it.

I drove around and around the windy streets of the cemetery. "Morgan's Grand Tour," "West Crawford," "McKeller Ave." When I saw the sign for "Road of Honor" I felt like this must surely be it.

If anyone had been watching me, I know I must have looked like a clown car just riding in circles. It was like that moment in *National Lampoon's European Vacation* when Chevy Chase is trapped in the traffic circle in London and he simply cannot get into the outside lane to exit. Round and round I went, looking for the little green sign.

I finally stopped right at the end of "Road of Honor" and opened Google on my phone. Surely there was a map. Every so often on the road, there was a little sign that marked a stop on the audio tour. I didn't want the audio tour, but there must surely be a map that showed all those little stops, and surely one of them was for the *Sultana* monument.

On the Elmwood Cemetery website, there was a place to purchase and download the audio tour, including the map, for ten dollars. It was definitely worth ten dollars to *not* go around the circle again. I downloaded the map and discovered that tour stop number 16 was for the *Sultana* Monument.

It wasn't hard finding the little sign by the road for #16, but the monument was not where I could see it from the road. I had to park, and Margaret Mary and I wandered up the hill, looking for the little green sign.

That was the problem though. I did finally find the *Sultana* memorial, and there was no little green sign. It was definitely there in the photo from the internet, but not there anymore.

This memorial was taller than the one in Knoxville; at its peak it came up to the top of my nose. Otherwise, it was smaller in every way: narrower, thinner. It was also a much more modern structure, having been erected in 1989, and laser engraved rather than the bas-relief work on the much older monument. There were no names engraved on this one except for the names of the people who had dedicated it and the historians who had contributed. The text on the monument told briefly of the disaster. It ended by saying "We salute their memory, and for the agony and terror of that night, we bid them God's mercy."

It bothered me a little that the engraving of the *Sultana* on the monument was wrong. It was a picture of a classic steamship with the one big paddlewheel on the back, whereas the *Sultana* had the two side paddlewheels. It did feel like they might have gotten that part right. Maybe if

I'd seen this one first, before the greater emotional impact of the monument in Knoxville, it wouldn't have bothered me. Still, it was a lovely gesture, in a lovely setting.

After the hour and a half in Elmwood Cemetery, it was a shock to find myself back in the industrial ghost town. My next stop was to be the Memphis National Cemetery where I'd read there was a large section of graves for the unknown victims of the *Sultana*. Again, I had the experience of searching for a manicured lawn in the middle of a dirty city, and again, I found it: a perfect haven that offered no hint of the drab outside world.

Unlike the Mount Olive Cemetery and the Elmwood Cemetery, which were eclectically filled with stones and monuments of all shapes and sizes, the Memphis National Cemetery was a garden of neat rows of perfectly matching stones. It wasn't difficult at all to find the section I was looking for, populated with hundreds of stones engraved with the words "Unknown U.S. Soldier."

Parked in the shade, I got out without Margaret Mary this time, and walked across the sidewalk to the first row of stones. I don't know what I had thought I would do in that moment, or what I thought I would feel, but I found myself meandering between the stones, touching each one as I passed, and simply whispering, "Thank you. Thank you." A mist of tears blurred the scene before me, but I continued to walk slowly between the stones, offering my gratitude to these young men, barely more than children, who had fought for the only nation I had ever known...and had never made it home.

When I turned to make my way back toward my car, I saw something off to my right, and I stopped still. Sitting cross-legged on the sidewalk, facing the headstones about seventy-five yards from where I stood, was Troy Bowden.

Even from that distance, I knew it was him, and I stood, terrified that I was having a hallucination. He was sitting exactly as he'd been sitting in my dream, only in the dream, it had been a different cemetery. What did this mean? What was about to happen to me? I stood absolutely still, waiting for whatever was coming.

But then the vision of Troy stood up, turned, and saw me. He, too, stood perfectly still for a moment, and then began walking toward me. As he drew nearer, he waved and smiled, though I could tell he was as surprised to see me as I was to see him.

The look of surprise, and the little wave, broke my spell of fear. This wasn't a hallucination. This was the real Troy Bowden walking toward me in the Memphis National Cemetery, a thousand miles from either of our homes.

"Trista?" he said, as he came within a few feet of me, his voice filled with surprise. "What are you doing here?"

It was a valid question, and one I wanted to ask him as well. I did my best to answer. "I came on a kind of a pilgrimage, to see the cemeteries here, and in Knoxville. I'm driving home tomorrow." I know I sounded pathetic, like a lost little girl. Funny how I had been so very sure of myself until Troy showed up. "What are *you* doing here? They...they told me you were going home for a few days."

Troy beamed. "I did! I am! This is home! I grew up here in Memphis, and every year I come back to visit my family. I always find a quiet time to come here, to sit and think, to visit the boys." He swept his hands toward the gravestones, and I understood what he meant. I knew what he was feeling, because I had felt it too, as I wandered through the stones. If I'd grown up in Memphis, I like to think I would have regularly visited these young men as well, tried to be their family.

I thought he might press me further about what I was doing in Memphis, Tennessee on a Wednesday afternoon, but he didn't. I also thought there might be some awkwardness due to the circumstances of our last parting, but there wasn't. He just grinned that grin of his and said, "Have you had lunch yet?"

"No," I said, "But I was definitely thinking about it."

"Well, let me take you to my favorite place!"

I started to agree, then remembered. "Oh, wait...I'm sorry. I have my little dog with me, and it's too hot to leave her in the car...I mean, in a parking lot. It's really cool and shady here."

"That's no problem," he said, enthusiastically, "My favorite place for lunch has a shady back yard where your dog can play while we eat."

I looked at him blankly, trying to understand, and he clarified, "My favorite place for lunch is my Aunt Lavinia's house. She makes an amazing salad with fresh strawberries and walnuts."

"Oh," I said, "I can't just show up uninvited..."

"You're not uninvited," he called to me over his shoulder as he strolled toward my car, clearly intending for me to follow. "I just invited you!"

Troy beat me to the car, and held the door open for me as I approached. "My car is parked just over there," he said, indicating a late-model rental on the sidewalk across the lawn from where we stood. He tapped on my back window and waved at Margaret Mary, who was waking up with an impressive yawn. "You ladies just follow me...it's about a fifteen-minute drive out to Cooper-Young."

Cooper-Young turned out to be an artsy neighborhood with a lot of interesting looking shops I would have loved to crawl through. The neighborhood stood in contrast to both of my earlier snapshots of Memphis. Perhaps I needed to give the city a more thorough look. I was seeing it in a very different light, now that I knew Troy had grown up here.

Troy was an excellent leader. As someone with a lifelong irrational fear of being lost, I hated following drivers who seemed to forget entirely that I was following. Drivers who would glide through a late yellow, with no consideration that I was going to be stuck at the red, and then wouldn't be able to find them. Or who let two cars get between us and then turned at a stop sign, such that by the time I could make the turn, they had already made another turn or two. Following, for me, could be a nightmare, and often ended with me parked on the side of the road in tears.

But Troy was clearly aware of me. The first time he came to a full stop at a yellow light so that we wouldn't get separated, I knew I was in trouble. This is someone I could fall in love with.

Troy turned onto Manila Street and pulled into the driveway of a sweet little house on a corner lot. I pulled up to the curb, not feeling confident enough to pull into the driveway. Instead of going to the house, Troy got out of his car and walked back to mine. He opened the back door and picked up the end of Margaret Mary's leash, sweetly coaxing her out of the car. I got out and came around to the curb.

"Ready to meet the folks?" Troy asked, and winked at me, even as he made kissy noises at Margaret Mary, who prissed beside him through the yard and to the front door.

By the time I caught up with them, the door was being held open by a woman who couldn't have been more than 45, but as Troy introduced me to his Aunt Lavinia, she was beaming at him like a mother.

"Troy told me about you, Trista—how you bought the little island everyone says is haunted." Troy and I had settled at a little table in the kitchen, while Lavinia finished the salad.

I laughed at the good-natured ribbing. "Well, Margaret Mary certainly finds enough phantoms to bark at. Or squirrels. It's all the same to her." I looked out the sliding glass doors at my little Wookiee, who was, at that moment, barking up a giant pine tree where she had just treed...something. Or nothing. She was happy either way.

Conversation through lunch was comfortably lovely, and I could see that Troy had a radiant relationship with his Aunt. They made several references to Lavinia's husband, Charlie, but he was at work, and I was not going to meet him.

Troy volunteered that Lavinia and Charlie had raised him after his parents died. I didn't feel ready to ask probing questions, so I just accepted what they told me, and understood that, despite some early tragedy, Troy had grown up loved and cherished.

"So, Vinny," Troy said, stretching back in his chair once the salad bowl was empty, "I'm not going to be home tonight...OK?"

"Well, of course it's OK," Lavinia laughed, "But where will you be?"

"I'm taking Trista on a road trip."

"You are?" she asked.

"You are?" I asked, simultaneously, turning in my chair to look at him. Was he teasing? I didn't know how to tell.

"Yep," he grinned at me. "I'm taking her up to Franklin. I want to show her something."

"How is that going to work?" I asked, both intrigued and confused. "I mean, didn't you fly down here for the week?"

"Sure, but I was going to fly home tomorrow anyway, because I have a roofing job on Saturday for a difficult customer I've already had to put off once." He winked at me. Dammit. "So, I was thinking that if I cancel my flight, and we leave this afternoon, we can get to Franklin by this evening, and make the rest of the trip between Thursday and Friday. I can still get back to Milton in time for the roof job. What do you say?"

Lavinia attempted to come to my rescue. "You're hard to resist, Troy," she said, "But Trista probably has other plans. That's a really long trip to commit to unexpected company."

"I know you're right," Troy said with a furrowed brow, and then he brightened. "How about this: We'll go up to Franklin this evening—it's like a three-hour drive—and then, after dinner, I can hitch a ride back to Memphis and catch my flight out tomorrow."

Committing to the whole trip back to Maine in the car with this man who so conflicted my emotions did seem like an awful lot—but I could probably manage three hours alone with him. Besides, if I was trying to open myself up to the signals I was being sent, the incredibly unlikely coincidence of meeting Troy in the Memphis National Cemetery certainly could be viewed as a nudge I should pay attention to.

"What do you say to that?" He asked me with that grin.

"Well," I said tentatively, "It's Margaret Mary's day to pick the music, and she wants nothing but Madonna all day...if you can handle that then, OK. Let's go to Franklin."

Troy and Lavinia both laughed aloud, and I warmed in the feeling of family.

The new plan meant that Troy needed to go pack, and that left me alone with Lavinia.

"I don't want to overstep," I began, carefully, "But I can't help but be curious about how it came to be that you and Charlie raised Troy. You're very young to be a Mom to a grown man."

Lavinia smiled at my compliment. "We were pretty young," she agreed. "Troy's mother, Julia, was my older sister. Charlie and I had just gotten married when she and Will died. It was very sad for the whole family. Troy was ten years old, and I was only twenty-one, but there was no way Charlie and I were going to let him go into foster care. He was such a bright little boy, and even with the loss of his parents, he pushed himself to recover, to grow. We're just so proud of him."

"I can see that," I said. "It's clear how much he loves you."

"He's obviously very taken with you as well," Lavinia smiled at me. "He's found several opportunities to bring your name into conversation over the past few days."

"I hardly know him," I confessed, woman to woman, "but I'd be lying if I said he doesn't occupy more of my thoughts than I'm comfortable with."

She clattered some dishes into the sink, and said, "Well, I can't think of any better way to get to know someone than being cooped in a car on a road trip!"

"I'm trying not to be nervous..."

"Who's nervous?" Troy said, coming into the room with a backpack slung over his shoulder and a rolling suitcase behind him.

"Me!" Lavinia jumped in. "Charlie is going to be so bummed when he gets home and finds out you left early, and then I have to spend all evening with him. Why don't you give him a quick call to say goodbye?"

"I'll call him on the road," Troy said. "I don't want to lose any more daylight. Besides, he can feel my presence when he takes my rental back to the airport tomorrow. I'll let him know I'm extending that unique honor." He turned to me. "You ready to go?"

"Just have to lure my mighty hunter back into the car."

"No problem!" Troy opened the sliding glass door and made his kissy noises at Margaret Mary. She came running excitedly and stood remarkably still while Troy clipped her leash to her collar.

"There we go," he said at last, and began leading Margaret Mary, along with his luggage, to the front door. "Come kiss me goodbye, Vinny...you'll regret it if you don't!"

Lavinia met Troy at the door for a quick hug and a peck on the cheek. Then she turned to me with another hug. "It was lovely to meet you," she said warmly. "I hope we'll see you again."

"Thank you so much for the lunch and the company. So much better than my original plan: Taco Bell in the car."

"Well, you're always welcome," she said sincerely.

"Let's go," Troy called, already out the door. "Time's a'wastin'!"

By the time I got to my car, parked on the street, Troy already had Margaret Mary loaded into the back. I watched him ease himself comfortably into the drivers' seat.

"I've gotta drive," he said, as I settled into the passenger seat, "because you don't know where we're going!"

"Should I be worried?" I asked, handing him the keys.

"Of course not. Look at this face." He grinned at me as he started the car. "I'm totally trustworthy."

If there was a period of awkwardness, it was gone by the time we'd gotten out of Cooper-Young. Troy made conversation easy, talking about Lavinia and Charlie, about their quirks and hobbies and the things he'd learned from them. I chimed in about my Mom, and the relationship we had developed in my adulthood. I told him the story of how Margaret Mary came into my life, and he shook his head over such a precious creature having such a terrible start. Troy told me about the dog he had growing up, a mutt he called Larry. Larry had been adopted at the shelter as a puppy when Troy was eight and had died during Troy's senior year of high school.

"I just never did think I had it in me to fall in love with another dog." He looked into the rearview mirror to take a peek at Margaret Mary in the back seat. "Maybe I was wrong."

After about an hour on the road, conversation was settling into comfortable periods of silence, and Troy turned on the radio. I had previously had the radio set to a satellite station that was a mix of pop hits from the past three decades, but Troy quickly switched it over to a station that was all country.

"Ugh!" I said as the first strains of Conway Twitty assaulted my ears. "What the hell is this? You like country music??"

"Hey now," he said, "Aren't you the girl from Texas?"

"Yes, and I spent my whole life trying to avoid this tear-in-your beer crap! Turn it off!"

"Tear-in-your-beer crap? Seriously? I think you just haven't learned how to truly appreciate the artform."

"Artform. It's a form of art where all the lyrics are about drinking and cheating and rain. Oh, and my favorite kind of country music: the songs that are about how great it is to be a total hick from the sticks."

Even over the crooning nausea of Conway, Troy started singing in a redneck twang, *"We're from the country and we like it that way! Ever'body knows ever'body. Ever'body calls you friend. You don't need an invitation. Kick off yer shoes, come on in…"*

I threw my head back and laughed at his rendition, but then I sang my own rendition with new words: *"You cain't get an education, and ever'body marries kin!"*

Now he was laughing, and we drowned out Conway. The next song was John Michael Montgomery's ballad, *I Love the Way You Love Me.* Troy started right in singing along, and I groaned in dramatic fake misery.

Troy turned the radio down so that John Michael was just soft background music. "Now, what's wrong with this one? This is a nice song. He *loves* her!"

"It's not real love," I argued.

"How is it not real?"

"Just listen to him…every single line is something that's just physical, something about the way she touches him or kisses him, or how pretty she is…and the ultimate is that he loves the sex. *'Strong and wild, slow and easy'*…it's all just superficial and sexual."

"For someone who has spent her whole life avoiding country music, you sure do know all the words." He was grinning at me, and suddenly the car was very, very small.

"I said trying to avoid it. There's no actual avoiding country music in Dallas, Texas."

"Ok," he challenged me. "What would you write? I mean, if you were writing this love song for John Michael Montgomery to sing, about all the reasons he loves his girl, what would you have him say so that the song is 'real'?"

"Well...how about something like, *'I love that your credit score is 780.'* That's the kind of thing that makes a relationship last."

"Totally romantic. Is your credit score 780?"

"Yes! And I worked really hard to get it there! I think it says a lot about my character, which is way more important than the way *my eyes dance when I laugh.*" I said that last bit in a sing-song sarcasm that brought out Troy's guffaw.

I was encouraged to continue. "I think he should say, *'I love the way you held the Pringles can for me to pee in that time I threw out my back and couldn't get out of bed for two days.'*"

"Oh my god! You did that?? I could totally love a woman who did that!"

"See what I mean? That's *real* love."

"OK, I've got one," Troy said thoughtfully. "How about *'I love the way you cleaned up the kitchen all by yourself after the party.'*"

"I would add to that and have him say, *'but of course I know that was a one-time thing and next time I'll totally be in there with you.'*"

"That may be a little difficult to work in with the rhyme scheme."

"It will absolutely be worth the extra effort."

By now, John Michael was finished and then Reba was telling us about the Night the Lights went out in Georgia. I knew every word to this one as well, and I sang along loudly, just for the pleasure of making Troy Bowden laugh. Margaret Mary chimed in with her own version of accompaniment, and the car was a haven of laughter and music.

"You've gotta like that one," he said, wiping the tears from his eyes when Reba and Margaret Mary and I were finished. "You couldn't memorize a song like that without liking it!"

"Yeah...me and Reba have a silent agreement. As long as she never ages, I'll keep singing along."

"She's certainly keeping up her end of the bargain!"

And then the self-congratulatory satellite radio break ended, and the car was filled with the beginnings of *Boot Scootin' Boogie*...and Troy snapped the radio off.

"Ohh...?" I teased. "That's not an acquired taste you think I should have by this point in my maturity?"

"I'm not sure anyone is mature enough for that one."

★ ★ ★

We arrived in Franklin proper at about five o'clock. Still plenty of daylight for whatever Troy was planning. It had become clear he wasn't going to tell me where we were going, so I had long since stopped asking.

Franklin was a pretty town like Knoxville. Very green, shady, and welcoming. I was enjoying the scenery, wondering when we would actually get "into town" when Troy said, "Here we are!"

On my side of the road, there was a long, long wooden fence. A very unique fence that was at once rustic and also looked like something from a battlefield. This assessment was justified when Troy slowed the car and turned right into an entrance with a big stone marker that said, "Eastern Flank Battlefield Park."

"Is this a Civil War battlefield?" I asked, intrigued.

"Yes, it is," he explained, "The Battle of Franklin. It was one of the final battles, just before the Battle of Nashville. They say the Nashville Campaign, which began with the Battle of Franklin, along with Sherman's 'March to the Sea,' were what really ended that war. So, this spot is of great historical importance...but also it's just really beautiful."

It was. As Troy drove slowly through the park toward the welcome center, I looked out my window at the lush green lawn with winding sidewalks. Ahead of us, I could see a tiny fenced graveyard shaded by oak trees so large they were likely there at the time of the battle. It was an absolute picture of peace...and I recognized the irony of that at the site of what had to have been a horrible, bloody battle.

"I'm guessing the welcome center is closed now," Troy was saying as he parked the car in the empty lot. I looked at the clock on the dash; 5:17. He was probably right.

"It's OK, though. I didn't mean to give you a history lesson. I just wanted you to see this place. I bet Margaret Mary is ready to take a walk, aren't you, Sweetie Pie?"

Margaret Mary was already on her feet and wriggling in anticipation of getting out to stretch her legs. Troy took the key out of the ignition and pocketed it as if it were his own. I climbed out of the passenger side and stretched as Troy opened the back door and took the handle of Margaret Mary's leash.

Coming around to my side of the car, he said, "Let's walk over there; you see that big wooden signboard? That's kind of a 'You Are Here' map that shows the lines of the battle itself. It's hard to imagine what happened here," he said as he began leading us down the sidewalk, "but it was a massive defeat of the Confederate army. Historians say the Rebels shouldn't have tried to take on the Union here. They were grossly outnumbered, and the attack was almost senseless. The Union army had every advantage, and the Rebs basically walked straight across this huge open field to where the Yanks were already set up for battle... it was just suicide."

He was right, it *was* hard to imagine. This lawn was now just towering oaks and green grass, with shafts of evening sunlight pouring through like poetry. There was not another person around that I could see. We had all this beauty to ourselves.

As if thinking the same thing, Troy said, "You think it might be OK to let this little lady off her leash? She's been cooped up for hours."

"I'm sure that's fine," I agreed as he stooped down to unclip the leash. "She's pretty Mama-centric."

Freed from her string, Margaret Mary bounded ahead of us, then turned and bounded back, beginning a series of little circles back and forth, proving my point.

As we walked slowly up the path, Troy pointed off to the left. "You can hardly see it right now, because they keep it really protected, and you have to buy a ticket to get in, but there's a house over there that was here during the battle. The tour guide can show you where there are still bullet holes."

"Wow..." I said softly.

"The family was hiding in the basement for the whole battle. No one was hurt. But then after it got dark, the

Yanks moved out toward Nashville, and they left this battlefield strewn with wounded of both uniforms; a lot of them got dragged into that house for treatment. Many of them are buried in that little cemetery over there.

"That must have been a horrible experience for the family."

"Those were horrible times for everyone."

I realized I had lost track of Margaret Mary, and when I stopped to look around, I saw that she was on the lawn, off to my right, sniffing at something on the ground. "Come on, baby!" I called, and she looked up, but then returned her focus to whatever was holding her attention on the ground.

Embarrassed that she was misbehaving in front of Troy, I stepped off the sidewalk toward her, and that's when it happened.

It felt as though the whole world caved in on me. The sky and the sunlight just crashed down on top of me like a building collapsing, and suddenly it was dark, and I was surrounded by smoke and the sound of gunfire. There were bodies everywhere, reaching up to me, grabbing at my legs. I had no gun. Where was my gun? I had to help these people, but it was absolute mayhem. I heard orders being shouted that I knew I should follow, but I couldn't leave these people. These men who were blown to pieces, crying out to me in the darkness and the smoke. I saw other men on their feet, men in gray uniforms, and I knew they would shoot me if they could, and I didn't know where I had laid my gun. So many bodies, so many mangled dead bodies, and so many mangled men, still alive, clawing at my legs. I could hear the drums. My regiment, everyone that I knew, they were all retreating toward the woods, and I should go. I should go with them...but the men. I couldn't leave them. I had to help them. But if I stayed, I would be separated. I would be lost, and I desperately didn't want to be lost...but I couldn't leave.

The whole experience may have been five seconds. Maybe not even that long. And then it was like Troy grabbed my hand and pulled me through a doorway back into the beams of sunlight through the massive trees on the peaceful lawn. I grasped at his hand as I grasped for the ability to breathe, and I was still coughing, choking on the smoke and the terror of the moment I had just experienced.

I stumbled backward and sat down hard on the ground. The choking turned to sobbing, and Troy was on the ground with me, holding me, rocking me in his arms like a child, kissing my forehead and murmuring softly to calm me.

"What is *happening* to me?" I choked and cried, and Troy just held me tighter.

"I'm so sorry, Trista. I'm so sorry. I thought something like this might happen. I mean, I thought being here, on this land, might help your memory, but I didn't know it would be this hard. Oh, god, I'm so sorry...I'm right here. You're OK, I promise."

I looked up at him, shocked, and pulling out of his embrace. "You knew this would happen? I don't understand! I can't make any sense of any of this! My husband left me, and I bought an island to...I don't know...to run away from everything...and my whole life is turned upside down! Why was I here on this battlefield? Why was I on a doomed steamship?" I pounded on his chest with my fists. "And why are you here at all? What do you have to do with any of this? What do you know that I don't know?"

Troy took my hands in his to stop the pounding, and he smiled at me and spoke very softly.

"I'm here because you told me to meet you. To meet you at the temple. I've been waiting for you for a very long time."

I looked at him, struck dumb for a moment, and then I said, "No...I didn't tell you to meet me. It was Samuel that said..."

Troy's soft smile broadened into his trademark grin, and he didn't need to answer me. In that moment, I knew.

I had been reading it all wrong. I saw the images in my dreams and the history they connected to, and I saw myself as Marilla Sutter, in her long ivory dress with her brown hair piled on her head. When Troy, in my dreams, said, "I think you already know her," I took that to mean that I knew her as in having *been* her. When Troy, in my dreams, said, "She belongs to me," I took that to mean that Troy had been Samuel in a previous life, and Marilla belonged to him as his wife.

But that was all wrong. The memories I was having were not Marilla's. They were Samuel's memories. I had not lived the life of the woman in the ivory dress. I had lived the life of the man on the battlefield. The man who couldn't leave the wounded behind. The man who was crushingly aware that he was going to be lost...a crushing fear that had followed me into this life.

I grasped again at Troy's hands as the realization sank in. "I'm...I'm Samuel," I said almost blankly. "I *was* Samuel."

He just grinned that grin at me.

"But...then that means that you were..."

"Now you're getting it." he said softly. "Can you imagine what it was like, being a pre-pubescent boy having the memories of a nineteenth century woman?"

We just sat there, on the grass, and I relaxed into Troy's arms. Margaret Mary had come back over to us, and she stretched out in a patch of sunlight. Now that the initial terror, and then shock, had passed, I was able to more calmly process through the images in my dreams.

When I had heard Samuel's voice, calling for Em in the water...it had been my voice. When I had seen Samuel's face, looming close into mine just before I hit the water, that was my reflection. When I wrote about thin soldiers on the *Sultana*...I was among them. My unreasonable fear of being lost, my fear of fire...these were Samuel's fears.

So many images tumbled over me...and I finally asked him softly, "Why did you know to bring me here?"

"I wasn't sure," he said, and kissed my forehead again. "I didn't know how much you remembered, or if you remembered anything at all. I didn't want to push you. I mean, I knew I couldn't say, 'Hello! Yes, that's a lovely color of green for your front door. By the way, in a past life, you were a Civil War soldier and I was your wife...how neat is that??'"

I giggled.

"So, I had to let you find your own way," he continued. "But then when I saw you in the cemetery, and you said you'd been to the other cemeteries...I knew it. I just knew it. You were figuring it out. You were looking for answers. There were answers in those places, but Samuel was never there. I thought if I brought you here, where Samuel had this traumatic experience, I thought maybe the connection would be made. I just didn't know it would connect quite so... hard."

I pulled back so that I could look him in the eye. "But...how did you know it was me? I mean...from the beginning?"

He hugged me in again. "Well, honey, I Googled you."

"What?"

He laughed. "I kind of finessed your name out of Lisa. I mean, I told her that I figured you'd be coming into Vincent & Son soon, and I'd like to know right away that you were the one who bought the island so that I could be the most help. So, she told me, and I went online, and I looked you up on Facebook, and I learned about your business."

"You stalked me?" I said with a laugh, and I smacked him on the arm playfully.

"Not anything that wasn't easily accessible online. I didn't like, get your social security number and your bank statement. I swear I didn't know your credit score until today when you told me."

"So, you figured out I was the one you were looking for by looking at my Facebook page?"

"Well, no. I had a hunch, because here you were, out of nowhere, buying Simple Island."

"Temple Island," I corrected him, and settled back into the curve of his body again. A perfect fit.

"Oh…you know that part? You're farther along than I thought! Anyway…I moved to Maine eight years ago, and in all that time, I've been waiting for you. When the married couple moved in and started renovating, I helped them out and got to know them, but I knew they weren't right. I mean, even when they were divorcing, there was not part of me that thought the wife was the one I was looking for. And then they left, and it stood empty. And I watched your friend Ian come out over and over, and I met the older couple when they came out...and then Lisa told me there was a single woman who'd taken out a contract and she needed my help with the inspection...and I don't know. I just knew. And then I met you. That first day in the store, when I looked at you...that's when I was sure. I felt it."

"I guess I felt it too," I mused, "only I didn't know what *it* was. It just annoyed me!"

"Annoyed you?"

"Yeah...it felt like you were picking on me, like a brother."

"Wow. Great. A brother."

"You know what I mean. Like you knew me too well, and that was...it was annoying. So," I changed the subject, "when did you first realize...I mean, when did you start having memories?" I asked, and Troy shifted his body, stood up, and offered me his hand.

Helping me to my feet, he said, "It's starting to get a little chilly now that the sun is going. Let's go find another place to talk. There's a lot to discuss."

Chapter Twenty-Six

August 30, 1859

My Dearest,

If your heart swells to write those words, can you imagine the bonfire that explodes in mine upon reading them?

Here as well, talk constantly turns to the coming war with our own countrymen, and like your mother, many people try to pretend that the argument will pass without anyone taking up arms, but this is a foolish assessment. Perhaps I should not have called it foolish when in that same sentence I am talking of your mother, and I do not mean that your mother is foolish, of course. As you said, your mother is delicate, as is mine, and this talk of war must be unspeakably frightening, and so the delicate people of our world attempt to put it away from themselves.

The foolish that I speak of are the citizens and the politicians who are not too delicate to consider the darker issues, but who choose not to consider them anyway. More and more, I can only see the inhumanity of the people who have the means and the intelligence to work on solutions to the problems inherent in slavery, and who instead spend their time and resources on selfish endeavors, as though their own comforts and petty pursuits are more important than the suffering of our global neighbors.

The relief of suffering is the reason that I chose to study medicine. In our little town, there is but one doctor, Dr. Brady, and he is elderly and limited in his education to modern methods and treatments. Once you and I are well and truly wed, I will set about establishing my own practice so that Dr. Brady can retire (this is a discussion he and I have had, and he welcomes that day), and then I will be the doctor here.

I am telling you this because you did not ask, but I know that you must be experiencing your own fears that I may also don the uniform and fight. That is not my plan. My best purpose will be to remain at home, the only doctor in town, to tend to the women and children and elderly people who are left behind by the men who do choose to don the uniform. Whether the conflict is six weeks or six months, there will be babies born and illnesses contracted and accidents and injuries of all levels of severity, and the town will need a doctor more than the army will need another single soldier.

Still, there is guilt in that decision, and I comfort myself by knowing that this was my decision long before I knew you, before I planned to marry you, before I felt that I could never leave you behind. Those things are all very true now, but even before you beckoned me to join you on the train of life, my plan to stay was set.

My Dearest, my "M.S." ...we will very soon be together, and I promise you that we will always be so.

Chapter Twenty-Seven

When Troy came back to the car from the hotel lobby, he handed me a little sleeve with an electronic room key card inside. Handwritten on the sleeve was the number 217. Troy tossed his own sleeved key on the dashboard, and I saw that it said 219. Separate rooms.

He drove us around to a centrally located parking spot and turned off the engine. "I'm not trying to take advantage of your weakened state," he said, winking at me. "But we need quiet and privacy to talk this out, and this seemed the best idea."

We carried our luggage up the elevator and then to our separate rooms. As soon as the door was open, Margaret Mary ran in and made herself comfortable on the armchair in the corner. After all of our recent travels, she knew the drill.

I put my luggage on the bed, and then turned right around and left the room. Troy's door was no more than two feet away from mine in the carpeted hallway, so I knocked softly.

He opened the door with a smile. "Is the Princess resting?" he asked, welcoming me into the room that was almost an eerie mirror image of my own.

"In her throne," I assured him.

I perched myself on the armchair in this room that matched the one Margaret Mary was occupying in mine, and Troy opened the little refrigerator to display the mini bar.

"I'm not sure if this will help or hinder this discussion, but either way, I'm going to have a drink. What's your fancy?"

"Coconut rum," I said, "if you've got it."

"Indeed, I do!" Troy brought me the little bottle. "Should I go get ice?"

"Not necessary," I said, and then wondered if I sounded like a liberal. "I like it just like this."

Troy sat cross-legged on the bed with his tiny bottle of bourbon, and he looked at me for a long time. Then he broke the silence to answer the question I'd asked in the park.

"I was ten. That's when it started. Specifically, it started on September 30, 1994. That's the night my parents died in the house fire."

"Oh, I'm so sorry..."

"They had made absolutely sure that I knew what to do if there was a fire. They drilled me on how to get low to the floor and crawl to the front door. When the alarm went off that night, I woke up, and I did exactly what they'd told me to do...and so I stood outside in my pajamas and waited for them. But they didn't come."

"Troy..."

"Watching the fire, and feeling so scared, that's when it started. And then over the next few nights, I think I must have dreamed Marilla Sutter's whole life."

"That must have been...overwhelming."

"I don't know," Troy reached up to ruffle his hair. "I mean, not so much. I think kids are just more resilient. Kids are more...accepting."

I thought about what Jennifer had said about acceptance being the hallmark of an *old soul*, and I looked at the man sitting across from me...the man I hardly knew, and yet knew so well. Just then, I fully understood what Jennifer had been saying.

"Anyway," Troy continued, "I think I just inherently knew not to talk openly about it. I didn't think I was going crazy or anything, and I didn't want anyone else to think so either."

"You mean, you've kept this to yourself until *now*?"

"Yes. I saw it as the only option...but it was OK. In high school, I was the absolute authority on the *Sultana* disaster. I was ready to write any research paper. So that was a bonus."

I knew he was trying to lighten the mood, a little comic relief. We sat quietly again for a minute, and then I thought about something he had said.

"Wait...the house fire was on September 30 of 1994?"

"Yes...?"

"And that's when your memories of Marilla started?"

"Yes...what...?

"That's it then!"

Troy looked at me blankly, waiting.

"Troy, in October of 1994, just a few days after this all started for you, I wrote a poem that my fourth-grade teacher entered into a contest..." and then I added, slyly, "I won third place."

"Congratulations!"

"It was a poem about the *Sultana*...only I didn't know it. And I don't remember writing it, and I don't remember having the memories, but I obviously had them, at least just in a flash. It had to have been tied to the fact that you were suddenly getting all of *your* memories!"

I quoted the poem for him, and he sat very quietly when I finished. I don't think either of us knew how to express what we were experiencing, but in fact the moment didn't need words. Troy Bowden and I had been tied together all our lives, each of us gradually making our journey to be together again. And here we were, in a hotel room in Franklin, Tennessee, finally putting together the puzzle pieces of our lives to make one perfect picture.

I drained the last sip of the tiny bottle of coconut rum. "Troy...I understand why I was there, but why were you on the *Sultana*?"

Troy stood up and collected my little bottle, and threw it, along with his own, into the trash can under the bathroom sink.

"First of all, let me give you a little bit of advice." He settled back onto the bed. "This is not like an expert opinion or anything, but in my experience, it's a lot easier if you don't use the words *you* and *me*. Yes...yes...we lived those lives, but those are not our lives now. As your memory comes back, more and more, it's important for you to be able to keep it separate. No matter what or how much you remember of Samuel's life, you are Trista Maybrey. You run a business, you have a kick-ass credit score and a funny little dog, you have parents and friends and hobbies and dreams and memories that have nothing to do with Samuel Sutter. I *want* you to remember with me...I've waited almost all my life for this...but I also want you to be Trista Maybrey. Does that make sense?"

I felt the tears come into my eyes, but I didn't let my gaze waver from his. "It makes perfect sense. Thank you. I'm so sorry you didn't have anyone to guide you the way you're able to do for me."

"Let me answer your question by telling you Marilla's story, as I remember it. But can I ask you a favor?"

"Sure..."

"Come over here with me...lie beside me while I tell you. I just want to be close to you."

More than anything I could ever remember wanting, I wanted to be close to Troy Bowden just then. Without hesitation, I crossed to the bed, and stretched out on the left side as he lay down on the right. He put his left arm under my neck so that my head rested on his shoulder. Lying there together, gazing up at the ceiling, Troy began telling me Marilla's story.

Marilla Danvers grew up in Cincinnati with her older brother Joseph and her younger sister Autumn. Marilla and Autumn were only eighteen months apart in age, but Joseph was five years older. Joseph worked for their father's railway company, and he traveled to New York often. He promised the girls that when they were old enough, he would take them with him to the city for a holiday.

In the Spring of 1859, that magical time finally came. Joseph took Marilla and Autumn on a train to New York City, and showed them a grand time. Fine dinners in fine restaurants, wonderful shows in the theaters. He let them shop for new dresses. It was a momentous week for the girls.

One night, the reason they had come to New York at all, Joseph was to have dinner in the home of a wealthy man who had invested heavily in the Danvers' railroad company. The guests included many other business associates, as this wealthy man wanted all of his companies together to discuss the difficult business happening in the Southern states, and to talk about how this might affect their profits.

Not interested at all in the talk of business, Marilla and Autumn were just excited to be in such a lavish home. They tried to hide their girlish giggles and behave like young women.

Among the guests that night were two young men whose family ran a lumber company in Maine. They were, of course, Samuel Sutter and his younger brother Jonathan. Although they were engaged in the discussions of business, it became obvious that they were more interested in the Danvers sisters.

"I don't remember any of this," I said, incredulously.

"It's OK…you will. If not, we can put the pieces together. You may remember things that I don't."

The next afternoon, Samuel and Jonathan Sutter paid call on Joseph Danvers at his hotel. They invited Joseph, and his charming sisters, out to dinner. And then, after dinner, they all went for a walk in the newly opened Central Park. Joseph could see what was coming to be between his sisters and these brothers, and he felt himself wise enough to know that having Marilla and Autumn marry into the Sutter family would be pleasing to his parents. It was a good match.

That evening, he walked several paces behind the two blooming couples, allowing them the opportunity to get to know each other, and the next afternoon, he invited the young men to tea before he and his sisters boarded the train for home.

Marilla and Autumn were quite sad to wave goodbye to their suitors at the station, but Joseph told them he was sure they would be hearing from them soon. Indeed, not three days after arriving back in Cincinnati, there came a letter from the brothers, addressed to Mr. Danvers, expressing their desire to pay formal suit to his daughters with the intention of marriage.

Just as Joseph had predicted, this match was quite acceptable to Mr. and Mrs. Danvers. Mr. Danvers, through mutual industry contacts, was familiar with the Sutters' business dealings and reputation. He responded to the letter favorably and suggested that he and his wife should meet with Lawrence and Helena Sutter to discuss the arrangements.

Once dowries and details had been agreed upon, the date of the wedding was set, a double wedding in September. But as the young women prepared their bridal trousseaus in anticipation of the big day, Autumn began to feel anxious about leaving home and living so far away from her parents. Joseph stepped in again, this time writing a letter to Jonathan, expressing Autumn's heartsickness over the prospect of moving so far away. It was decided, rather quickly, that after the wedding in Cincinnati, Samuel would take his bride back to Maine, but Jonathan would stay in Ohio and work for his father-in-law's business, thus further tying the two families together.

The only one who wasn't completely comfortable with this plan was Helena Sutter, because Jonathan was her baby. He was a grown man, of course, at twenty-four years old, but he was still Helena's baby, and she was grieved that he would be so far away.

Her husband Lawrence, not wishing to see her sad, tried to make up for it with an idea. As part of the family property, there was a little island, Temple Island, just off the coast, and Lawrence proposed that he would have a little house built and gift the island to Samuel and Marilla as a wedding present. That way, Samuel would have his own home, but still be very close so that Helena would not feel she had lost both of her sons at once.

So, after the wedding, and a honeymoon trip to New York City where they had first met, Marilla and Samuel came home to the surprise of their own little home on their own little island, and there they were very happy.

★ ★ ★

"It starts to get patchy here," Troy said. "I don't actually remember much about their early life together."

"You remember a lot more than I do!" I said, and Troy squeezed me closer.

"I know, historically, that the war began, and everything changed in the nation. I know, like from Wikipedia, how many Mainers joined the Union army, but...not Samuel."

"He was a doctor." I said, remembering what Calvin Barstow had told me. "He stayed to be a doctor...but also...I think he stayed because of Marilla. He couldn't leave her."

"But he did leave her. Like at the very end of the war, he joined the army and I don't know...I don't remember why."

"Keep going," I encouraged him. "Maybe that's part of the puzzle that I'm supposed to put together."

Samuel left for the war in the fall of 1864. He knew Marilla was safe with his parents. Marilla knew this as well, but she was deeply grieved to see Samuel go. Thus far unable to have children, Marilla was so afraid of losing Samuel as she had seen the war create so many young widows. She was almost relieved when they later received word that Samuel had been captured on November 30, at the Battle of Franklin, in Tennessee, which seemed so very far away.

Samuel was able to get a letter to them, telling them he was at the Cahaba prison...

★ ★ ★

"Castle Morgan!" I interjected.

"Yes, that's what they called it. Look! You're remembering!"

"It's ironic that Marilla felt relieved. It seems like the soldiers were far more likely to survive the battlefield than the prison camps."

★ ★ ★

...and rumors were that they would be released soon.

Those rumors were prevalent throughout the winter. Surely this eternal war was over, and the boys could come home. Newspapers predicted the end, and also described the horrible conditions in the Confederate prisons.

In early April of 1865, Marilla Sutter could bear it no more. Sitting in a sewing circle with her Mother-in-law, listening to the women cluck their tongues about the conditions the Boys in Blue were being treated to, which was called Southern Hospitality, Marilla made a decision. That night, at low tide, she left her island in secret, and began a journey South. She was determined to bring Samuel home, whatever it took.

"This part is also patchy," Troy admitted, "And you won't be able to help me. I remember that part of the trip was by train, part was by steamship, and I think there were long treks of walking involved. I have vague images of people who offered assistance along the way. She had money, so that was helpful. I remember that there were long periods of difficulty, and short periods of ease. I remember that, during her journey, she learned that the war had officially ended, and then, later, learned of Lincoln's assassination. It was a long trip, and I'm sure it was mostly unpleasant, but I really have tried to remember it in more detail...but I can't. At least not yet. Maybe I'll bore our grandchildren with detailed stories of Marilla's journey South, but I can't do that yet."

I winced inwardly at his mention of "our grandchildren." Not because I wasn't ready to think of us as a couple...that was an easy given...but because he had no way of knowing that I couldn't have biological children. I had a heavy sigh and let him continue.

Marilla arrived in Memphis on the evening of April 25. She booked a room in an inexpensive hotel and spent the night and most of the next day sleeping. On the evening of the 26th, she went to the hotel restaurant and was seated at a small table for dinner.

While she was waiting to be served, Marilla was approached by a starkly thin man in what appeared to be a very new Union uniform. He seemed so out of place in the hotel restaurant, but he spied her—a woman sitting alone—and he pulled out a chair at her table and sat down.

At first, she tried to kindly rebuff his attentions, but he was loud and coarse, and she didn't want there to be a scene in the restaurant. She offered to buy him dinner, and he ate ravenously, explaining between mouthfuls that he had just been released from Castle Morgan, and was only on shore while his ship unloaded the cargo of sugar, then he'd be headed back north with his fellow parolees.

Marilla was shocked to learn that the Cahaba prisoners had not only been released, but that they were right there, in Memphis, on a Steamship headed to Cincinnati...her family home!

She hatched a plan. Spending the last of her precious money, she bought the soldier one drink after another, encouraging him to tell his stories of the war, until his words slurred, and his eyelids were too heavy to hold open. Knowing he was very close to passing out, she helped him to his feet and walked him out to the alley as though they were old friends.

In the alley, Marilla did something daring. She propped the very drunk soldier against the back wall of the hotel, and she stripped him of his uniform and boots, leaving him sitting there, passed out from liquor, in his long underwear.

Quickly, in the darkness of the alley, Marilla Sutter removed her dress and donned the uniform. It was too big for her, sagging off of her as it had sagged off of the half-starved man, she'd taken it from. No womanly curves could be seen.

She stuffed her hair under the soldier's cap and darkened her face with dirt from the alley. With a quiet apology to the sleeping man, Marilla Sutter ran toward the docks to find the Sultana.

It was after eleven o'clock, and several other men were boarding the steamship. No one even noticed or questioned the young woman in her stolen uniform. Once on board, Marilla was stunned by how many men there were, in all states of health and wholeness. They were sitting or lying everywhere, everywhere she could see. She could hardly make her way through them without stepping on someone.

At that hour, they were almost all asleep. Marilla found a tiny space against the rails of the top deck and curled her body into a tight ball for sleep. She would have to find Samuel tomorrow, when everyone was awake and standing.

But tomorrow didn't come for the Sultana. At about two o'clock in the morning, Marilla awoke to the horrible explosion. The ship was on fire! The men were on fire! The whole world was chaos. Men were ripping up boards of the deck and throwing themselves over, hoping to float to safety. Marilla was defenseless. She didn't know how to save herself in this situation. She didn't know what to do.

And then the decision was made for her. A very large man rushed past her to jump overboard, and in doing so, he broke off a section of the deck railing that Marilla was pressed against. Helpless to catch herself, she fell, screaming, into the cold water.

Moments later, just as she was surfacing, she could see a man on the deck throwing bales of hay and other floating parts of the ship overboard, for anyone who might reach them. One of the bales landed right behind Marilla, and she clung to it, as others struggling in the water also latched on. It was too many people, and more people were grabbing on, pushing others under the water in their effort to save themselves. Marilla was dragged by the feet away from the bale, and when she came up again, she knew she couldn't go back. She would die faster trying to float on something than if she tried to swim away from the panicked masses.

And then she saw him. Samuel was there, and he was calling to her. How he found her in all of this turmoil, she would never know, and would not have time to find out. He was floating on a shingle, and desperately trying to steer his small vessel to where she was struggling in the water. But, as she watched, he was also taken over by drowning men, and his shingle was swamped. Samuel was pushed under the water, but he resurfaced and called out to her. "Em! Em! We are lost! Meet me at the Temple! Come and find me at the Temple!"

Samuel Sutter was pulled under the cold water again and didn't resurface.

★ ★ ★

"That's all I know," Troy said. "I imagine Marilla died very shortly thereafter. If her body was ever found, there was no way of identifying it. No one was looking for her in the Mississippi River."

★ ★ ★

We lay there quietly for a while. It was almost midnight, but neither of us was ready to sleep. At last, I broke the silence to say, "I can't have children."

"What?" Troy asked, and I knew I had kind of blurted it out.

"I mean, I need to tell you that I can't have children. I don't have a uterus."

Troy was silent for a moment, taking in the meaning of what I was telling him. "I understand," he finally said, softly. And then, "Neither do I...in this life."

That struck me as hilarious, which was probably compounded by the late hour, and I laughed roundly.

When peace settled over us again, Troy asked, "Do you think you're ready?"

"Ready for what?"

"Ready to tell Samuel's story."

"I...I don't know. I don't feel like I know very much. Most of what I know now is because you just told me."

Troy rolled toward me and propped up on one elbow. "I think, now that you've reconciled to the truth of what's been happening, it will come easier. Not all at once, probably, but if you relax and beckon to the memories, I think you'll find a lot more of them than you realized you had. Maybe just...close your eyes. Try to focus on the pieces you do remember."

I reached into the collar of my shirt and pulled out the little obsidian crystal Jennifer had given me. "My best friend, Jennifer, gave me this crystal. She's very spiritual, very connected to the earth, and she said this would help me regain the memories. Of course, she said I should place it on my third eye...should I try that?"

"You have a third eye?? That's even cooler than that Pringles can thing!"

"Not an actual third eye, silly! It's..."

"I know what the third eye is. It's the...sixth chakra, right?"

"Nice! I'll have to introduce you to Jennifer. She'll be very pleased."

I lay flat on my back and placed the crystal between my eyebrows. "How do I look?" I asked. "Spiritual? Connected?"

Troy laughed. "Even if all your memories came back clearly tonight, I'm not sure I could take you seriously with that thing on your face."

"OK, then," I agreed, tucking the obsidian back into my blouse. Then I laid back, closed my eyes, and turned my attention to relaxing my body. I focused on the peaceful images of Marilla that I had seen in my dreams. Marilla standing on the little beach of Temple Island, in her ivory dress with her hair pinned up. Marilla in my bedroom, making love with Samuel. Marilla in Central Park, holding Samuel's arm and laughing.

When I realized that was a new memory, I focused very intently on remaining relaxed and letting the memories flow. I couldn't let my surprise jar me out of the moment. More images came, and then they were crowding in on each other. I don't know if it was being with Troy, or Jennifer's obsidian, or if it was just *time*...but the crowding settled down, and the pieces of the story began coming together. Not as cohesively as Troy's story of Marilla, but he'd had many years' head start.

With my eyes closed, and remaining as relaxed as possible, I began telling Samuel's story.

✲ ✲ ✲

The first time Samuel Sutter saw Marilla Danvers, he knew she would be his wife. It wasn't just that she was beautiful, which she was, but something in the way she carried herself was markedly different from the girls he knew in Maine. She was young, but not coquettish in the silly way that a lot of men found intriguing. Everything about her, her voice, her facial expressions, her enthusiasm for her surroundings...it was all so refreshingly honest, and Samuel spent that evening, which was supposed to be about business, intently inventing ways to find himself close to her.

At the end of the evening, his brother Jonathan couldn't stop talking about Autumn Danvers, and Samuel was amused to realize he hadn't even noticed the younger sister, nor had Jonathan paid much attention to the older one. It felt like two perfect matches.

For months, as the wedding date approached, Samuel and Marilla wrote heartfelt letters to each other, talking about their dreams, their plans for the future, their love for each other. Samuel told Marilla that, although he had always worked for his father's lumber business, he had also studied medicine, and he planned to devote himself full time to medicine once they were married.

"I don't remember the letters," Troy said. "I mean, it makes sense that they were communicating, but I don't have any memory of that."

"That's my piece of the puzzle," I said, pleased that I had something new to contribute.

Samuel was sad to learn that Jonathan was going to establish his life with Autumn in Cincinnati. He knew that he had always appreciated his brother's presence and his contribution to the family and the business, but until he knew Jonathan was moving so far away, he didn't realize how much he loved him.

When Samuel brought Marilla home to Maine after a month in New York City for their honeymoon, they were thrilled and surprised to find that Samuel's parents had built them a snug little home on Temple Island, a tiny island off the coast of their property that had never been used for anything before. Samuel opened a little doctor office in town, and after hours, he and Marilla worked together to create the perfect home. Marilla enjoyed gardening a little patch, and Samuel dug a small root cellar to help keep her vegetables cool.

They were disappointed that they didn't have a child right away, but when the war broke out, they decided perhaps that was for the best. The face of the country changed dramatically as everything began to be focused on the war effort.

Samuel did not plan to join the army. He knew that Milton needed a doctor at home, and he knew that when wounded soldiers came home, they would need care. He also didn't want to leave Marilla alone. Jonathan wrote to them from Cincinnati, saying that he wanted to join the army, but that the Danvers' railroad company was crucial to the war effort, and his Father-in-law needed him at home, so perhaps his work was enough of a contribution to saving the nation.

Helena was deeply relieved that neither of her sons were going to fight.

But in the summer of 1864, Jonathan telegrammed to say that Joseph Danvers had been killed at the battle of Chickamauga, and that he had decided to join the army in order to help bring this terrible war to an end. Helena Sutter was beside herself to think that her baby was going to war, and she pleaded with Samuel to go and take care of him, to watch after Jonathan and keep him safe.

Samuel knew that this war was almost over, and that his services as a doctor could be helpful on the battlefields. On his thirtieth birthday, he said goodbye to a tearful Marilla, and took a train to Cincinnati, where he and Jonathan mustered in with the Ohio 175th Infantry on October 11, 1864.

★ ★ ★

"OH!" I said, brightening to this memory, "That's why!"

"That's why what?" asked Troy.

"That's why he was on the *Sultana* when they said no troops east of Ohio were lost in that disaster! Also," I was breathing heavily with the excitement of realization, "that's what Ohio $175 means. It was the number of his regiment!"

Troy laughed softly at my excitement, but of course, he didn't understand what I was talking about, so I had to explain to him about the dream, the man in the shop selling tattered uniforms, all with the same price. I also described the chair full of bloody kittens that the man was tending, and the alligator that was quietly eating them. "I think I understand those bits as well but let me work out some more of the story."

The Ohio 175th was sent directly to Tennessee, where they spent a month performing routine garrison and guard duty. Jonathan was given special assignment for guarding the railroad, and the generals counted on him for his knowledge. Samuel's services as a doctor were greatly appreciated, though he was not listed as an army doctor. Disease was rampant. Samuel was painfully aware that twice as many men died of disease than in battle. There was no glory in this war.

In late November began the Nashville Campaign and Samuel and Jonathan were marched to Franklin, where they arrived, along with the rest of the Army of Ohio, several hours before the Confederate troops. It was a terrible battle, a slaughter of the gray army, but there were places where the Confederates broke the Union lines and the fighting was hand to hand. No amount of drilling and training could have prepared Samuel, a healer by trade, for the carnage he was expected to contribute to on that battlefield.

My breathing was becoming labored, and I backed away from the memory.

"Are you OK, Trista?" Troy was stroking my hair.

"I don't want to remember the battle. I don't want to know any more than I already do."

"I'm not sure you can choose *not* to have the memories, but you certainly don't have to dwell on that part. It's OK...you can skip it."

I tried re-centering myself and slowing my breathing, relaxing again.

As darkness fell on Franklin, Tennessee, the Union army fell back. Not in defeat, but because the ultimate goal was to take Nashville, and this had been the Confederates' last effort to keep that from happening. In the darkness and in the intensity of the importance of reaching Nashville, they left their dead and wounded on the battlefield. Samuel knew he should go, but he waited. He didn't know if Jonathan was among these wounded. He stayed with the men. He helped carry men into the house, men in both uniforms. He helped triage the most wounded and comfort the ones who were dying.

"Samuel was tending the kittens," I said, and Troy nodded in understanding.

He kept thinking that he might have time. Armies move slowly, but a single man can move very fast. He could catch up with them...but when he finally decided he absolutely had to go, he realized they were too far gone, and he didn't know

where they were. He was lost, completely alone in the cold darkness.

And then a Confederate Lieutenant, almost with a kindly smile, came to him and said the war was over for Samuel, he was now a Confederate prisoner.

★ ★ ★

"There's a gap," I said now, after a minute of trying to recall. "I don't really remember much about the prison camp. I remember something about a flood, the men were all standing in knee-deep water. I remember that some of them had been there a long time. I've read about the terrible flood at Cahaba prison that spring, but...I don't actually remember. I don't remember the details. I kind of don't want to."

"It will come when it comes...if it comes. I've been working on this for almost a quarter of a century now, and there are still gaps for me."

★ ★ ★

When the day of release came, the men who were held at Cahaba Prison were moved out with the goal of Camp Fisk, near Vicksburg, Mississippi. The journey was partly by steamship from Cahaba Landing, but the last thirty-five miles was a terrible long march, wet with the spring rains.

When they finally reached Camp Fisk, the men who had survived the journey were suddenly treated to something like comfort. Yes, it was still an army camp, but Samuel was relieved to find that there was enough food for everyone—

hard tack, to be sure, but at least it was enough that no one was starving—and medical care, and new uniforms.

It was explained to them that they would all be taken by steamship to Cincinnati to muster out of the army. For some of the men, that meant going far north of their actual homes and then having to find their own way back. The government bureaucracy was likely going to mean many more men would die before reaching home.

Thousands of men were transferred the four miles from Camp Fisk to Vicksburg to wait on the docks. There were three ships that Samuel could see, but it appeared that everyone was being relegated onto the Sultana.

"I'm sure you've read about the greed and the corruption that led to that decision, to overload the *Sultana* so terribly," I said to Troy. "Of course, Samuel didn't know. He just wanted to go home."

"I told you I was the local high school expert on the *Sultana*," Troy reminded me with a smile. "Someday I'll tell you all the conspiracy theories about Confederate bombs and other reasons involved in the explosion. I don't believe them, but I know them. At the heart of it, you're right. It was greed and corruption."

The deck of the Sultana was filled not only with the men from Castle Morgan, where conditions had been relatively tolerable—relatively, because conditions had been terrible,

especially during the flood—but compared to the parolees from Andersonville, the Cahaba men looked positively fat.

For two days, the beleaguered steamship chugged upstream in the Mississippi River which was swollen to as much as three miles wide, covering the tops of trees that usually stood tall on the banks. Days were long, but most of the men were in excellent spirits, happy to be going home at last.

When the Sultana docked at Memphis on the evening of April 26, some of the soldiers were anxious to get off the ship and wander the town like free men. Samuel felt that was just an opportunity to find trouble, gambling, and alcohol. He didn't begrudge the men their desires, but he didn't want to join them.

He found a place to sleep on the inner part of the top deck and was already fast asleep when the Sultana began steaming away from Memphis. He awoke briefly with the motion, but then slept again.

The next time he awoke, he found himself flying through the air. It was a sensation beyond description. It seemed like a dream, which quickly became a nightmare, which quickly became a reality that was worse than either of those.

He saw the water closing in on him almost in slow motion. There was no way to slow his fall, nothing to grab or hold—just the night air, and the dark river. When he hit the water, it felt like hitting a city street, and it knocked the wind out of him. Underwater, not knowing which way was up, Samuel struggled with empty lungs to find the surface, guided only by *the light...which turned out to be the* Sultana, *engulfed in flames.*

Samuel was one of the first ones in the water, because the initial explosion had thrown him, dramatically, into the swollen river. Treading water, catching his breath, he looked up at the pandemonium before him...and then he saw her.

Standing against the rails at the bow of the top deck, wearing a Union uniform, except for the cap, such that her beautiful hair was flying in the wind, was Marilla. It was impossible, it was unimaginable...but it was her. He called to her over the din of the flames and the cries, but there was no way she could hear him. And then, as he watched, she fell. The deck railing gave way, and she fell to the sea.

Samuel was about halfway down the starboard side of the burning ship, and someone on the second deck was throwing out shingles and closet doors from the cabins, anything that might float. Samuel grabbed on to a piece of...something...and began desperately swimming toward the bow where Marilla had fallen.

But now more and more people were in the water. And more than that, he was horribly aware that every movement in the dark water might be the alligator.

"Yes," I interrupted my own flow. "The alligator! The crew kept a pet alligator in a box, and Samuel thought it might be in the water!"

"It wasn't," Troy said bluntly.

"Oh, I know. I read that one of the soldiers killed it—with a sword! —and used the box to float to safety. But Samuel didn't know that. Couldn't have known."

He was kicking people away from him. He knew he was probably causing the deaths of some of his comrades, when he had so terribly hated causing the deaths of his enemies. But he had to get to Marilla.

In the chaos, he couldn't see her…and then he did. She was holding on to a bale of hay and he could see that others were swamping her. She couldn't fight them off the way he had. As he swam toward her, he saw her dragged away from her spot on the hay, and then he searched the water, frantically, until he saw her resurface. He called out to her, and she turned to him. Their eyes met across the water, and he knew he wasn't going to make it to her. Already, there were too many people vying for his shingle. He was being drowned.

But if there is a God in heaven, if there is any sense to the cycle of life on this planet, then Samuel knew in that moment that he and Marilla would meet again. The best he could do was to offer a plan, a plan that they would meet again, someday, in some other time, on their little island. He knew that nothing could keep him from it. And so, he called out over the noise of the screaming, the noise of the flaming hulk that had been his promise of home, he called out to Marilla to meet him there, at Temple Island…and then the water claimed him.

Chapter Twenty-Eight

September 12, 1859

My Darling Samuel,

Here on the eve of our wedding, I wanted to write one last letter, and I will have it delivered to your hotel so that you can have one more communication from me before we stand together at the altar tomorrow morning. In a way, it seems that the time has passed so quickly between our meeting and our marriage, and in another way, it feels that I have known you for all of my life and have been breathlessly awaiting this day for as long as I can remember.

Perhaps I have dreamed you as you say you have dreamed of me over the years. Perhaps the sense that I was bound to you since I emerged from my mother's womb comes from this. I am overcome with emotion to think that, from tomorrow forward, we will have our whole lives to discuss this, to define the parameters of our past as we build the foundations of our future.

As much as I have wished to hurry this period of waiting before our marriage, I have also cherished this time of letter-writing. I feel that I know you so well now, my Samuel, that we have become the dearest of friends as we move toward becoming husband and wife.

Minette Bryant

And so tomorrow I will stand before you in a dress which, thanks to my Mother's indefatigable insistence, has more French lace than can be found in the whole of France, and despite my exhaustion from carrying that entire dress down the aisle to you, I will still manage to say all of my vows and to mean every one of them with my whole heart. And then I will belong, body and soul, to you.

I imagine I will need to exchange my bridal gown for more practical attire before we embark for our honeymoon, as the sheer weight of the dress would no doubt break the back of the elephant you promised to provide for me.

Chapter Twenty-Nine

I was in tears telling the last of the story. It was such a strange sensation, remembering those moments as one who had been there, and also grieving that experience as if for someone else. Troy held me as I cried softly, partly from the story, and partly from the exertion of the flow of memories.

I finally got up to go to the bathroom for a tissue to blow my nose. Reality, intruding upon the period of magic. When I came back, Troy was sitting up on the side of the bed, and I sat beside him.

"You're probably exhausted," he said. "And I bet the Little Princess is thinking you've abandoned her."

"I know...I'm a terrible mom. I've dragged her all over the country inside a month, one place after another. Maybe we're ready to settle down now."

"Maybe so." He patted my hand. "Do you need me to walk you to your door?"

"That's OK," I smiled. "I think I can find my way the half-yard from your room to mine."

He stayed seated on the bed as I got up, threw away my tissue, and then walked to the door. I opened it, took a step out into the hallway, then turned around and said, "Troy?"

He turned. "Yeah?"

"Please ask me to stay..."

I don't think he ever actually asked, he just came to me, pulled me back inside, and closed the door behind us.

This was not at all like the first time we were together, in my cabin. That first time was hurried, frenzied, almost like we needed to finish before our reasoning selves could fully realize what was happening. This time was not an accidental flame which might die if we slowed down. This time was a harmony of flesh and spirit, the culmination of the lifetime it had taken to find each other.

That night in Franklin, we were Troy and Trista, but we were also Samuel and Marilla. When Troy murmured that he loved me, I knew it was his newly discovered love for me, and also Marilla's love for Samuel. When I responded with my own words of love, they were not meant lightly, a product of the moment, but the most deeply felt love I had ever known.

This was the connection of lovers who knew, without question, that they would spend the rest of their lives together, and when we finally lay, wrapped in each other's arms in the darkness of the early morning, we whispered to each other, amazed at how this had all come together.

"I wonder how John Michael Montgomery would write a song about this," Troy wondered. "*I love the way you* remember your past life and then jump on me at two in the morning..."

"Mmmm..." I mused. "How about '*I love the way you rigged it so that we would have this life changing conversation in a room with a queen-sized bed*'?"

"That works."

"And don't think I didn't notice the switcheroo you pulled back at Lavinia's house."

"What's that?"

"You said you would take me to Franklin, then hitch a ride back to Memphis to catch your plane...but then you packed all your stuff and told Charlie to return your rental car to the airport. You never actually thought that we were going back to Milton separately."

"No...no I didn't. But I had to pretend I was offering you an out."

We lay there, quietly, just feeling the moment...and then I decided it was time to test the waters of this new relationship.

"Troy," I said softly into the dark room. "I need to ask you something important."

"What is it?"

"I need to know if you love me enough to let me use the address of your store to have some things delivered. Stuff I want to buy online. I don't exactly have a delivery address."

"Wow..." Troy breathed. "That's a biggie. Let me think. Let me think..."

I laughed at the seriousness in his voice.

"How about we strike a bargain. Instead of the store, why don't you just have your stuff sent to my home address. I have a feeling you'll be keeping a toothbrush and a pair of pajamas there anyway."

"And my pet iguana," I said flatly. "And I gave your number to my contacts in the drug cartel."

"That's fine...but you have to consult with me before buying dish soap. I'm very particular."

Suddenly, I sat up, remembering. "Hey!"

"What?"

I turned to look down at him. "*Astra inclinant!*"

He grinned up at me and responded, "*Sed non obligant.*"

"What is that? I obviously know it..."

"It's the language on the Sutter family crest. It means *The Stars Incline Us, They Do Not Bind Us.* It seems more appropriate than ever now."

I looked at my watch. "I really should go," I said, hoping he could read the disappointment in my voice. "I need to take Margaret Mary out, and I'd love to get a few hours of sleep before we hit the road for home...I have a feeling that won't happen if I stay here. Do you mind?"

"Are you kidding? I was thinking you'd never leave!"

I leaned over to kiss him goodnight, a brief kiss that lasted half an hour...and then I was back in my own room, where Margaret Mary glared at me accusatorily. "I know, I know, I'm sorry" I told her. "I swear I didn't forget you. I just got caught up. Wanna go out?"

"Out" was the one word of my apology that she understood, and she immediately jumped down from the chair, shook herself, and began sneezing in excitement. When we came back into the hotel room, it was almost six o'clock in the morning. I tightly closed the blackout drapes and set my alarm for eleven, thinking that Troy Bowden had better not come wake me up any earlier than that.

The long drive back to Milton, Maine from Franklin, Tennessee was a fantastic voyage of discovery. With all the walls down, Troy and I were able to get to know each other on brand new levels. We shared stories, we shared fast food, we shared painful memories, and we shared the driving.

We stopped very late on Thursday night just outside New York City, and spent the next day there, just enjoying the city, and enjoying each other. Saturday, we drove the rest of the trip to Milton; we planned to spend that night together on the island, but Troy wanted to drop his luggage off at his house and pick up a few things before heading to Parson Point.

Driving through Milton, it felt like years since I'd been there, but it had only been a week. So much had happened, so much had awakened inside me, I felt like I definitely understood the concept of "New Trista" now.

Jennifer. I hadn't spoken to her since I said goodbye in the airport drop-off zone. Wow, did I have a story to tell her now.

Troy turned left off of the main road just after we passed Vincent & Son. The road winded back into the forest, and then he turned onto his driveway, which winded even further. It was almost dark, but in Troy's headlights, I could see the house nestled in a clearing with the forest close behind it.

It was beautiful. Classic, but masculine, with high peaks and stonework in the walls of the front porch. It looked like a combination of cozy woodland cabin and old money.

"Oh, Troy," I breathed. "It's gorgeous!"

"Well thank you, ma'am," he said proudly. "I built it myself."

I stared. "You're kidding," I said, though I knew he wasn't.

"It took me five years to finish it, a little at a time as money allowed, because I wasn't going to take out a loan. I lived in the back room at Vincent & Son while I worked on this."

"The back room? Like, the stock room?"

"Sure! I made it really cozy."

It was chilly outside, and I was shivering now, outside the warm car, regretting the shorts I had chosen for the journey home. In Maine, May is still early Spring.

Troy unlocked the front door and invited me inside. I stood, looking around me in awe—at the high-raftered ceilings, the open staircase leading to a loft where I could see his bed, the bar behind which was a fabulous stainless-steel kitchen—while he hustled around gathering together a small bag of things to bring to the cabin.

"Got your toothbrush?" I asked, as he trotted back down the stairs.

"I thought I'd just use yours," he teased as he opened the front door and turned out the light.

"We will never know each other well enough for that," I assured him with one eyebrow raised.

It was dark now, but according to the charts, there was just about another hour for low tide. We got back in my car, where Margaret Mary was waiting patiently, and Troy drove us back to the main road, and then across to the turn out to Parson Point.

When he got out of the driver's side of the car, I heard Troy swear, low under his breath.

"What is it?" I asked, helping Margaret Mary out of the back seat.

"Looks like the Beardens are home," he said in a husky whisper. "Let's not disturb them, shall we?"

We practically tiptoed down the gravel drive past their black suburban. Lights were on in the house, and we did our best to make no noise as we crossed. Troy employed his own Maglite so that we could find our way down the wooded path, and then he lighted our way down the stone steps, handing me the light so that I could shine it for him.

We kept our voices down as we crossed the mud, not wanting the sound to carry back and incur the wrath of Mr. Bearden. Once on the grassy slope leading up to Temple Island, we again did our best to help each other with the light while we found the trail that led to the cabin.

Surrounded by the safety of the trees, I exhaled loudly and said, "It sure is good to be home!" ...and then promptly fell into a hole.

This was not like the hallucinations I'd had, this was a real hole right in my path, and when I fell in, I twisted my knee and had to sit there for a minute, in the pit the size of a horse trough, until I felt like I could risk trying to stand.

Troy shined his light on the hole, and said, "What the...what is this?? Are you OK?" he began shining the wide beam of the Maglite in every direction all around us, and we could see that there were at least four other holes just like this one.

I thought maybe I was ready to stand, and Troy reached down to offer me his hand, but just then, out of the darkness, there came a disembodied shovel that hit Troy over the flat of his upper back, and Troy fell to the ground, unconscious.

Unable to comprehend what I was seeing, I stared at Troy on the ground at the edge of the hole, and then the other end of the shovel came into view from out of the darkness, and there was a very large man attached to it.

It was no one that I recognized. He had thick, rumpled, dark curls, and black eyes. He looked like he might have been a man in his thirties, but a hard life had left him with baggy pockets under his eyes, which made his glower down at me seem even more menacing.

He dropped the shovel by the hole and pulled his cell phone out of his pocket. He pushed one button, then said, "Boss...we got a problem. Little lady came home. And she brought company."

He never took his eyes off of me, and I never looked away from his gaze, but I also couldn't find my voice to say a word. My world was turned upside down once again, and whatever this man wanted, I had no doubt he would kill us both to get it.

"Go in the house," he ordered gruffly, pocketing his cell phone, and I struggled to get myself out of the hole. Once back on level ground, holding my knee against the stabbing pain, I knelt down beside Troy and touched his face.

"Leave him!" the man ordered. "I'll bring him in."

Wincing with every labored step, feeling the pain of my knee and the several places where my bare legs had been scraped, I made my way back up the path, mortified to be leaving Troy behind, but I could feel the large man close behind me, making sure I followed his orders.

The cabin door was unlocked, and I imagined this meant the man and his "boss" had already been inside. It was dark and cold, but, as I passed, I turned on the LED lantern that was sitting on the bar.

The man ordered me to sit down in one of the dining chairs, and then he began binding my hands behind me with the pink duct tape I had so recently used for a happier purpose. When my hands were bound together, he then taped my bare ankles to the legs of the chair. I didn't struggle. What was the use? I just sat there, running with silent tears.

He left me then and went back outside. He was gone for about ten minutes before he came back, with Troy. Troy was on his feet, stumbling, but walking...awake and alive. My tears came harder with the relief of seeing him. Blearily, Troy lolled in the chair as the man pink-taped him in just as he had me.

Once satisfied that Troy was sufficiently bound, the man walked back to the door, then turned and pointed a finger at us. "Now you wait," he grunted and moved off into the darkness.

Finally, able to speak, I called to Troy, "Troy...are you OK? Are you hurt?"

Troy remained slumped in the chair, not raising his head to look at me, and said, "This is gonna hurt in the morning."

"Troy, what does he want? Do you know him? Did he say anything to you?"

"No," Now Troy raised his head and turned toward me. "He didn't say a word to me, not until we got in here and he said *now you wait*. I don't know him. Never saw him, and I know nearly everybody in town."

"It looks like he's...digging for something. All over the island."

"Yeah, I saw that. I don't suppose you know what for?"

"Of course not! I've got a few pieces of jewelry here in the cabin that might pawn for enough to stay high all weekend, but there's nothing else of value here."

"I don't think this guy is looking for a quick high."

"No...and after he hit you, he called someone to say we had come home. So, it's not just one thug looking for something to steal."

"Well, Thugly better watch himself," Troy said blearily. "If he comes back in here, I'm gonna get out of this chair and teach him a lesson."

I knew Troy was trying to make me feel better by making light of the situation, but there was no light side *to* the situation. I was sitting in my own home, with the only man I'd ever really loved, and we were both pink-duct-taped to dining chairs in the dim blue light of an LED lantern, helplessly waiting for *someone* to tell us our fate.

Within another ninety seconds, that someone showed up. It was Ian Andrews.

Ian jogged up the front stairs and stood in the open doorway, looking at us with a face of mock pity. "Well, this is sad," he said, clucking his tongue as we squinted up at him. "Couldn't have stayed away just one more night? We might've had all this mess cleaned up by then, and no one would be the wiser. But...here you are. Let's just hope you can be of help."

"Ian," I said, pleading, "Please just tell me what this is about! Whatever you want, you can have it! Nothing is worth all of this."

Ian laughed loudly, then said, "Oh, sweetheart...you have no idea. You have something that is worth far more to me than this island. More than ten islands! Are you playing dumb, or does it just come naturally?"

I looked at him blankly. There was no right answer to that question.

Ian reached into the bag he was carrying, and he pulled out a small, but very thick, book. "It's in here," he said, and he tossed the book on my lap, as though I would be able to thumb through it with my hands taped behind the chair.

But the moment the old book touched my bare legs, I felt a wave of emotion and memory come back to me, washing over me bodily as it had when I touched the earth of the Franklin Battlefield...but this wave wasn't frightening or violent. Instead, it was a warm rush of love and family and childhood and devotion. I almost choked on a sob that was joy, not pain, but Ian misread me.

"I didn't throw it that hard," he said, taking the book off my lap roughly, and thumbing carelessly through the pages to the center.

Troy was looking at me intently. He knew the nature of what had just happened, but not the substance. Just then, Thugly called to Ian from out in the yard, and Ian tossed the book on the table and left us alone.

"That's...that's Helena Sutter's Bible," I whispered to Troy. "When it touched me, I had all the memories of Samuel's relationship with his mother. That Bible was always with her. Oh, god...what does this have to do with anything?"

Troy would have, of course, told me that he didn't know, but he didn't tell me because Ian was back.

He picked up the book again, thumbing again to the middle, and he held out the page he'd chosen for me to see. The LED lantern was slightly behind me, so if I moved my head to the left, I could see the page clearly with no shadow.

It wasn't a page of the Bible text itself; it was the center section where the Bible's owner might write the names of family members and the dates of births and weddings and such. But on the page for weddings, it only said, in what I recognized as Helena Sutter's tiny handwriting (and again, I felt the rush of devotion that Samuel had for his mother):

Buried at Temple Island: wedding jewelry, grandmother's revered silver

I looked up at Ian in confusion, as he passed the open Bible in front of Troy as well.

"Do you know how long it took me to figure out what the hell Temple Island is?" he challenged me, ranting. "When that little Bible came into my possession, about three years ago, I must've spent five thousand dollars just on investigators to find out where Temple Island is, and then when I found it...it was for sale! I thought the gods were smiling on me! I came up here, made an offer, and they turned me down! I made another offer, and they turned me down! I didn't even know if what I thought was here was actually here...I tried just snooping around with a metal detector, but they ran me off. And then, lo and behold, *you* show up, offering the asking price, sweeping it out from under me."

Ian was pacing now, like a nervous cat. "But I'm too invested. I've spent almost everything I have saved just trying to get a shot at finding it. I tried to finesse you nicely, Trista...I did. But then Mister Fix-It shows up and spoils my chances...truth is, though, if anyone knows where it is, it's probably him. You think he's dating you because he's sweet on you? He wants the same thing that I want...but it's too late."

With that, Ian rushed back out into the night, leaving Troy and me agape.

"Were you able to read what it said?" I asked him.

"I was."

"So, do you think there's some piece of jewelry in there that's worth a fortune? How would he know? It just says "wedding jewelry" ..."

"It's not the jewelry," Troy said flatly. "It's the silver."

"Silver? What would that be worth? I mean, antique silver would be interesting to a collector, polished up it might sell nicely in an antique store..." I trailed off, remembering what Ian had said about his passion being antiques. I knew he didn't have a yardwork service...the bit about loving antiques must have been the only honest thing he had told me on our date. Helena's Bible "came into his possession" through, what...an estate sale? An auction? Maybe it was just in a box of junk he bought on speculation.

"Tell me what it said, Trista," Troy encouraged me.

"It said, *Buried at Temple Island: wedding jewelry, grandmother's revered silver.*"

"No," Troy corrected me gently. "Not "revered silver" ... "revere silver" ...Revere. As in Paul."

"You mean Paul Revere like, *the British are coming,* Paul Revere?"

"Yes, but also, the noted Boston silversmith, Paul Revere."

I blinked at him, trying to make sense of it.

"If there's a set of Paul Revere silver buried somewhere here, it's worth...I don't know. It's priceless. It's certainly worth more than this island...and more than our lives."

"But, why would it be buried here?" I asked, incredulous.

"I wouldn't know, Trista...but Samuel might have. Can you try to remember?"

With Ian gone, the cabin was silent except for the sound of Troy breathing beside me. I tried to recapture what I had done before. I closed my eyes and centered on softening my breathing and relaxing my muscles. I turned my focus to the feeling I had just encountered upon touching Helena's Bible. The love between a mother and her oldest child. I could feel her, close to me, I could hear her soft voice, humming to me...and then it came.

★ ★ ★

Helena Sutter was a proud woman, and deeply devoted to her family. She would never have gone against her husband's wishes, as she trusted him to always make the decisions that were best for herself and the children, even after the children were grown.

But when the horrible war broke out, and the government was calling for everyone to do their part for the effort to preserve the Union, Lawrence, it seemed to Helena, was going too far in his service to his country.

Lawrence was dictating that boxes upon boxes of family valuables be donated to the Union cause. Nothing was too large or too small to be of value. On the day he boxed up all the flatware, Helena knew she had to act.

She came to Samuel in his office and asked for his help and his utmost discretion. She understood and supported her husband's fervor for the war effort, but she wanted to preserve some things from his frenzy of enthusiasm.

She asked Samuel if he would hide a few things that were of sentimental value. She said that, to the government, her grandmother's silver and her wedding jewelry were just trinkets to melt down, but to her, the jewelry would always be the cherished remnant of her wedding day, and the silver represented her childhood memories of sitting in her grandmother's parlor in Boston, drinking tea and listening to the stories of life in the old days.

Helena knew that, one day, this terrible war would end, and she didn't think Lawrence would be angry that she had sought to preserve these treasures. Always anxious to comfort his mother, Samuel agreed, and when Helena brought him her prized possessions, they buried them in a chest, in Marilla's little root cellar, to wait for the war's end.

But the war raged on, and then Samuel went off to join Jonathan, and nothing more was said of the little buried chest...

★ ★ ★

Ian came bounding back into the room, and my flow of memories was broken. I looked up at Troy, hoping to communicate to him that I had found some answers, but Ian gave us no time, even for silent communication.

"Tide's all in, now," he said, too loud for the small room. "Looks like we're here for the night. This would be a good time for *somebody* to start talking!"

When Ian said *somebody*, he kicked Troy, hard, in the shin. Helpless to move or defend himself, Troy took the booted kick squarely, and cried out in surprised pain.

In that moment, a tiny white avenger, my little albino Wookiee, came flying in through the doorway, barking loudly, and grabbed Ian by the pants-leg. Ian kicked her off of his leg and she flew across the room and hit the bedroom wall. Stunned for only a second, she got back on her feet and launched herself at Ian again...but this time, he had taken the gun from his bag and he fired once.

The report of the pistol was impossibly loud in the cabin. In a momentary deafness, I saw Margaret Mary fly back with the impact of the bullet. She landed in a heap on the rug behind the sofa, and a red carnation bloomed on her side. The silent movie ended, and I heard screaming. It was my screaming. I couldn't *stop* screaming.

Ian stopped me. With a face of rage, he stepped over and put the hot muzzle of his gun against my forehead. "Shut up or I'll do it for you!" he said angrily.

"Get away from her!" Troy was shouting. "Get away from her, you son of a bitch!"

I choked on the sobs. With the hot metal of the freshly fired weapon burning my skin, I couldn't even turn my head to look at Margaret Mary.

Ian lowered the gun and took a few breaths to calm himself down. "Look," he said, "The only way anybody's getting out of this is if I find what I'm looking for. Then we might make a deal."

Troy looked at me, and I knew what he was thinking. There would be no deal. Ian had gone too far now; he couldn't let us live.

"But if you don't help me find it," he continued, "It will be really easy for me to make you disappear. Nobody knows where you are. Nobody will even report you missing for...what?...a week or so, at the least. That's the beauty of living on a private island, right Trista? So nobody knows your business."

I took a deep breath. He was right. In my world, only Jennifer had a vague idea of where I had been going, and no timetable. She might not try to call me for a month, even. My mother would call or text, but it would be several days before she became truly concerned. My employees had grown accustomed to my being AWOL over the past few weeks. If Troy's fill-ins at the store wondered where he was, who would they call? If someone knew how to get in touch with Lavinia, she would assume we were still on a road trip.

Troy sat silently, no doubt thinking through the same scenarios I was. We were lost.

"Look," Troy said finally, "I don't know much more than you do. I tried to find it while I was tending the place, but I never could. You've obviously discovered that metal detectors don't work. It may be wrapped or boxed in something that blocks detection."

I looked at Troy, agape. He turned to me for less than a fraction of a second...and there was that wink. A wink that I caught squarely, but Ian didn't see. He was trying to buy time. I decided to play along.

"What? All this was because you wanted to play Pirate and hunt treasure? You said you loved me!"

Ian laughed gruffly. "This is rich," he said. "You might need to learn a lesson here. Take a good long look in the mirror, Miss Maybrey...when men start coming out of nowhere trying to be with you, you need to check yourself. You're not that great."

"Hey, wait a minute," Troy said, dropping the act to defend my honor.

And then the windows of the cabin flooded with a powerful searchlight, and a loudspeaker blared at us: "THIS IS THE COAST GUARD. YOU ARE SURROUNDED. COME OUT WITH YOUR HANDS UP!"

Ian ran to the window in a panic. "What the fuck is this?" he asked, in a high-pitched voice, suddenly *not* in control of the situation. Two men in Kevlar vests came through the front door holding very big guns. At first, they looked at us, taped to the chairs, obviously not the bad guys, and then they turned toward Ian, and he threw his gun on the floor and put his hands over his head, a coward after all.

★ ★ ★

We watched as the armed men cuffed Ian and ushered him out the front door, and then another man came in to free us from our chairs. He was gentle.

"Are you hurt? Do you need medical attention?" he asked us each, in turn, as he cut through our duct tape with a knife.

"She hurt her knee when she fell," Troy said.

"He was hit over the head with a shovel!" I insisted, certain that his was the greater injury.

"We'll get you both to the ER for a good work up, make sure you're OK."

Once free, I went quickly to the rug where Margaret Mary was lying, so still. Tears welling in my eyes again, I put my hand on her and could feel that she was still breathing.

"What've we got here?" the officer asked, standing over me.

"Do you think we can save her?" I asked him, like a child hoping for a miracle.

"We will certainly try," he said. Carefully, he lifted the tiny body and placed her on one of my sofa cushions, and then he lifted the whole cushion and carried it out the front door.

Troy held my hand tightly as we followed the soft-spoken man and his precious package outside. We could see two Coast Guard boats anchored on the west side of the island, their searchlights still piercing the trees like daylight. In that false sun, we could see Ian and Thugly being fitted with life jackets and loaded into one of the boats. I supposed the other was for us.

I stopped and put my free hand on the arm of our rescuer. "How did you know?" I asked sincerely. "How did you know to come?"

"Your neighbors called," he said, indicating the direction of Parson Point.

We continued walking toward the waiting boat, and Troy mused. "I guess they must have heard the gunfire..."

"Actually, no," the officer said. "The cops were already here when they heard the gunfire, and some screaming, and they called the Coast Guard."

"Why were the cops already here?" I asked, as Troy helped me down from the rocks into the boat.

The officer gingerly handed down the cushion with Margaret Mary, and I took it carefully onto my lap.

"Well, I guess the neighbors called to complain about a car parked on their property, wanted it towed. Police got here to check it out and heard the commotion."

I sat confused as the boat engine started. Why would they be calling about towing my car? We'd already had that conversation, and they knew I had the right... and then I realized, and I laughed out loud, my voice ringing across the water.

"Ian's car!" I said to Troy. "He did this to himself!"

"Remind me to give Mr. Bearden a big wet kiss!" Troy said, and the boat pulled away from the shore of Temple Island.

"Only if I can watch!"

Chapter Thirty

September 12, 1859

My Darling M,

I hope that it is not so late that the courier has awakened you, but I could not restrain myself from writing back to you on this last night that we will ever have to spend apart. How I will ever find sleep on this night of nights, I cannot say, my mind is so racing with dreams and ideas and excitement.

My greatest desire is to wander out into the night and stand under your window, throwing pebbles like a child to get your attention and then reenact the balcony scene of Romeo and Juliet, but depicting our own story, and probably without the element of iambic pentameter, as I do not believe myself capable of such a feat in my current state of mind.

But do not worry. I will not be throwing pebbles at your window tonight. I will wait until I see you coming into the church in all your French lace and the love in your eyes which will mirror mine.

Still, in lieu of being able to see you this evening, I think I will instead share with you a secret that I have learned. My brother, Jonathan, who will tomorrow become your brother as well, has learned—and shamelessly told me, though he was sworn to secrecy—that my parents are giving us a quite extraordinary gift to celebrate our marriage.

Just off the coast of my family's property is a tiny island, which is called Temple Island. It is heavily wooded and therefore beautifully private, but still close enough to the mainland that moving back and forth is not difficult. They have apparently already contracted for the workmen to build us a small house on Temple Island such that it will be completed by the time we return from our honeymoon.

It may sound daunting to you to think of living on our own little island, but please have faith that, as I have said before, the sea will become your dear friend, the tides your trusted confidant. We will learn this life together, Dearest M, and our love will see us through into forever.

Chapter Thirty-One

Margaret Mary spent the night at the Animal Medical Clinic in Milton, where they assured me that she would survive. The bullet had grazed her hip...it was a deep wound, but not a mortal one.

Troy and I, after being thoroughly checked out in the emergency room, and thoroughly interviewed by the police, spent the night in his loft. I could hardly believe that we had awakened that morning in a hotel in New York City, and now we had been through this incredible ordeal together.

Finally at peace, snuggled close in his bed under the sloping ceiling, wearing a pair of Troy's boxer shorts and a t-shirt, I told Troy about the memory I'd had, what I had learned about Helena Sutter's grandmother's silver, and why it was buried on the island.

"I guess no one ever came back for it. Samuel didn't come back at all, and I don't know what happened to Helena. No one else knew it was there."

"But," Troy asked, "Where is *there*. Do you know where they buried it?"

I shook my head, frustrated, in the darkness. "No. All I know is that it's in the root cellar, but..."

And then it came to me. I sat straight up in bed. "I *do* know! I know where it is! Oh, Helena has been trying to tell me all along!"

From the first time I saw Helena in the dream about all the people on the island, through the two waking visions, she had been repeatedly burying me in that root cellar. In the first dream, she pointed me down a hallway with a sign for "Fresh Blueberries" and then both of the visions had happened when I was sitting in my chair in the overgrown blueberry patch on the west side of the island. Why, that meant that, as the Coast Guard was putting the handcuffed Ian into his life jacket earlier that night, he'd been standing right over the spot where his treasure was hiding!

Troy was waiting for me to tell him, and I did my best to explain what I thought were the clues in my memory as to where we would find Helena Sutter's hidden chest. And then, exhausted from the day, and from the night, and from the collision of two lives...I slept.

✶ ✶ ✶

The next morning, with the first low tide, we made our way back to Temple Island, and with shovels and hoes, we cleared the blueberry thicket, and the decades of detritus under it, until we found the wooden boards that were the rotted door of Marilla's root cellar. Troy pried at the boards, and they gave way with barely a sigh.

Inside the small, symmetrical hole, we could see nothing but the tree roots that had snaked their way in over the past century. We worked together all day, cutting back those roots and clearing a path to the bottom of the cellar.

Once cleared, we discovered only the thinnest layer of dirt covering a hard object at the bottom of the hole. With a shovel, a lot of sweat, and an hour-long stream of profanity for which Troy later asked my forgiveness, the steel chest was pried up from what might have become its permanent resting place.

The phrase "everything conveys" took on a whole new purpose.

Troy dusted off the top of the chest, and we stood over it, reading the words that surrounded the Sutter family crest: *Astra inclinant, sed non obligant.*

✵ ✵ ✵

Now, Troy and I live in the cabin on Temple Island from April through September, and then we spend the winter months at his house in town. *Trista Maybrey and the Mysterious Island*: in this chapter, Trista chooses to winter with central heating.

We talk often about Samuel and Marilla, what we remember of them, what we've learned from them. But we are not them. We are Trista and Troy, and we are building our own lives.

My business continues to grow, and Troy and I have talked about the possibility of having a child through surrogacy. We may, but for now, we are focused on each other, and the love that brought us together across a nation and over a hundred fifty years.

We go to Boston about twice a year, to visit Helena Sutter's Paul Revere silver tea service at the Boston Tea Party Museum. It still belongs to us, but it is on permanent loan to the museum; we never have to buy tickets. Besides, Boston has the world's greatest vegan restaurant, and Margaret Mary loves to run in Boston Common Park.

More important to me, though, than the silver, is Helena's Bible, which Ian left on my dining room table. It might not be worth anything to a collector, but to me it is the most valuable antique I could ever own. I can learn more about Samuel by connecting to his love for his mother than by any other collection of memories. Love cannot be quantified, and it does not fade over time. History has taught us many things about the war he fought, the work he did, the tragedy in which he died...but Samuel's love for his family cannot be contained in a history book. It's the love that lasts.

Sometimes at night, lying in the breathless stillness of the island, I imagine I can hear them, Samuel and Marilla, laughing softly and talking together in the firelight of their little house. I know that I am living the life they planned together, and I am honored to have that responsibility.

And then I roll over and put my arms around this man that I can't imagine my life without, and the breathless stillness holds us all until morning.

About the Author

Minette Bryant is a lifelong lover of words and word-craft. Having been born into a musical family, she has used her love of words to write music and lyrics ever since childhood. To date, she has written and produced six musical theater productions and one non-musical stage play.

Minette and her husband live in the Piney Woods of East Texas, but they also own a tiny island off the coast of Maine where they spend their summers. Minette calls the island her "creative space" and it was this island which inspired the story of *Seeking Samuel*.

A long time vegan and animal welfare advocate, Minette lives with a menagerie of rescue animals, and has taught them all an appreciation for cheesy sci-fi and Broadway soundtracks. Minette holds a master's degree in Counseling, and a Doctorate in Literature.

Seeking Samuel is available on Amazon, Barnes & Noble and fine bookstores everywhere.